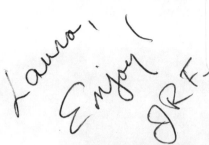

PARADISE: DISTURBED

BY JAMES ROBERT FULLER

A Myrtle Beach Crime Thriller
Book 1

DEDICATED TO MY MATERNAL
GRANDPARENTS, JAMES, AND
MAUD FULLER, WHO WITHOUT, I
SHUDDER TO THINK WHERE OR
WHAT I WOULD BE TODAY.

A TREMENDOUS THANK YOU TO MY WIFE,
BARBARA, FOR THE COUNTLESS HOURS SHE
SPENT EDITING AND RE-EDITING THIS NOVEL.
YOU WOULDN'T BELIEVE THE MISTAKES SHE
CAUGHT!

A BIG THANKS TO ALL OF MY GOLFING BUDDIES
WHOSE NAMES I HAVE INCLUDED IN THIS BOOK.
PURELY COINCIDENTAL!

PARADISE: DISTURBED

BY

JAMES ROBERT FULLER

FIRST EDITION

ISBN: 978-1-387-96573-1

PROLOGUE

June 25, 2018 – Myrtle Beach, South Carolina

Tonight, his name would be Jim.

This wouldn't be his first kill, or his second, or even his third. It would, however, be his first since arriving in Myrtle Beach 10 months earlier.

If successful, it would raise his count to 35. Now, as satisfying as 35 may be, it paled compared to that of Gary Ridgway, who was better known as "The Green River Killer."

Convicted for the deaths of at least 49 proven victims, Ridgeway had confessed to the murders of at least 71 women. The true number, however, is likely closer to 90. Ridgway strangled his victims and dumped the bodies in remote locations from 1982 to 2001.

Jim was a far more gruesome killer than was Ridgeway and far more ingenious. Although he had never met the psychopathic Ridgeway, he regarded him as his true mentor. His ambitious, but deadly goal, was to better Ridgeway's proven total by the end of the summer.

He had moved to Myrtle Beach from Fairmont, West Virginia, where he added seven victims to his growing resume. Previously, he had accumulated kills while living in many California towns, and in Vancouver, British Columbia. A new job opportunity in Myrtle Beach provided a reason to leave Fairmont, where, in his opinion, the police were inept. They, like the cops in all previous locales, were not worthy of answering the challenges he presented.

Born in 1980 in Long Beach, California, he spent the first 24 years of his life taking on challenges and winning them all. He considered even obscure challenges, like never being found while playing hide-and-seek in the

1

dense June fog of Long Beach, a triumph. Conquered with relative ease were even bigger tests, like the perpendicular hike through Squamish Indian country at Lake Lovelywater near Vancouver, a test toughened even more by having to carry a week's worth of provisions in a backpack.

Bored with winning each challenge thrown his way, he reversed roles in 2004 and became both a challenger and a serial killer.

Over the past 14 years, he had accumulated 34 kills. At each of those kills, he would leave a clever partial clue. The combined clues, if solved, would lead authorities to his doorstep. No one, in those 14 years, had knocked on his door. He remained undefeated.

Maybe Myrtle Beach or "paradise," as referred to by the locals, was the spot where a true challenger would step forward, although he doubted the worthiness of a tourist town's law enforcement. But he was ready to give the "paradise cops" a shot at the title.

They would have their first clue sometime early Tuesday morning.

His next victim, a vacationer, was a college girl only 19 or 20, beautiful and carefree, yet careless. She came alone to this bar on the now famous Myrtle Beach Boardwalk promenade. The bar, Dirty Don's, had a 15 foot by 30-foot patio set up outside the eating establishment. Patrons could sit at the makeshift bar and pretend to watch the ocean while surveying the crowd for someone to catch their eye.

That's why he was here, hoping that someone would catch his attention. He had already taken his position on a stool at the end of the bar. From this vantage point, he could see everyone who entered.

The moment she stepped onto the patio, she caught his eye and vice versa. Offered a seat at the bar, a dozen or more stools from where he sat, he watched as potential suitors surrounded her. Drinking gin and tonics like they were lemonades; she was losing touch with her surroundings. Guys were hitting on her like she was a dart board–plying her with drinks–hoping on this warm summer night to get lucky.

They are wasting their time, he thought. *She's having a great time playing them along.*

Waiting until she was well over the edge, he made his move. Sliding from his stool, his 230-pound muscular frame elbowed its way through the young lions that had surrounded his target.

As he stood at her side, he heard, "Hey, what the hell is this, buddy?"

Asking was a young man with an impressive tan, a chiseled body, and who carried a pittance of cash, and an expired condom in his wallet.

"It's called Main Event Time, sonny," the stranger hissed through clenched teeth, his face mere inches from that of the wannabe tough guy.

"My name ain't sonny. It's Keith!"

"I don't give a rat's ass what your name is. Now go home and beat it off, sonny. Tonight is not your night."

Keith, not quite 20 years of age, gave thought to challenging the tall, well-built stranger, but thought better of it after seeing something in the man's eyes he had never encountered. It frightened him, and he knew he was over-matched.

Backing away, he put on a brave show by uttering, "Next time, mister. Next time."

"Yeah, okay. Next time. Go home and do what I suggested. You'll feel much better in the morning."

The young man's friends felt no compulsion to challenge the stranger, because as Keith walked away, the other young studs followed.

Turning to her, he said, "Hello. I'm Jim."

"Hi, Jim," she slurred. "That was impressive. You scared away all my free drinks."

"Hmm, sorry about that."

"I've seen you watching me all night from that lonely spot at the end of the bar. You took a while to say hello."

"It appeared you were having a good time. I didn't want to interrupt."

"What made you decide I had stopped having a good time?"

"You looked hungry. How about we get something to eat?"

"Now that's a novel approach," she said, giggling.

"Oh? How's that?"

"Trying to get in a girl's pants by buying her a hamburger."

Smiling, he replied, "I'm thinking of something a tad classier and more satisfying than a hamburger, maybe more like surf and turf."

"Wow! Aren't you a gamer!" she cried aloud, holding up her drink in a mock toast. Then, lowering her voice, she leaned in toward him, saying, "Does that do it for you? Buy a lady a steak and then–wham-bam–thank you ma'am."

Smiling at her remark, he gave a slight sideways nod before stating, "I'm starving. I know a place close by. Would you like to join me?"

"You don't even know my name."

"Matter of fact, I don't. How about we fill in all the blanks over two medium rare rib-eyes and two lobster tails?"

Taking a sip of one of the three full drinks sitting before her, she said, "My name is Sara and I could go for a nice surf and turf dinner, but don't think for a minute, Jim, that I'm easy. I'm not one of those girls who loses her head and drops her panties just because some guy offers to buy me a fancy dinner."

"I'm sure that's true," said Jim.

As they headed south down the boardwalk, he took her hand in his, and smiling asked, "Ever been on a golf course, Sara?"

Sara, unaware that the grilled cheese sandwich she had made herself for lunch would be her last meal, answered, "No. Why?"

"Just wondering, is all."

Tonight, he would satisfy many hungers. Sara's though, would not be one.

CHAPTER 1
Beer and Pretzels

May 8th, 2016

   It would be his last case as an Air Force Security Police officer. He had been in the OSI for 35 years, and he was ready for retirement. His name was Colonel Ron Lee.

   Lee had worked his way up through the ranks because of his amazing ability to solve cases in record fashion. Nearing 55 years of age, Ron's physical health had eroded over the past couple of years. His weight had ballooned to 280, and it took a toll on his six-foot plus frame, especially on his knees.

   A good-looking man in his younger days, he remained so. Although his wavy hair had turned gray, his eyes still retained their piercing blue color and his complexion remained clear. His demeanor, however, had changed little. It still had a gruff edge to it that overshadowed a biting sense of humor.

   This last case was one of murder. A neighbor had found an Air Force captain's wife, Margie Buckner, murdered in the family's home in Pueblo, 45 miles from the base in Colorado Springs. Someone had strangled her from behind with a towel. They found no useful forensic evidence at the crime scene. The estranged husband, Fred Buckner Sr., claiming his innocence, was in base custody.

   Lee had set up an interrogation room in the kitchen. Mrs. Verna Beamon, the victim's next-door neighbor, would be his first interrogation. It was Verna's husband Harry who had discovered the murder scene earlier that morning. He had gone out to collect his Sunday paper from the driveway when he found his neighbor's copy in his hedges. Taking it over to the Buckner home, he discovered the front door was ajar. After calling out Margie's name and not receiving a reply, he entered the house and found the body.

"Morning, Mrs. Beamon. I'm Colonel Ron Lee. I'm with the Air Force's OSI."

"OSI?"

"That's the Office of Special Investigations, ma'am."

"Is this a special investigation?"

"Whenever a crime involves Air Force personnel, they call our office to investigate."

"Margie isn't in the Air Force."

"No, ma'am, she isn't, but her husband is. Therefore, here we are."

"I see, Sergeant."

"That's Colonel, ma'am."

"Why do you guys have so many damn titles?" uttered the woman with frustration.

Ignoring her question, Lee asked, "When did you last see Mrs. Buckner, ma'am?"

Verna Beamon was on the wrong side of 60. She was skeleton thin. Her hair was stark white, but thick. Her tired-looking eyes were a dull brown. She wore a print skirt with a white blouse. Verna wasn't wearing makeup, *but she should have,* thought Lee.

"Well, let's see, today is Sunday and Margie and I had lunch over here on Thursday. That was the day I helped rearrange her clothes closet and cupboards."

"Rearrange her cupboards, ma'am?"

"Yes, Major. She had so many extra settings of dishes and glasses, and living alone, she took some to a homeless shelter. I helped her pack away boxes of dishes and glasses, and then we rearranged everything to make it easier to access what she would need. We took the discarded dishes and glasses, along with a bag full of clothing she no longer wanted, over to the shelter on Madison."

"Tell me about the family, Mrs. Beamon, especially the relationship with her husband."

"Fred? Oh, they were a happy couple for the first ten years I knew them, Mr. Lee."

"Colonel Lee, ma'am."

"I keep forgetting, Colonel. I'm sorry."

"Do you know why they separated?"

"Can't say I do. Margie never confided in me about any differences they may have had. I'm guessing that things just went to pieces. We never saw it coming, Lieutenant."

"Colonel, ma'am. I am a Colonel."

"Oh, that's right. It's the other fella who is a lieutenant."

"That's correct, ma'am. What about the children? I understand the Buckners have a son and a daughter."

"That's correct, Captain."

Lee, raising his eyes toward the ceiling, let go a sigh of resignation.

"Jamie, that's the daughter, is the oldest, and she lives in Oregon. She married a fella she met while attending the university up there. She teaches at a school. Best I remember, they have two children."

"How often does she come home to visit, ma'am?"

"I don't think she's been here since Christmas."

Ron noted it was May 8th. *Five months,* he thought.

"Remember, Captain, she works and has two school-age kids, so it's obvious why she doesn't travel much."

"Yes, ma'am. What about the son?"

"Little Fred?"

"Yes, ma'am. What can you tell me about him?"

"He's eight years younger than his sister."

Then, lowering her voice to a secretive whisper, Verna bent forward toward Ron, and with darting eyes, said, "I believe Fred and Margie had a child who died at birth, so I'm thinking they waited a while to have another."

She then sat up straight, and continued talking in a normal voice, saying, "Fred's about 21. I think he's in his junior year at Colorado State or Colorado. I can't remember which one. It's the one in Fort Collins."

"That's Colorado State, ma'am."

"Okay, Captain, if you say so."

Surrendering to the woman's inability to remember his rank, Lee asked, "Does he come home often?"

"Quite the opposite, Colonel. He seldom comes to visit."

Lee smiled at her finally getting his rank correct. Knowing it was about a three-hour drive from Pueblo to Ft. Collins, he asked, "When was the last time you saw him?"

"I haven't seen little Fred since Christmas."

"Anything else you can tell me about the son, Mrs. Beamon?"

"I know he and Margie were often at odds, but Margie would never share the reasons with me."

"Excuse me, Colonel."

It was Lieutenant Rudy Foster, Lee's partner.

"Yes, Lieutenant."

"The son just arrived, Colonel. Would you like to talk with him now?"

"Yes, send him in, and then, if you would, please escort Mrs. Beamon home."

Helping the woman from her chair, Lee said, "Thank you for your time, Mrs. Beamon."

"You're more than welcome... I'm sorry, what was your title again?"

"It's Colonel, ma'am."

Five minutes passed before a handsome young man, standing six-foot and weighing around 165 pounds, appeared in the kitchen doorway. He had dark hair and dull blue eyes. A small scar, the result of a skiing accident when he was much younger, stretched for an inch across his left jawbone. Dressed in a pair of shorts, a blue T-shirt, and wearing a pair of expensive looking sandals, it was clear, based on his all-over tan, he spent a good deal of time in the sun.

Lee, still seated at the kitchen table, stood, and extending his right hand, said, "I'm Colonel Ron Lee. Sorry for your loss, son."

"Thank you, Colonel," answered the young man with a slight quiver in his voice. "Do you know what happened?"

"We're just getting started, Mr. Buckner."

"Please, sir, call me Fred."

"Okay, Fred. There are blanks that need filling. We're hoping you can be of some help."

"I'll do my best, sir."

"That's all we ask."

Before Ron asked a question, the college student said, "They say someone strangled her and left her lying on the living room floor."

It was a matter-of-fact statement, bordering on robotic. The son displayed no genuine emotion. Lee also took note he had referred to the woman as "her" and not "mom."

"That appears to be where it took place. There were no signs of a struggle. We're thinking she knew her killer."

"Was it my father?"

"Can't say."

"Where is he?"

"He's being held at the base until we can verify his alibi."

"Do you know how he is doing?"

"He insists he is innocent. Not that it matters, but I believe him."

"You do! Why?"

"I've seen husband-wife murder scenes before. This just doesn't have that look."

"I don't think dad would ever hurt mom. He loved her even though…"

"What?" asked Lee as he jotted something down in his notepad.

"Nothing."

"I need to ask a few questions. Can you sit for a few minutes?"

"No problem, sir."

Pulling a chair from the table, Fred Jr sat to Lee's right and tried to see what the colonel had written on the small pad.

"When did you last see your mother?"

"Last month. She drove up to campus on a Saturday."

"When were you home last?"

"Christmas."

"Why so long between visits?"

"Long story."

"I'm listening."

"I don't think it's relevant to what has happened, Colonel."

"Maybe, but I'd like to hear it, anyway."

While casting a look of "mind your own fucking business," in Lee's direction, young Fred stood, saying, "It was a long ride from Ft. Collins. Would you mind if I had something to drink, Colonel? Mom keeps a few beers in the fridge. Would you like one?"

"No, thanks, but you go right ahead."

Walking to the fridge, Fred Jr. opened it and searching the different shelves, reached toward the back and plucked out a can of Coors Light.

"Are you sure you don't want one, Colonel?" Fred said, holding up the can and giving it a slight side-to-side jiggle.

"Sorry, but no. I'm on duty. I'll pass, although, I must admit, a cold brew sounds mighty tantalizing."

Retrieving a bag of pretzels from the pantry along with a clean glass from the cupboard, he returned to the table and poured his beer.

"I love pretzels with a cold beer, Colonel."

"Did I ask you the last time you were home, Fred?"

"Yes, you did. I told you it was at Christmas."

"That's right, you said that. Tell me, Fred, how well do you know Mrs. Beaman?"

"Verna? I've known her for about 15 years."

"Was she and your mom close friends?"

"I'd say they were close."

"We were talking before you arrived. She was telling me about the last time they spoke."

"Oh?"

"Yeah. She said they had lunch here last Thursday."

"That's nothing unusual. They often eat at each other's home," remarked Fred as he dipped a pretzel into the glass of beer.

Seeing a quizzical look in the colonel's eyes, he smiled, saying, "Something my old man used to do. I picked up on it."

"I'll admit that I also do that," Lee said with a face that had turned serious.

"I saw that look on your face. I thought you were wondering what the heck…"

"How did you know, Fred?"

"I'm sorry, Colonel. How did I know what?"

"About the glasses."

"The glasses? What about them?"

"How did you know, Fred, where your mom kept the glasses?"

"I'm sorry, but I'm not following your question. The glasses are always in the cupboard," replied Fred as he lifted the glass toward his mouth.

Lee stood. Planting his hands down on the table, he leaned forward. His face, previously calm, was now grim as it moved ever closer toward Fred. Eyes that moments earlier were non-expressive now penetrated Fred's soul. Then, just inches from Fred's horrified face, he stopped. Now engulfed by something akin to fear, Fred froze.

Lee spoke, and his breath cloaked Fred's face like a wet towel. His voice had the sound of a death-knell.

"Your mom and Verna rearranged all the cupboards on Thursday, yet you walked straight to that cupboard to get that glass. How did you know they were in that cupboard?"

Fred, in slow-motion fashion, lowered his glass onto the table. His eyes drifted toward the cupboard from where he had retrieved the glass. Then they darted to another cupboard which Lee presumed had been the previous location of the glasses.

Fred's horrified eyes told all.

Exposed, he couldn't think fast enough on his feet to construct a plausible story, so he blurted, "She wouldn't give me money! The bitch wouldn't give me any more damn money and I needed it badly!"

"What did you need it for, Fred?"

"I needed stuff!"

"Stuff? What kind of stuff?"

"Drugs! Coke!"

"So, for that, you killed your own mother?"

"Yes! I strangled her! She had the money, but the bitch wouldn't give me a damn cent!"

Twenty minutes later, after getting a signed confession, Lee stood in the front doorway watching as Rudy led Fred Buckner Jr. to a Pueblo police cruiser. Seeing the college student being whisked away, he felt no sense of achievement. The kid was immature, a junkie, and stupid.

"Well done, Colonel."

"Thanks, Rudy."

"Nice job, Colonel Lee."

Offering the compliment was Brigadier General Bullock, his commanding officer.

"I'm glad you finally solved a case without shooting the suspect," he said with a wicked smile.

What an asshole, thought Lee. Two more weeks and I'm retired for life and won't have to put up with his shit.

The two weeks slipped by without incident and then Ron and his wife, Carol, were on a flight out of Denver to Charlotte where they would pick up a connecting flight that would take them to Myrtle Beach, South Carolina. They had bought a two-bedroom condo in a development called The Market Common, that had been a U.S. Air Force base until it closed. Stationed here for two years, Ron knew the area well.

The base closed in '93. Since that time, entrepreneurs had purchased the land and turned it into a gold mine while keeping intact historical remnants of the base itself.

Ron and Carol would live their lives enjoying all that the Grand Strand area offered: an abundance of golf courses, magnificent beaches, fabulous weather, terrific restaurants, entertainment venues, and plenty of shopping.

All of that, however, ended just 17 months later, on November 12th of 2017. That's when Carol suffered a fatal brain aneurysm.

Months later, retired Colonel Ron Lee's life would take a new turn, as would that of the stranger who wanted a challenge.

Soon, a deadly game would begin.

CHAPTER 2
Not Traditional

June 26th, 2018

It was a gorgeous Tuesday morning as the first foursome of the Hagan Hackers golf group, a troop of 40 golfers who had a regular Tuesday outing, approached the 7th tee box at the Tradition Golf Course.

The course lay in Litchfield, an area that had the Atlantic Ocean as its front porch and the Waccamaw River as its rear deck. In between there was an abundance of golf courses and beautiful residential areas. It was a small piece of the paradise identified as "The Grand Strand."

Playing in the lead foursome were Tim Taylor, an amateur photographer, John Hagan, the group's coordinator, John Bendele, a better fisherman than golfer, and Danny Ziolkowski, a popular player who would maintain his 20 handicap long after hell had frozen over.

Having teed off at 7:10, they reached the 7th tee at 8:30. The hole was a 368-yard par 4 that ran parallel to Willbrook Drive on its right. There was a good-sized pond fronting the green, about 280 yards from the tee box. No one in this group or any to follow would be in fear of driving their ball into the pond from the tee box.

After hitting their drives, they drove off to hit their second shots. Having hit the shortest tee shots, Bendele, using his rangefinder, zeroed in on the flagstick on the back right side of the green, near the small cul-de-sac where the carts would soon park.

"What do you have from there?" yelled Danny, some 15 yards in front of John's ball.

"I have 173, Danny. You'll have about 160."

"How far to the water?"

"About 135 from here."

Taylor, who had hit a long drive, some 50 yards past Bendele's, also had a rangefinder.

Waiting until Bendele had hit his second shot, which found the water, Taylor announced, "I wonder what the hell that is?"

"What's that, Tim?" asked Hagan, standing 20 yards behind Taylor's ball position.

"There's something lying against the base of the pin. It might be an animal. All I see is fur."

"It's most likely a squirrel," suggested Hagan.

After Ziolkowski had plunked his second shot into the water, Hagan and Taylor hit and found the green, but neither hit their ball near the pin.

Having hit their second shots in the water, both Bendele and Ziolkowski would take their fourth shots from the ball drop on the right side of the green.

All were eyeing the object lying at the base of the pin as the two carts followed the cart path toward the green. No one could determine the identity of the object from the moving carts.

Moments later, however, all would be clear.

They were only 15 yards from the pin's back right position when they exited their carts near the green's parking area. None, however, dared to take another step toward the green. Stopping their progress was a severed head lying at the base of the pin. The eyes were open and glazed. Dried blood, having trickled from the nose, resembled a frozen brown river as it ran down the upper lip and drizzled onto the chin. Protruding from the mouth was the tip of a tongue. Matted dark hair clung to the cheeks. The head, propped up by a ragged neck, sat about three inches above the ground. A semi-dried pool of blood, no bigger than a foot in diameter spread out from the torn neck.

"My God," said Danny.

Sara was right in one sense. She didn't lose her head over a steak dinner. The fact is, they never came close to a steak restaurant.

CHAPTER 3
New Career
January 5th, 2018–6 months earlier

It had been less than two months since Carol had passed when there came a knock at the condo door.

Ron stood amazed as he opened the door to see his long-time partner, Rudy Foster, now a Captain in the OSI, standing before him.

"Rudy! What brings you here?"

"Hey, Colonel. How are you doing?"

"To be honest, Rudy, I can't say I'm doing all that well."

"I'm sorry to hear about Carol and I want to apologize for not being at the memorial service. We had a whopper of a homicide back in Colorado Springs and I couldn't leave."

"I understand. I heard about that case. It appears our old commander was more than what met the eye."

"Yeah, he appreciated those call girls, but only until he finished his business with them."

"How many did he kill?"

"It's unofficial, but we believe he butchered at least seven. It's not unusual, as you well know, Ron, for those types of girls to disappear. There's no telling what really happened to them."

"He's not talking?"

"No. In fact, he acts like he's still in command," replied Rudy with a laugh.

"I'm guessing they'll be putting him to sleep."

"Most likely. It's too bad Colorado replaced hanging as their execution method. I would love to see that asshole dangling from a rope."

"I would have flown out to see it," added Lee with a grin. "Now, what brings you here?"

"You. I hear from my sources, Colonel, that you're not doing a damn thing with your life. That has to change."

"It's a tad premature for that, Rudy."

"Bullshit! It's never too early, Colonel. Why don't you get back into doing what you do best?"

"I'm retired. The Air Force won't take me back."

"No, but law enforcement could use a guy of your talents."

"You mean Myrtle Beach cops?"

"No, I'm thinking bigger."

"State Police?"

"Bigger, Colonel."

"Bigger? You're not thinking… Federal?"

"Listen, Colonel. I have a friend in the South Carolina FBI Field Office. His name is Greg Olsen. We went to law school together at the Academy. He's a big shot. I've talked to him about you… he knows your reputation…"

"And he still wants me?"

"Yeah, and he needs someone in this area full time. How about it, Colonel?"

Sitting in his favorite recliner, Lee spent a few moments digesting Rudy's offer. The abnormally cold and wet winter had impacted his golf. Tired of sitting in this lonely house, and feeling like a caged animal, he came to a quick conclusion.

"Okay, Rudy, but there are two stipulations."

"Like what?"

"I work out of my home and I get Tuesdays off."

"Tuesday? Why Tuesday?"

"That's when my golf group plays."

Smiling, Rudy replied, "I believe we can make Tuesday's happen, Colonel. The working at home thing… doubtful."

"I guess I can live with that. What about my rank?"

"I'm thinking, just to give you as much flexibility as possible, you'll be a Special Agent or a Senior Special Agent."

"Meaning?"

"You'll have jurisdiction over local, county, state, and federal investigations."

"That's broad enough," laughed Lee. "When do I start?"

"Olsen wants you to come to Columbia on Friday for the swearing in ceremony."

"What time?"

"One o'clock."

"I'll be there."

"Glad to hear it."

"Thanks, Rudy."

"You're welcome, Colonel."

CHAPTER 4
The Announcement

June 26th, 2018

"Colonel, where are you?"

It was John Hagan, the leader of Hagan's Hackers, calling group member, Ron Lee.

"I'm on number four. Why?"

"Get to seven green as fast as you can, Ron."

"Why? What's up, John?"

"There's a severed head lying next to the pin."

Five minutes later Lee's cart pulled into the parking area next to the seventh green. Billy Jackson, nicknamed AJ, a former South Carolina sheriff deputy, was in the cart next to him. They both left the cart and made their way toward the green. By then, the group playing behind Hagan's group had also reached the green. All ten players stood staring at the head. No one spoke a word. Nor was any thought given to approaching the green.

"No one has been up there, right?" asked Lee with a strong tone of gruffness.

"No," replied Taylor, now recovered from a severe case of the dry heaves. "I thought it was a dead animal when I viewed it through my rangefinder."

"Has someone called 9-1-1?" asked Jackson.

"Yeah, I did," answered Hagan.

Lee made his way up to the green, telling everyone, including Jackson, to stay put.

Not getting any closer than 10 feet, he scanned the area hoping to see any sign of how the head had gotten where it was.

He saw nothing but two balls on the green's surface.

They cut the greens early this morning. It's certain the mower guy would have seen the head. Unless it was the mower himself who did this. No, that would be too easy.

A dew covered green would have indicated the killer's foot-size, but that possibility, on this the fifth day of summer, evaporated with the green bathed in sunlight and already dry as a bone.

Ron surmised, based on the ragged and torn neckline, the killer chopped off the head, rather than slicing or cutting.

He must have used a spade shovel or an axe, thought Lee. *Whoever did this is a butcher. He has issues, that's for sure.*

Glancing toward the fairway, he saw Rick Geslain's group waiting to hit their second shots. Behind them, waiting on the tee, was the Gary Whittaker foursome.

Lee turned to the players standing in the cul-de-sac, saying, "I'm guessing that golf is over for today, men."

"I'll take a cart and go back and let the rest of the groups know what's happening," volunteered John Hagan.

"You'd better let AJ do that, John. Since you were in the first group, the police will want to talk to you."

Turning toward Billy, Lee gave him instructions to tell all trailing groups to return to the clubhouse by reversing direction. "No one else is to proceed this way. It's too damn crowded as it is!"

Moments later a half dozen state police and local sheriff deputies arrived.

The beginning of what was to become the crime of the century in Myrtle Beach, had unfolded.

It would be Ron's first major case since joining the FBI.

The first clue was staring him straight in the face, but he couldn't see it, and he wouldn't, not until the body count had reached a much higher number.

Someone had issued a challenge.

CHAPTER 5
Invisible Message

June 26th, 2018

"Who found it?"

"Those fellas," said Lee, pointing toward the Hagan group, huddled around their golf carts in the parking area.

Asking was Bill Baxter, Captain of the State Police barracks in Myrtle Beach.

"They were the first to arrive. I was about four holes back. They called me when they reached the parking area and saw the head. I was the only one to approach the green."

"So, you're Special Agent Ron Lee of the FBI. I've heard a lot about you. Spent quality time in the Air Force OSI, I hear."

"Please do me the favor of calling me either Colonel or Ron. I hate that Special Agent shit. And yes, I spent thirty-five quality years in OSI."

"Will do, Colonel. You can call me Captain or Bill. Makes no difference."

"Glad to meet you, Captain."

"I suppose you'll have jurisdiction over this matter, Colonel?"

"Wasn't planning on it, Bill."

"Oh, and why's that?"

"As of now it's a simple murder case. Nothing points to federal involvement. Although..."

"Although what?"

"Hopefully, I'm wrong, but I believe we may have a serial killer in our midst. If that's true, the FBI will take over."

"What makes you think it might be a serial killer?"

"You must admit this isn't your typical murder scene. Chopped off head, missing body, and no evident clues. Serial killers love to make statements. Wouldn't you say leaving a severed head on a public golf course is making a statement?"

"As they say in golfing terminology, that's a gimme," replied Baxter.

"You can bet we're gonna see more of this, Captain."

"Have you had previous dealings with serial killers, Colonel?"

"Yes, I've had involvements with serial killers in the past and this has all the indications of a serial killing. I'm guessing that within a week, we'll be investigating something similar, and then we'll know for sure we have a serial killer in our midst."

"Damn! I hope not, Colonel."

"If I'm right, and I believe I am, we can expect more of this up and down the entire Grand Strand."

"How do we catch this guy, Colonel?"

"Decipher the message."

"Message? What message?"

"These guys always have a message and they love telling it to you. They dare you to catch them. He's left us a message, no doubt. We need to decipher what it is he's telling us."

"What do you think he's saying in this situation?"

"I haven't the faintest idea, Bill, but believe me, it's here."

CHAPTER 6
The Feeding

May 5th, 2018–7 Weeks Earlier -

"Hey, Dad, it's nearing 1:00. They will feed them soon. Let's find a good watching spot," the 10-year-old said to his father.

The place was a park attraction in North Myrtle Beach called "Alligator Adventure." It consumed about 15 acres of land adjacent to Barefoot Landing, a popular shopping and restaurant center.

Featuring a wide variety of exotic animals, the park was primarily an alligator and crocodile exhibit. It housed the largest crocodile in captivity, a monster called Utan, that was 18 feet long and weighed over 2000 pounds.

Although there were attractions aplenty, the one most anticipated by the spectators was the feeding of the gators and Utan.

Walkways filled the park, giving patrons easy access for total viewing of all the creatures. One walkway, forbidden to the patrons, was the one that led to a platform from where the zookeepers would feed the crocs and gators. The deck flooring itself was only three feet above the water. A railing, fronted by a wire mesh screen, was another three to four feet above the water. Less than seven feet separated the zookeeper's hands from the grasp of a giant alligator.

Feeding by hand and using long poles, the zookeepers would dangle large chunks of meat, mostly whole chickens, out over the water. The crocs would then use their powerful tails to spring from the water, much like a breaching whale penetrates the surface of the sea, to snatch a meal.

Large groups of onlookers, three to four feet deep, would gather on boardwalks across from the feeding walkway. From there, they would "ooh and ah" as a reptilian beast would occasionally spring upward, four or five feet out of the water, to grab or be tossed a meal. The show, repeated multiple times during the day, lasted about 15 minutes.

The son soaked in the spectacle with boy-like glee, but the father had an epiphany that awoke an old need. A need, hibernating for nine months, had rejuvenated, and was alive once more.

As he watched his son's reaction to the feeding spectacle, his mind was addressing all the things that made him think he was a good husband and father... *never smoked, never drank, never did drugs, studied his bible daily, and made it a point to spend weekends doing things with his family.* Nodding his head, he concurred with his inner self that he was an excellent provider.

There was, however, this one small glitch that made all the rest just a facade... his need to kill.

His method of killing had two acts: the kill and the disposal. The second was the most difficult, but for him, it was also the most satisfying.

Soon he would embrace it once again.

CHAPTER 7
Hello Ernie

May 12th, 2018

Tonight, they would know him as Peter Bailey.

After witnessing the feeding of the reptiles, Pete knew he had found the piece he had been searching for, but before fulfilling his desires, he had work to do.

He watched the movements of all the Alligator Adventure employees from a parking spot that was only a hundred yards from the park's entrance. Closing time was 9:00pm, and he was here to observe the procedures of the nighttime security personnel.

The park was clear of all patrons and employees by 9:30. Only a single security guard remained. It was 9:45 when the guard made his initial round through the park, returning to the office at 10:45.

"So, you take one hour to make your rounds," Peter Bailey said aloud to no one.

He watched as the guard sat at a desk smoking a cigarette and drinking from a thermos. When 11:00 came, the guard once again entered the park and just as before returned to the office in an hour.

"Once again, it took an hour. I'd say you have it down to a science, Mr. Security Guard."

Then something unexpected happened. The guard gathered his thermos and jacket, turned off the office lights, locked the door, and made his way to his vehicle. He entered a red 2008 Chevy Malibu, and after stopping to close and lock the parking lot gate, he drove away. The lot was now void of any vehicles.

Peter Bailey followed.

The guard turned right on Route 17 and proceeded south. Driving to Surfside Beach, he exited 17 onto the renovated portion of Glenns Bay Road. Turning left, he made his way to where the road intersected with Business 17, the main drag in Surfside Beach.

Crossing the intersection, Glenns Bay became Surfside Drive. The first intersection on Surfside Drive was Poplar and on its left corner was the Sundown Sports Pub, a long-established bar known for its neighborhood appeal and solid food. The guard turned left onto Poplar and then parked in one of the half-dozen parking spaces hugging the restaurant's eastern side.

Having noticed an open parking spot in front of the restaurant, Pete made a sharp left turn around the traffic island that separated the right and left lanes of Surfside Drive. Pulling into the open slot, he waited until the guard had entered the Sundown before exiting his car. Walking toward the front entrance, he paused for a moment to peer inside through the large picture window next to the doorway. He estimated there to be a dozen or more patrons. Four older men sat at the U-shaped bar, couples sat at small tables scattered around the room, while others occupied booths. A dozen or more 60-inch televisions populated the bar's walls. A jukebox played country music. Two women, he estimated to be in their late forties, played shuffleboard.

He continued watching as the guard received salutations from every patron.

He must live close by.

Entering, he sat at the bar just 3 stools from where the guard had taken a seat. When asked, he ordered a ginger ale.

The female bartender gave him an unseen sneer.

"Hey, Ernie, how are the crocs doing tonight?" asked a patron sitting a half-dozen seats away. "Anybody get eaten today?"

The query triggered a few scattered snickers from those within earshot of the question.

"None today, Bobby, but if you stop by tomorrow, maybe Utan can have you for a snack."

Again, more scattered laughter.

So, his name is Ernie.

"Excuse me, sir, but do you come here often?"

"Every night after I get off work. Why?"

"Oh, sorry to interrupt, but this is my first time in this establishment and I'm looking for advice on the menu items. What might you recommend?"

"Establishment! Hey, Joyce!" roared Ernie. "Did you know you had yourself an 'establishment'? I thought this place was just a shitty bar! Who knew?"

"Really!" shouted the barmaid. "Well, thank you, stranger. Instead of a shitty bar, I have myself a shitty establishment!"

"Yeah, but what are you gonna do about it, Joyce?" asked a fella at the end of the bar.

"Since it is now an establishment, I guess I'll be classier and wear panties."

"Down with panties! Down with panties!" chanted the man named Bobby.

"Hey, Bobby. Even if you got my panties down, I doubt you could get your little hose up!"

Everyone, including the stranger, were chuckling at the banter between Ernie, Joyce, and Bobby.

"Sorry, fella. We mean no disrespect. We're just having fun. This is a friendly place."

"I'm coming to realize that," answered the smiling stranger.

"To answer your question, all the sandwiches are good, the wings are terrific, but my favorite is the cheeseburger."

"Cheeseburger it is! Thank you… is it Ernie? Is that what I heard the other patrons call you?"

"Patrons!" exclaimed Ernie with a mocking laugh. "Hey, fellas. This guy called us, patrons. Sorry, buddy, but we're more like a bunch of barflies."

30

"Screw you, Ernie," said a man near the end of the bar. "Please refer to me as 'Patron Sam' from now on."

"Back at ya, patron Sam!" hailed Ernie with a smile.

"Yeah, mister. The name's Ernie Cavanaugh. And you're welcome. What's your handle?"

"Pete. Peter Bailey. You must be a local, Ernie, if you come here so often."

"Oh, yeah. I live on Poplar," he said, pointing out the window toward the street. "Live on the corner of 14th Avenue South. Place called Ocean Pines."

"Ocean Pines? Sounds… tropical!"

"Not even close! It's a complex of apartments. There are four Ocean Pines complexes. I live in complex number one."

"I see. Is it one of those places that has units all connected?"

"You got it. Thankfully, I live in an end unit."

"Why, thankfully?"

"I only have one neighbor I can hear through the walls. I'm not talking about bed-banging either. Everyone that lives in those units is long past his or her bed-banging days, if you know what I mean."

"Ah, yes, I know what you mean."

Having gathered what he needed to know about Ernie's residence, Pete changed the subject, asking, "Did I hear you work at Alligator Adventure?"

Ernie, drinking a beer, replied, "Yeah, Pete, you did. I've been a security guard there for the past eight years. Easy job. Work from six to midnight."

"They have to make sure no one would be stupid enough to sneak in there during the night and get eaten. Right?"

"There's that, but the main thing is to make sure all the animals are secure. Not necessarily the gators, but the other exotic animals."

"Sounds like you have a good shift. I sure wouldn't want to work the midnight shift."

"There isn't a midnight shift. Video cameras record the park at night. There are plenty of alarms all around the place. Someone gets into the park and there are bells and whistles going off everywhere. The place would be crawling with cops in minutes."

"I guess you have to be careful when making your rounds, eh?"

"No. When I'm there, the alarms are off. I set them before I lock up."

"Ah, so you have the keys to the henhouse, so to speak."

"Right here," replied Ernie while patting a key valet attached to a right-side belt loop of his jeans. "I have the key to the office, the key to the park, and the key to the parking lot gate."

"They lock the parking lot?"

"Yeah, but there are no surveillance cameras out there. They figure that if someone wanted to break in, they wouldn't be dumb enough to park right outside the building."

"Yeah, that makes sense. You know, Ernie, I was there last week with my son. Great place! I loved the feeding of the crocs. That's an amazing exhibit."

"Ain't it though," replied Ernie. "Those beasts will eat you if given the chance."

I'm counting on it, Ernie.

"How many reptiles inhabit that feeding pond?"

"I don't know the exact number, but I'm guessing between crocs and gators, it's somewhere around 30 to 40."

"Do they feed them every day?"

"Oh yeah, but do you know what? Those damn animals take turns! Ain't that crazy?"

"Amazing is more like it!"

"Here's your cheeseburger, sir. Need any ketchup or mustard?"

"Thank you, ma'am, but I think I'll eat it as is."

"Ernie, your hot turkey sandwich will be out in a minute."

"Thanks, Joyce. No hurry. There's no one waiting for me at home."

"Not married, I take it?"

"I was, but she passed away ten years ago. We retired down here in 2005. Came from Philly. Anyway, they diagnosed her with breast cancer in 2006 and she passed in two years."

"I'm sorry to hear that. Didn't mean to dredge up bad memories."

"That's okay. Anyway, I found this job. Keeps me on my toes and I can still play golf with the guys a couple times a week."

"You were right, Ernie! The cheeseburger was delicious."

"Told ya."

"Well, it has been a pleasure talking with you," said Peter. Then, placing a twenty on the bar, he called to the bartender, "Joyce, I'll be taking care of Ernie's meal."

"Geez, thanks, Pete."

"Maybe I'll see you around again sometime."

"Never can tell," replied Ernie.

Oh, but I can, thought Pete.

CHAPTER 8
The Keys

May 12th, 2018

The man calling himself Pete had two objectives: find out as much as he could about the after-hours security of the animal park, and determine where the guard, he now knew as Ernie, kept the keys to the park entrance and offices.

Ernie provided plenty of information about the park's security and then was kind enough to pinpoint the location of the park's keys.

Like so many guys of his ilk, he had a key valet. His valet only had six keys; two of which were his car keys. Another was his home key, leaving the other three belonging to the alligator park.

Leaving the bar, he travelled south on Poplar looking for 14th Avenue. He came upon it after having travelled all but the final two blocks of Poplar's southern length.

He first came upon, according to the large sign posted in front of the complex, Ocean Pines 2. Pines 2 was on the north side of 14th, with Ocean Pines 1, his destination, on the south side. Passing through the intersection, he saw a similar sign for Ocean Pines 1.

He made an unobserved U-turn at the next intersection and drove back toward the 14th.

Large parking lots, big enough to hold 20 cars or more fronted each of the Ocean Pines properties. Turning right onto 14th Avenue, he drove ever so slowly, while observing the particulars of the Ocean Pines 1 property on his right. First came the parking lot entrance, followed by some nondescript shrubbery that ran parallel to the street side ditch. It ended abruptly a few feet from a small shit-brown colored shed, which housed the electric meters for each Ocean Pines 1 unit. Twenty feet beyond the shed were the condo units. Ernie's unit, number 101, was on the corner, as advertised. A sidewalk made its way from the parking lot, past the shed, and straight to Ernie's door.

Continuing down the street, he again made a U-turn and proceeded back toward Poplar. The parking entrances for both Oceans 1 and 2 were directly across from one another. Pulling into the lot for Ocean Pines 2, and seeing no lights in any unit, he parked in the closest spot he could find. It was, after all, 2:00am, and this was a senior citizens community. Having prepared for the success of his objectives, he extracted a blackjack from the glove box. Next, he lifted a small case off the passenger floor and placed it on the passenger seat.

Leaving the case, he exited the car. Walking through the shadows, he made his way down 14th for about 50 yards before crossing it. A shallow grassy ditch fronted the Ocean Pines 1 property. He traveled along the ditch until reaching the shed housing the electric meters. Crouching against the shed he waited for Ernie's arrival. Twice a vehicle came up 14th toward Poplar. Someone would have surely seen him had he stayed where he was, but having the advanced warning of the cars' headlights, he stepped around the corner of the shed until they had passed.

Twenty minutes elapsed before a vehicle traveled down Poplar from the direction of the Sundown. It slowed as it came to 14th and turned left. A moment later, Ernie's Malibu made a right turn into the Oceans 1 parking lot.

Having eaten his hot turkey sandwich, Ernie, while having two more beers, flirted with Joyce. Realizing his chances with the barkeep bordered on nil, he said good night.

Pete watched as Ernie parked in the first available spot. Seconds later he heard the car door open, then slam shut. A quiet click signaled the locking of the car and then footsteps followed; first across the parking lot, then onto the sidewalk. Seconds later, Ernie, having removed his key valet from his belt loop, was searching for his house key.

No sooner had he located the needed key, then his lights were put out by Pete's blackjack blow to his head. Ernie collapsed on the sidewalk with a muted thud. He would wake up in the Waccamaw Hospital many hours later, with a broken nose, wondering what had happened.

Pocketing the blackjack, Pete scooped up the key valet from the ground where Ernie had dropped it. Returning to his car he opened the case he had left on the seat, revealing a clay-like substance. Taking three keys from Ernie's valet, he made impressions in less than a minute.

Finished, he closed the case, exited the car, and made his way back to where Ernie lay. Placing the keys back in the exact spot where he had found them, he then took Ernie's wallet and pulled out the man's pockets.

"Gotta make it look like a robbery," he whispered. "Geez, Ernie, all you have is seven bucks! This won't even pay for my gas!"

CHAPTER 9
Ernie Talks

May 13th, 2018

"How long has he been awake, nurse?"

"It's been about 20 minutes, officer."

"Can we talk to him?"

"As soon as the doctor clears him, I'm sure you'll be able to speak with him."

Mrs. Sadie Elkins, while walking her dog who had an urgent need to empty his bladder at 3:15am, had found Ernie, his nose broken and bleeding, lying on the sidewalk. Thinking she had found a murder victim, she screamed until a neighbor rushed out to see what was wrong. Someone called the police, and the Surfside Rescue Unit rushed Ernie to the Waccamaw Hospital in Murrells Inlet, just three miles away.

It was 5:30 in the morning when Ernie regained consciousness and after mandatory medical procedures, the attending doctor allowed the police to speak with him.

"Mr. Cavanaugh, I'm Officer Bales and this is my partner, Officer Jenkins. We are from the Surfside Police Department. What can you tell us, sir?"

"What the hell happened to my nose?" screamed Ernie.

"It broke in your fall onto the cement sidewalk," answered Dr. Williams, the attending resident.

"Damn, that hurts!"

"Sir, what do you remember about the attack?" asked Officer Bales for a second time.

"Remember? Hell, I remember nothing! I parked my car and was walking to my door and then… nothing. God, my head hurts."

"Someone slugged you on the back of the head," stated the physician. "I'm afraid you will have a lump for a few days, to go along with some severe headaches you'll be experiencing."

"Why would someone do this?"

"When we found you, sir, your wallet was lying beside you, empty of money, and someone turned your pockets inside out. Do you know how much cash you were carrying?"

Laughing, Ernie replied, "I had less than ten bucks on me. I don't wear a watch and I still have my wedding ring, so all they got was a few measly bucks."

"What time was it when you came home, sir?" asked the officer.

"I left the Sundown restaurant around 2:15, maybe 2:30. I had a sandwich, a few beers, and I shot the shit with some 'patrons'," he laughed, "and then I left."

"Why the emphasis on the word 'patrons,' sir?"

"Oh, there was a guy I was talking with that referred to the guys as patrons. We all laughed."

"Have you ever seen this guy before?"

"No. He stopped by to get something to eat."

"Was he there when you arrived, or did he come in later?"

"Later, but only by a couple of minutes. Why?"

"Who did he talk to, besides you?"

Giving it some thought, Ernie responded, "Now that you mention it, other than giving his order to the bartender, he never spoke a word to anyone else."

"What did you talk about, sir?"

"He asked about the menu. I told him what I liked. Then we talked about work…"

"Your work or his?"

"My work. He never mentioned what he did."

"What else?"

"I told him…"

"Told him, what, sir?"

"I told him where I lived."

"Did he leave before you left?"

"Oh, yeah. He left well before I did. Do you think it was him?"

"We're just trying to get the facts together, sir. It could have been kids. We have a lot of visitors in town now. It is Bike Week."

Each year Myrtle Beach hosts two Bike weeks; Harley Week, which was now in progress, and Bike Fest, a black biker extravaganza that always took place on Memorial Day weekend.

"Anything else you can tell us, Mr. Cavanaugh?"

"Sorry fellas, but no."

"Thank you, sir. We'll keep you posted."

The officers left the room, leaving Ernie, Dr. Williams, and a nurse together.

"I want you to rest for a few hours, sir. I'll look in on you again later. You'll be able to go home this afternoon."

"Thanks, Doc. Do you know where my clothes are?"

"They're hanging in the closet," answered the nurse, pointing at a closed door on the opposite side of the room.

"Could you check to see if my keys are there? I think I had them in my hand when…"

"I'll look."

Opening the closet door, the nurse found a clear plastic bag that had two articles in it, Ernie's keys, and a wallet.

"Yes, sir. They're here."

"Could I have them? I feel more comfortable if they are in my possession."

Handing Ernie his keys, the nurse turned to leave the room, saying, "Get some rest, Mr. Cavanaugh. I'll be back around 9:00."

Ernie hadn't heard a word the nurse had said. He had been examining his keys. An unfamiliar residue covered three of them.

"I must have dropped them into some mud when I got nailed."

His condition being what it was, it didn't occur to Ernie that the residue only affected his work keys.

Moments later the keys slipped from Ernie's hand as he fell asleep.

Had he mentioned to the police officer, he had his keys in his hands when knocked out, it's possible it would have saved lives.

Possible, but not probable.

CHAPTER 10
Replay

The kill had been easy. He once again felt good about himself. It had been 10 months since his last kill and he missed this feeling.

A smile filled his face as he replayed the night in his mind, while driving the body to its disposal location.

****

"What's the name of the restaurant?" asked Sara.

"Angelo's," he answered. "It's on business 17 down near the airport."

"I don't know the area. I came down from Richmond for the week."

"Did you come with anyone?"

"Drove down by myself."

"Where are you staying?"

"There's a place over on 8th North called the Midtown Inn. It's decent and only a block from the boardwalk promenade. Rented it for a week for just $400."

"That's a good deal, for being that close to the beach."

"Yeah, I thought so. Say, I thought the restaurant was only about a mile away?"

She hadn't noticed that they had passed Angelo's about a minute earlier.

"We'll be there soon. I need to stop at my place for a second."

"Your place?"

"Yeah, I need cash. I didn't plan on spending money on a fancy meal for two."

"So, you live close by?"

"Just around the corner," he said as he turned onto Farrow Parkway.

"That sign read Market Common. Is this where you live?"

Ignoring her question, he asked, "Hey, how would you like to see Air Force fighter planes up close?"

"Fighter planes? Not really. Why?"

Turning into Warbird Park, he said, "Market Common used to be an Air Force base some 25 years ago. They have three fighter planes on display in this park."

The entrance led to an oval drive that encircled two of the jet fighters. He drove around the oval until he was behind the two planes. The entire lot was empty as he hoped it would be. They had placed a marker entitled WARRIOR under a mature Bradford Pear tree that was now displaying its summer foliage. Adjacent to the tree were three indented parking spots. Backing into the parking spot nearest the tree, so that its branches hung over his vehicle, he cut the engine and turned off the headlights. Exiting the car, he said, "Let me get your door, Sara."

Circling the car, he stood outside the passenger door without opening it.

Taking a moment, he glanced up and down Farrow Parkway. Two cars were coming. He waited until they passed. Opening the door, he said, "C'mon Sara, let me show you these planes."

She reluctantly stepped from the car, and as he closed the door, he turned her toward him. Moving closer, as if he were taking her in his arms, he instead caressed the left side of her face with his right hand stopping as he reached her jaw. Then with his left hand he grabbed the back of her head and while lifting her jaw with his right, he twisted her head violently to the left, snapping her neck like it was a chicken bone. There would be no dinner for Sara.

Reopening the door, he sat her back in the seat. He had hung an elastic headband around the passenger headrest. Taking it, he pulled it over her head and placed it on her forehead. Her head, held in position by the headband, was now straight. He took her hair and covered the band around her ears. She looked normal. A beautiful girl, wearing a black headband, staring through the windshield, out into the never-ending darkness.

"Good girl, Sara. Now we have a ride ahead of us, so I want you to relax."

Moving to the driver's seat, he started his vehicle, but waited until a car had passed on Farrow before moving. Pulling out of the dark parking spot with his headlights off, he drove toward the exit. Looking both ways and seeing no oncoming headlights, he turned his on and made a right turn onto Farrow.

Driving through the Market Common area, he made his way to Route 17 and turning right, headed north. He drove carefully but not too carefully. His destination was 17 miles away and he could hardly contain his excitement. The sickness had reached another level since Fairmont.

If his dead passenger, knowing what was to come, could scream, she would have.

****

Turning right onto 46th Avenue South, he turned off his headlights and turned into a driveway that ran behind The Kitchen Table Restaurant. A hard-right turn would take him to the restaurant's front parking lot, but that was not his destination.

Straight ahead was the entrance to the rear parking lot where the restaurant's employees parked. A concrete island running parallel with the rear of the restaurant, split the uneven parking area. The left side of the lot could accommodate 20 cars or more. The narrow right side could only accommodate three parking spots. Turning to the right side, he parked in the first available spot. Blocked from sight by some huge scraggly bushes and a big green dumpster, his car was invisible to anyone who might enter.

"We have privacy back here, wouldn't you agree, Sara?" he said with a sick giggle.

It was dark and void of disturbances. There was no one to either see or hear. The restaurant, only ten yards away, had closed hours ago.

After popping the trunk open, he removed heavy black plastic sheeting he had folded. It opened into an 8x8 square which he spread out on the ground. Opening the front door on the passenger side, he lifted Sara out of the vehicle, and after placing her on the plastic sheeting, removed all her clothing. Returning to the car, he opened the rear passenger door and removed a plastic bag that contained a complete set of hospital scrubs, including a shower cap. Stepping out of his shoes, he slipped into a pair of shoe covers. After donning the scrubs, and putting on a pair of rubber gloves, he announced, "I'm ready, Sara. Chop, chop."

Grabbing an axe from the trunk, he went to work. The head was first.

Thirty minutes later he finished. He placed the head in a cooler of ice he had stored in the back seat. Two 33-quart garbage bags would suffice in holding the parts of her body. He placed the arms and legs in one bag and the chopped-up portion of her torso in the other. Using zip ties so they would not leak, he placed the bags in the car's trunk. Gathering her clothes, he stuffed them, along with the hospital garb he had worn for the occasion, into another bag. Showing no signs of being rushed, he strolled to the dumpster and disposed of the bag.

Returning to his car, he carefully folded the four corners of the now bloody plastic sheeting. After tying the four corners together with a zip tie, he carried it to the dumpster for disposal.

Taking one final look around and seeing that all looked okay, he entered his vehicle. His next destination was directly across the street from the restaurant.

Leaving his headlights off until he was sure there were no oncoming cars, he exited left from the parking lot onto 46th and drove to the Route 17 intersection. The light was red.

Checking his watch, he saw that it was twenty minutes past midnight.

"Perfect."

The light turned, and he scooted through the intersection to the other side where the road's name became Barefoot Resort Bridge Road.

As his car crept past the Alligator Adventure building, he gave it a thorough going over to verify that Ernie had left the premises. Seeing all was quiet, he stopped at the parking lot entrance, exited the car, and hurriedly opened the gate with one of the three keys he had made. Driving into the lot, he again exited the car to close the gate, but he didn't lock it. After parking in the darkest spot he could find, he exited the car.

"So far, so good," he whispered.

Opening the trunk, he grabbed the two 33-gallon garbage bags holding the decapitated body of a girl named Sara.

Leaving the bags near the park entrance gate, he made his way to the office where he shut down the surveillance cameras and alarms.

Rushing back to the gate, he unlocked it and picking up the two bags, entered the park, closing the gate behind him. Making his way to the feeding dock, he set the two bags down, and peering over the railings, stared into the dark water just seven feet below. Seeing no indications of any reptilian beasts, he recalled how the zookeeper had banged on her bucket to call the animals to the feeding site. He had no bucket, but he had rubber gloves. After slipping them on, he slapped his hands together a half-dozen times. He heard the stirrings; they were here.

Reaching into one bag, he extracted Sara's left arm.

Maybe I should have chopped this in half, he thought to himself. *Next time for sure.*

Imitating the zookeepers' procedure of feeding the gators with chickens, he held the arm out over the water and jiggled it.

Nothing.

No stirrings.

His eyes searched the dark waters as he held the arm out over the feeding pond.

Vroom!

Without warning, the water erupted and a gator he swore was the size of a truck, exploded out of the water with jaws wide open. Using the toes of its front feet, it clung to a wire-mesh that covered the lower portion of the railing. Once his shock had dissipated, he dropped the arm into the beast's jaws, then watched as the animal fell back into the water and disappeared.

He stood there, shaking. Cold chills ran up his back and he quivered. Moments later, he laughed with great fervor. This was the most thrilling thing he had ever done, and he had done many unspeakable things. He was giggling like a kid on Christmas morning. *What a rush*!

Grabbing a leg, he looked down to see movement in the darkened waters. He held out the leg and two gators rose from the water as one. Frightened by the unexpected encounter, he jumped back while dropping the leg. He didn't know if either animal had caught it or if it fell into the water. Looking over the railing, he saw the water stirring violently, and he assumed the thrashing animals had missed and were scrambling to see who would get it first. He giggled again.

Laughing as each piece of Sara disappeared into the jaws of these prehistoric monsters, he realized that he hadn't had this much fun since Terre Haute where he dissolved the bodies with acid.

He took thirty minutes to dispose of the butchered corpse. All that remained was Sara's head, on ice in the cooler.

"I'll be taking care of the head first thing in the morning," he said to no one.

His plan was to arrive at the Tradition golf course early and park on Tradition Club Drive right behind the 7th green. Although he wouldn't be able to see the mower, he would hear it. Once the mower moved on, he'd take the head and place it at the foot of the pin.

Although there was no one to hear, he felt it necessary to continue talking.

"Then I'll grab breakfast before teeing it up. Damn, I'd sure like to be there when the first group arrives. I'll bet they will shit their pants!"

Grabbing the two empty bags, he left the park, locking the gate behind him. Returning to the office, he turned on the surveillance equipment. After locking the office door, he returned to his car and left the parking lot. Congratulating himself on a job well done, he locked the entrance gate and drove his car across the street.

Returning to the dumpster behind The Kitchen Table restaurant, he disposed of the two garbage bags and then drove straight home.

It was 1:35 when he climbed into bed. His wife, awakened by his entrance, mumbled, "Working late, aren't you?"

"Yeah, you might say, I was really up to my ass in alligators."

CHAPTER 11
Murder Info

June 27th, 2018

The FBI granted Ron's request of having Tuesdays as a day off, but they were emphatic about his working out of the FBI's office on 38th Avenue. Since his residence in Market Common was only a 15-minute drive away, Ron offered no resistance.

Ron arrived at the office at 7:30. It was always quiet early in the morning. It gave him a chance to read the Sun News, Myrtle Beach's only paper, and to have a few moments of quiet time to himself. He would scan the news and sports sections, and then, while drinking a second cup of coffee, he'd work on the Jumble and the Sudoku puzzles found on the comic page.

It was Wednesday, the morning after the discovery of the head at the Tradition Golf Club.

"Morning, Ron."

It was Tim Pond, Ron's newest partner.

"How are you doing, Tim?"

Tim was a 20-year veteran of the Bureau and his career was on a treadmill to nowhere. Stationed in field offices across the country, none of which had been criminal hot spots, his resume lacked glamorous cases. The closest thing to a highlight happened eight years earlier when he brought down a small-time drug lord's operation in Pensacola, Florida. Since then, he has been biding his time till retirement. He had five years to go.

Although Tim's resume was nowhere close to that of Ron's, they had become best of friends where personal verbal exchanges became comedic moments. It made for a perfect partnership.

"I'm bored. How about you?"

"I doubt we'll be bored much longer, Tim."

"Oh, and what makes you think boredom will no longer be an issue?"

"I caught a murder yesterday."

"On your day off?"

"Yeah, ain't that a kick in the ass."

"I heard they found a head on a golf course."

"That's the one. A foursome, about five groups ahead of my group, found it."

"Our group found the head!" gasped Tim.

Tim was also a member of the Hagan golfing group, but, due to a dental appointment, didn't play on Tuesday.

"Yep. The first group, Taylor, Hagan, Bendele, and Danny Z found the head on the 7th hole."

"So, what's it going to mean to us?"

"I think it's just the beginning, Tim. This sicko has been doing this for a long time."

"Where did you come up with that hypothesis?"

"Just the way someone had set it up. Take, for example, leaving someone's head you just chopped off at the foot of a pin. If it were one of your everyday type killers, they would have tossed it into the woods or a trash bin. No, this guy is making a statement and I'm betting he has a lot more to say."

"So, you think there is a serial killer in town?"

"I do. He has announced his presence with this kill. When another head shows up, we will take over the investigation."

"When? Not, if?"

"Oh, there's no doubt in my mind this is just the first. Question is, can we stop him before we have a panic on our hands?"

"Well, chasing a serial killer beats sitting around this office scratching my ass all day."

"That's something I've wanted to talk to you about," said Ron with a shit-eating grin.

"Screw you, old timer."

The phone rang.

"FBI. Special Agent Lee speaking."

"Ron, this is Captain Bill Baxter."

"Hey, how are you doing, Bill?"

"Shitty, since you asked."

"Now why's that?"

"We have had no chance to ID this head."

"No one has filed a missing person's report?"

"None. I spoke with the Myrtle Beach police. They have had no reports of a missing woman."

"Well, it's only Wednesday, Bill. Maybe something will come in before the turnover."

During the summer, a reported quarter million people would come into town each Saturday while the previous quarter million were leaving. They called it "the turnover." Locals had other names, most unprintable, for the two-way exodus.

"Yeah, if we don't get an ID by Friday, then anyone who may have seen something will be in the wind."

"Most likely you're right, Bill."

"I have a few things of note, Ron."

"What might they be?"

"An autopsy of the blood found traces of gin."

"Okay, so she had been drinking. The question is, where? There's only about 10,000 bars in town. What's the second thing?"

"She had a sunburn on the back of her neck."

"Wow! How unique! There can't be more than another quarter-million new arrivals just like that. Not much to go on there, Bill. Anything else?"

"This may sound crazy, Ron, but my lab guy says the neck showed frostbite. Severe frostbite."

"Frostbite? Did your man say how long skin would need exposure to get frostbite?"

"It depended on how cold the environment was."

"Can a dead person get frostbite?"

"According to my man, yes."

"Does your man think she died of exposure?"

"He doesn't have enough information to make that call, Ron. Are you thinking he kept her in a freezer?"

"I'm not sure what I'm thinking. He may just have kept the head on ice after he killed her. No disrespect toward your guy, Bill, but would you send the head to our lab in Columbia?"

"I'm sure their means to analyze are much better than ours, Ron. I'm sure our man won't feel disrespected."

"Great. Tell him I said he did a great job."

"Will do."

Hanging up the phone, Ron turned to Tim, saying, "Would you like to get a head start on this investigation?"

"Can we? It's not even a federal case."

"I have jurisdiction over any case I feel warrants our attention. My intuition tells me that this case will warrant our attention, real soon."

"Okay, what do you want to do?"

"I've been thinking about when he placed the head on the green."

"What are your thoughts?"

"There's little doubt he put it there after they had cut the green that morning, which means he had to be there watching the mowing."

"I'll buy into that, Ron, but he wouldn't be standing around holding a severed head."

"No, but he could have been sitting in his car. Let's drive to Tradition. Maybe someone saw a car parked where it shouldn't have been."

"Great idea!"

"Why are you so damn excited about driving down there?"

"I haven't had breakfast," explained Tim, "and the Applewood Pancake House is right there next to the Willbrook entrance."

CHAPTER 12
Millie Strange

June 27, 2018

"Did anyone talk to the guy who mowed the green, Ron?"

"Yeah, the local cops found him mowing on the backside. He said he mowed the seventh green around 6:15. Claims he saw nothing unusual."

"Sounds like he lied."

"Now, Tim, why would you say that?"

"I don't believe 6:15am even exists."

"You're an asshole," Lee said with a grin.

As they turned onto Willbrook Boulevard, Pond shouted, "Hey, Ron, you passed the damn pancake house!"

"To hell with the pancake house," snorted Lee. "Do I look like I need a stack of pancakes?"

"You! What about me?"

"Pancakes make you stupid, Tim. I think you've had your quota."

"Screw you! You're a big dick."

Smiling, Lee replied, "I'll stop for lunch after we check out some homes around the seventh hole. Maybe someone saw something."

"I wanted pancakes."

"Have pancakes for lunch."

"It's not the same. Pancakes are for breakfast, dumbass."

"There's the seventh tee box. There's a road right behind the green. I'm guessing that's where he parked while watching the green being cut."

Turning left onto Deacon Drive, Lee drove about 50 yards passing a faux security structure that had eye appeal but served no useful purpose. After passing the structure, the road split with Deacon continuing to the right and

Tradition Club Drive veering to the left. Ron went left for about a hundred yards and then did a U-turn and parked in front of a sign that read CART CROSSING.

The cart path from the seventh green to the eighth tee box crossed Tradition Club Road at this spot.

"I'll bet you lunch, this is where he parked."

"No bet," Tim said, who from his passenger seat caught glimpses of the green through the foliage to his right.

Remarkably, Ron's parking spot was a mere five feet from where the killer had parked on Tuesday morning.

Leaving the car, Ron directed Tim to interrogate the inhabitants of the homes on Deacon Drive while he did the same on Tradition Club Drive.

Looking down Tradition Club Drive, Tim saw only two homes that would be in view of their parking spot. Conversely, there were at least nine such homes on Deacon.

"Equal distribution, apparently, is not part of your management style, Ron."

Viewing his workload, Ron nodded in agreement.

"Rank has its privileges, Tim-o-thy."

Tim started toward his assignment, but not before flashing the senior agent the bird.

While smiling at Tim's gesture, Ron proceeded toward the two homes he had assigned to himself. Millie Strange lived in one of those homes.

Going from house to house, they asked if anyone had seen a car parked where their car now sat.

"What time would that have been?" asked most inhabitants.

"I'd say between 6:00 and 6:30 in the morning."

"Who the hell gets up at 6:00 in the morning?" was the normal reply - except for that of Millie Strange.

"Well, Mr. Lee," voiced Millie, "I can tell you I saw a car parked there on Tuesday morning. I cannot, however, tell you the make of the car."

Millie Strange may have been a frail 80-year-old widow who couldn't have been a centimeter over five-foot tall, but her mind and eyes were still sharp. Although it was a warm summer morning, she wore a winter jacket with its hood up over her head and gloves.

"Tessie, that's my little beagle, and I like to walk early in the morning. I walk out my backyard and through my friend Meg's backyard over on Deacon. I make my way up Deacon and then come back down Tradition to my house. It only takes about 15 minutes. I was on my way back to the house when I passed this dark colored four-door car sitting there. It looked new, but I can't say it was for sure. There was a man sitting in the driver's seat, but he turned his head away. I couldn't see his face. He appeared to be a big, tall man."

"What makes you say that, ma'am?"

"His shoulders were well above the window rest."

"You didn't see him get out of his car, then?"

"Can't say I did, Mr. Lee. Tessie likes to get back for her breakfast as soon as possible."

"Tell me, ma'am. Could you hear one of the golf course mowers when you saw the car?"

"Oh, yes. I could definitely hear a mower on the green that's on the other side of the trees."

"Anything else you can recall, Mrs. Strange?"

"Please call me Millie."

Crossing her arms, Lee watched as the woman appeared to be struggling with her memory. Then, with an unexpected flourish, she raised her right hand with her gloved index finger pointing skyward, saying, "There is one other thing, Mr. Lee, but I doubt it means all that much."

"What's that, Millie?"

"He had a white golfer's hat. I could see the brim. It was one of those... oh, what's the name they give that hat... kinda floppy with a chin string..."

"An Aussie hat?"

"Yes, that's it! I knew I'd remember."

"Ahh, yes, ma'am. You did great."

Handing her a card, he asked if she remembered any other details, regardless of how insignificant they may appear, to call him immediately.

"I'll do that, Mr. Lee. I enjoyed our talk, sir."

"I took pleasure in the experience, Millie."

Meeting back at the car, Tim asked if he had any luck.

"If we weed out all the guys in Myrtle Beach who drive a dark colored 4-door sedan and who wear a white Aussie hat, our killer will be in that pile."

"Well, okay then! This case is just about cracked. C'mon, Ron, you owe me lunch."

"Pancakes?"

"No, asshole. Pancakes are for breakfast. That ship has sailed."

CHAPTER 13
The Half Shell

July 2, 2018

"I'll have a dozen of the Buffalo shrimp."

"What would you like to drink with that?" asked Chelsea, the barmaid on duty during the six to midnight shift.

"I'll have a ginger ale."

"Comin' right up, mister."

He was on the hunt again. This was his third visit to this out-of-the-way bar in Murrells Inlet. Each visit required a different look. Tonight, he wore jeans with a black T-shirt and a corduroy jacket. A baseball cap covered a gray wig that matched a fake mustache.

The Half Shell, a modest hole-in-the-wall bar, used to be a secret, but no more. Not only were the drinks cheap, but the food was also good. The crowd was older but not old. The women who came here were good-time girls who didn't stop by for the food or the drinks. Divorced, many were, to paraphrase a Frank Sinatra song, looking for a "stranger for the night."

He planned on leaving with a good-time girl.

Five minutes later, she walked through the door.

Having seen her on two previous visits, he had calculated she was in her forties. A brunette with brown eyes, she had a rough edge, but still had charisma. Although she wasn't tall, weight was not a problem, unless one was to be critical of a slight midriff bulge.

Tonight, she had on a pair of tight jeans and a sleeveless red blouse that had trouble holding her ample breasts in place.

He decided that she would be his second kill.

As she walked by, he said, "Buy you a drink, ma'am?"

She stopped and turned his way.

"You must have been reading my mind."

"How's that?"

"You're the first thing I saw when I came through the door and I know you gave me the once over twice routine. Ain't that right?"

"You got me. But then again, what man wouldn't?"

"Boy, you are a charmer."

"I take it then I can buy you a drink?"

"I'll have a Jack and ginger."

"Chelsea! A Jack and ginger for... sorry, you haven't told me your name."

"Laura."

"... for Laura."

"And yours?"

"It's John."

"Hello, John. Would you like to get a table where we can talk?"

"It's true!"

"What's that, John?"

"Great minds think alike. We must have a mental connection going here."

"You think? I have thoughts going through my head, John. Any chance they're coming through to you?"

"Oh, yes, darlin,' I believe they are!"

"I believe you have a hunger, John, which needs fillin'."

"Appetites do need filling. Don't you agree?"

"You think I'm the woman who can fulfill a guy's hunger?"

"Laura, I think you're the appetizer, the main course, and the dessert all wrapped into one."

"What a crock, but I like it."

Croc? Well, if you like croc, then I'm your man, thought the man calling himself John.

CHAPTER 14
Satisfying Hungers

July 2, 2018

"So, John, tell me about yourself."

Having left the Half Shell around 10:30 after eating and drinking for over 3 hours, they were now in John's car driving north on Route 17.

"What would you like to know, Laura?"

"Where are you from originally? What is your line of work? Where do you live? Those would all be good starting points."

"Let's see… I've been to a lot of places, but I grew up in Sacramento, California. I teach at Coastal Carolina."

"Oh, what is it you teach?"

"Anatomy."

"Mmm, so you know the human body," she said while giving him a large grin that didn't hide her meaning.

"Yes, I know it well and I'm hoping to know yours in ways you can't even imagine."

"Oh, I don't know. I can imagine a lot of things."

"Look, I live in Market Commons. Would you like to see my place?"

"I had been wondering when you'd get around to asking. I'd love to see your place."

"Hey, have you ever been over to Market Commons to see the warplanes in Warbird Park?"

"I've driven past them a few times, but I never stopped to see them. Why?"

"Being ex-Air Force, I find them fascinating. Call me sentimental. I'd love to show them to you! Would you like to drive over and look at them before we head to my place?"

Reaching across the seat, she put her hand on his knee and quickly moved up his leg until contacting something unexpectedly flaccid.

"I thought you'd be more interested in showing me your cockpit, but apparently your joystick doesn't appear to be responding."

"Oh, no! Believe me, it works! Give me some time and I'll be doing things with your body you have never experienced. I guarantee it."

"Now that's what I like to hear. Okay, let's go see these planes and then let's get to your apartment. I have a hunger badly in need of being fed."

"I'm sure we'll satisfy many hungers tonight, Laura. Many hungers."

****

The drive from Alligator Adventure to Indian Wells took 40 minutes. Even though it was 1:15 in the morning, the number of tourists in town for the July 4th week, had the roads crowded even at this late hour.

Approaching the Surfside Beach and Garden City area, he saw that traffic had become negligible.

This is the area where families stay on vacation, he thought. *They're all pooped from being on the beaches all day. Almost all will be in bed by this time.*

As he made his way down Route 17, he passed his destination on his left. He had to stop at the light for the Garden City Connector and when he did, a Sheriff's cruiser turned left off the Connector and drove south on 17.

"I hope he didn't take notice of my car," he said aloud.

The light changed, and he turned left onto Connector Road. Having no cars trailing nor any approaching, he made a quick left turn onto what was not a road but a driveway that led to two senior care centers. The oldest of which, NHC Healthcare, was at the driveway's termination point.

While making the turn, he switched off the vehicle's headlights. Driving slowly through the pitch darkness, he reached the driveway's end, parked, and cut off the vehicle's engine. He saw a light in the lobby of the Healthcare facility but saw no activity.

Reaching for a knob on his dashboard, he turned off the interior lights before exiting his door.

Opening the back door, he grabbed the cooler that had been resting on the floor behind the driver's seat.

Closing the door, he stood silently in the dark staring at his destination approximately 100 yards away. It was the 15th green on the Indian Wells Golf Course. Most of that yardage was in the open. The short, but treacherous, journey included crossing a small bridge, under which the overflow from the large pond fronting the 15th hole passed. Having crossed the bridge, only a climb up a steep embankment remained to reach the green. During the daytime, the entire green was viewable from the road, but that wouldn't be the case in the darkness. The lack of a moon was a factor in his favor.

Standing in the trees for a moment, he watched the traffic on Route 17. It was sporadic. Seeing the nearest southbound car was at least a mile away, he made his move. Sprinting through the trees, he covered some grassy ground until he reached the cart path near the tee box of the 16th hole. Making his way back along the cart path, he crossed the ten-foot bridge and found himself behind the 15th green.

His heart raced as the car that had been a mile away forty seconds ago, rapidly passed. Remaining still, until assured no other cars would pass, he then sprinted up the embankment and onto the green. His eyes, although adjusted to the dark, still had trouble finding the pin. Then he saw it. It was in the lower left corner.

Hmm, he thought, *I don't recall ever playing this course when the pin was in that position.*

Checking the road once again, he could see oncoming headlights in both directions. Seeing that the front of the green sloped dramatically away from the road, he raced toward it. Reaching the sloped area, he flattened himself on the ground where he remained until all vehicles had passed.

Rising from his prone position, he checked the condos to his right. A large stand of pines stood between the green and the condos, narrowing the chances of being seen in his favor. After thoroughly scrutinizing the condos and not seeing a single light, he assumed that all inhabitants were in bed. It was a safe assumption given it was approaching 2:00am.

Feeling safe, he opened the cooler, reached into it, grabbed a hank of hair, and extracted the head. It was still warm. The cooler he had filled with ice ten hours earlier now contained an inch of cool water. He hadn't expected it would take almost six hours to woo a victim to the Air Park.

Turning the head so her eyes, still open, were looking at his, he said, "Didn't I tell you, Laura, that you would satisfy many appetites tonight? I've never seen so many hungry alligators, but then again, this was only my second time."

Carefully, he placed her head on the ground facing west.

"You can watch the cars go by, Laura."

CHAPTER 15
Ichabod

As they sat on the 11th tee box at Arcadian Shores, waiting for the par 3 green to clear, they saw to their right a course ranger frantically waving. He was heading their way on the cart path that encircled the pond between the 10th green and the 11th tee box.

Moments later, as he neared their location, he called out, "Agent Lee! You're needed!"

"Son-of-a-bitch! That asshole has killed again!"

"What the hell makes you think that, Ron?" asked Gary Whittaker, Ron's cart partner.

"Intuition, Gary. Believe me when I tell you that this guy has only scratched the surface."

The ranger, pulling alongside their cart, asked, "Are you Special Agent Ron Lee?"

"I am." Then, without waiting for the ranger to say anything, he asked, "What course?"

"Indian Wells, sir. Agent Pond called. He said you'd know why."

"Can you take me back to the clubhouse?"

"Hop on, sir. Don't forget your clubs."

"This is two weeks in a row now I've missed golf. If this bastard keeps killing, I'd like him to pick a different day of the week."

"Maybe he's tied up with work the rest of the week, Ron. Monday might be his off day."

"Yeah, Gary, maybe so. I'll see you next week."

"Good luck, amigo," hailed Whittaker as Lee rode off with the ranger.

****

"How many holes did you play before I called?"

"One, dammit! We started on hole ten. We were sitting on the 11th tee when I saw the ranger hightailing it my way. I knew immediately, Tim. I knew it!"

They were in an Indian Wells provided golf cart, heading toward the crime scene.

"Sorry about that, Ron."

"Okay, where's the head?"

"It's out on the 15th green."

"Fifteen! That's the one right out by Route 17."

"Yeah, that's the one. Some guy walking his dog around 6:00 saw something he thought strange and called the local police. They were on a shift change so they called the State Troopers. By the time the troopers arrived, the guy mowing greens was there. The troopers said it rather shook him up. Captain Baxter called our office. I had just walked in and took the call."

"You mean you were on time for a change?"

"Yeah, I was just 15 minutes late."

"You said a guy reported the head?"

"Not exactly, Ron. He reported something strange."

"Where was he when he saw this 'strange thing'?"

"In the trees next to those condos. That's where he lives."

"How could he see something lying at the bottom of a flagstick from way over there?"

"Well, I can't say how he did, Ron, but the fact remains he saw something."

"How far from those trees to that green, Tim? A hundred yards?"

"I'd say 75 yards."

"Okay, 75 then. Do you think you could spot a head at the bottom of a flagstick from 75 yards away?"

"Look for yourself. There's the green. We're about 75 yards away, maybe even further."

Tim had stopped at the tee box of the 16th hole. Visible, across an expanse of water some 60 yards wide, was the 15th green and on it, a head, lying at the base of the flagstick, facing route 17.

A moment later they had pulled up behind the green and made their way to the pin.

"Any clue who she is?"

"None, sir," answered a state trooper.

"Didn't think so," muttered Lee.

It wasn't until the previous day they uncovered the identity of Sara Carson. They only discovered it after the manager of her hotel complained about her car being in his parking lot two days after she was to have checked out of her room.

When told, Lee had replied, "Yeah, unfortunately for her, she permanently checked out on Tuesday."

"This one looks older, Ron."

"Yeah, I think you're right, Tim."

"I'm guessing he's nondiscerning about age."

"Is that what you're thinking, Tim?"

"Yeah. What are your thoughts?"

"First, it's undiscerning."

"What is?"

"You said nondiscerning. It's undiscerning."

"Yeah, yeah. Tomato, potato. Who gives a shit? You knew what I meant."

"Maybe you were thinking of non-discriminating."

"Maybe I non-wasn't."

That drew a grin from Ron.

"How do you think he placed the head here without being seen?"

"Now that's the $64 question, Timothy."

"I hate being called Timothy."

"I know."

This time Pond physically gave him the middle-finger.

"You're welcome," snickered Ron. "Do you have any thoughts on how he got the head out here?"

"Well, he had four choices."

"Do tell."

"The least likely is that he came up the 15th fairway. He would have too much ground to cover, and if caught, his retreat through numerous fairways would have been difficult. Besides, I'm thinking he had to park in the immediate vicinity."

"I agree with everything you said, Tim. That's the least likely choice, and it's not likely at all. What's your second scenario?"

"It's also a slim possibility, but he could have parked out there on 17, which isn't over 50 yards away, then ran up here to do his dirty work."

"Negatory, Tim-o-thy! It is a definite no to parking the car on the main road. That would require jumping a ditch filled with water. Uh-uh. Ain't no way."

"Cut out the Tim-o-thy crap, Ronald."

"You can call me Ronald. I like Ronald. My mom named me Ronald. What? You don't like your mom?"

"Screw you, asshole."

"Okay, now you're getting somewhere. What's behind door number three, Timmy?"

"You're pissing me off, Ronnie."

"Never mind that. Give me door number three."

"He parked in the condo parking lot, then made his way up here."

"Hmm, a good possibility, but also a good chance he could have an unexpected encounter with a resident."

"Also, my thinking."

"Okay, so what's our fourth option?"

"Over there," said Tim, pointing to the left. "That's the parking lot for the Alzheimer's healthcare facility."

"Hmm, I wonder if they ever forget where they parked."

"That was sick, Ron," said Tim with a big grin.

"Sorta like one of your jokes, heh?"

"Well, yeah, it has a resemblance. Anyway, the driveway entrance is off the Garden City Connector and it dead ends right there at that tree line. He parks his car. Then he walks through those trees, past the next tee box, down the cart path, over that little bridge, up onto the green, and places the head at the base of the flagstick."

"I like that option, Tim. All he had to worry about were the cars passing on 17, and since he did this in the dead of night, traffic is near nonexistent."

"Might that be inexistent?"

"No chance, Shakespeare. Stick with nonexistent."

"You're just an Oxford-fucking dictionary, aren't you?"

"Something like that."

"What makes you think he did this in the early hours, Ron?"

"The ragged edges of her neck still look supple. I'm betting she died an hour either way of midnight. Let's take a walk over to the healthcare center."

Minutes later, they were standing just a few yards from where "John," holding a cooler containing a severed head, had milled about just a few short hours earlier.

"Tim, see if they have any surveillance cameras. I see none but…"

While Tim went inside to check on surveillance, Ron poked about in the tree line. Trying to play the part of the killer, he positioned himself in a spot to give him the best chance to make good on his delivery.

Talking aloud to himself, he began, "The first thing he'd be worried about is the traffic on 17. He would have to be in a place where he could see headlights coming from either direction."

Lee moved about the pines until he found the perfect spot. It was, in fact, exactly where the killer had stood. Being careful not to disturb anything, Lee checked every inch of ground in a twenty-foot radius but found nothing.

"Where did you park your car, Ichabod?"

Lee, without thinking, had given the killer a nickname. A name synonymous with the headless horseman, from "The Legend of Sleepy Hollow."

Walking back toward the parking lot, Lee stayed amongst the trees while searching the pine straw.

The straw, however, gave up no clues.

"No surveillance, Ron," reported Tim.

"Nothing here, either. This guy is careful."

"He'll make a mistake, Ron. They always do."

"Yeah, but I have a feeling this guy has been doing this for a long time."

"If so, how come we haven't heard of him?"

"This guy is cunning, Tim. I'm thinking his M.O. changes as he moves around the country."

"But no one does that."

"Yeah, you're right, Tim, and that's why they get caught."

CHAPTER 16
Autopsy

July 3, 2018, 7:30pm

"What do you have for us, Charlie?"

They sent the woman's head to the FBI labs in Columbia. Ron and Tim were talking, via Skype, with Charlie Spencer, the FBI's chief forensic man in the state of South Carolina.

"I believe she was in her late forties, guys."

"How did you come up with that?"

"Her teeth."

"What about her teeth?"

"They're worn down from grinding over the years. Her tongue also has wear and tear also associated with a forty-something person."

"How was she killed, Charlie?"

"Broken neck. Just like the other girl."

"Anything else?"

"Well, she didn't die hungry. It's either that or she didn't brush her teeth much, but I'm going with the first diagnosis."

"What the hell does that mean?" asked Tim.

"Found plenty of food stuck in her teeth."

"Oh? What kind of food?"

"Chicken. Most definitely chicken wings."

"Wow, Charlie! You have narrowed it down to about a thousand restaurants," remarked Ron.

"She also had shrimp…"

"Shrimp and wings! Thanks to Charlie's findings, Tim, we're on the verge of solving this case!"

"Up yours, Ron."

"Just kidding, Charlie. What else do you have?"

"She ate mussels and cheese bread."

"Sounds like she was a fan of the buffet," snickered Tim. "Find any mac and cheese?"

"What about the other girl, Charlie? Any food?"

"Nope. She died hungry. Either that or she flossed just before he broke her neck."

"What about makeup, Charlie? Anything there?"

"She didn't wear much makeup, Ron. A light shade of red lipstick and some eye makeup. Her earrings were nothing special. Something you could get at a Dollar General. Nothing out of the ordinary."

"She was ordinary, then."

"What do you mean, Ron?"

"Older gal, ordinary makeup, cheap earrings, eats a lot of finger foods. Likely the gal you wouldn't run into in one of our finer pickup joints. She most likely hung around neighborhood bars, where they drink lots of beer, play country music, scratch their balls, and spit on the floors."

"How many of those in Myrtle Beach, Ron?" asked Charlie.

"I don't know. A million, maybe?"

"Well, that should keep you busy for a day or two."

"Yeah, it undoubtedly will. Say, Charlie, could you make her look presentable, and take a picture, without the neck carnage showing, and send it over?"

"No problem, Ron. You want it with her eyes open or closed?"

"How about one of each?"

"I'll have them your way in about two hours."

"That will be fine, Charlie."

Lee was about to hang up when he said, "Charlie! Wait!"

"Yeah, Ron? What is it?"

"One more question. When I saw her neck, it still appeared to be supple. Did you find any signs of frostbite like there was on the previous girl?"

"No. But her head was definitely on ice. But not long enough for frostbite."

"How long, possibly?"

"I'd say two, possibly three hours."

"Hmm, that's strange but then again... maybe not. Okay, Charlie, thanks. I'll be waiting for those snapshots."

After hanging up, Ron turned to Tim, asking, "Know any bars where they spit on the floor and eat chicken wings."

"Can you narrow it down for me, partner?"

"The girls wear cheap earrings."

"A little more information, please."

"They listen to country music, drink beer, and the girls get their asses pinched a lot."

"You should know them, Ron. I'm told that's where your mama hung out."

"Hey, wait a minute there, Tim-o-thy. My mama's ass is off limits."

"I hear tell back in the old days that wasn't the case," grinned Tim. "Besides, where do you think I picked up my wife?"

CHAPTER 17
Cornhole

July 4, 2018

"Sorry you had to miss golf yesterday, Ron. I heard you had another murder on a golf course?"

A bunch of the Tuesday golfing group had gotten together at Rick Geslain's house for a 4th of July cookout.

Ron, awaiting his turn to get into a cornhole game, had been sitting in the shade enjoying a beer and a dog, when Steve Morris, one of the more intrusive members of the group, approached.

"No, Stevie, it wasn't a murder on a golf course. That's just where some evidence made itself known."

"Evidence? You mean her head?"

"Yes, I mean her head."

They had kept the news media in limbo as to the exact specifics of the crimes. They only told them they had found two decapitated women.

"Surely you can divulge something more than what we see on tv or read in the newspaper."

"Surely, I can't."

"Have you located their bodies?"

"Not at liberty to say, Stevie."

"How were they killed?"

"Can't say, Stevie."

"What leads do you have? Are there suspects?"

"That information is not for sale, Stevie."

"Why not? C'mon, Ron, just give me a tidbit."

"I can't give out that kind of info. I wouldn't even tell my wife, if she were still alive, so I'm obviously not telling you."

"You don't think I'm the killer. Do you?"

"Hey, now there's a thought. Do you have an alibi for the nights of June 25th and July 2nd?"

"I was with my wife both nights. Speaking of whom, would you like to see pictures of the fish she caught?"

"Ah, no. Say, Steve, are you familiar with that commercial where they say, 'What's in your wallet'?"

"Yeah, I know it. Why?"

"Someone asked me that once and do you know how I replied?"

"How?"

"I said, 'a naked picture of your wife'!"

"My wife? You'd said you had a naked picture of my wife?"

"No, no, Steve. Apparently, you weren't following too closely. Just forget it."

Steve was about to embark on some dissertation when Gary Whittaker, a winner of the cornhole game just completed, asked, "Who's your partner, Ron?"

"A.J.! Oh, thank you, Jesus!"

"Action!" yelled Mike Haase to Bill Jackson, known among his golfing friends as Action Jackson. "You and Lee will play against Gary and me."

"Who do you want, Mike or Gary?" asked Ron as A.J. approached.

"I'll take Haase. I whip his ass every time we play this game… and most other games too now that I think about it."

"Like hell, old man," responded Haase with a non-humorous chuckle.

With the game tied at 4 apiece, Gary turned to Ron, asking, "Any leads yet, Ron?"

"Some, but I can't say anything more than that, Gary."

"I understand."

"You got us two points, Action!" yelled Ron as he collected his blue bags. "We're up 6-4."

"Do you think he's a serial killer?"

"Possibly. He's a psychopath if nothing else."

"Why do you say that?" asked Gary as he tossed his first corn-filled bag long.

"It's what he does to the girls. The way he cuts off their heads."

"That was a disgusting display he left at the Tradition."

"Yeah, he chops them. He treats them like a piece of meat. Hey, look at that, I put one in the hole."

"I have a bag left, Mr. Lee, and I will cover yours."

"Be my guest."

Gary let the bag fly, and it didn't even touch an edge as it fell into the hole.

"Lucky dick."

"Oh, no, that's skill," laughed Gary. "Been honing it for years."

"Give us a point, Gary," announced Mike.

"6-5. We still be up," announced Jackson.

"That won't be the case much longer," yelled Mike as he deposited his first bag in the hole.

"Well, partner," drawled Action, "it appears as if the youngster is learnin' the game. Trouble is, I learnt it a long time ago," added the ex-deputy sheriff, as his first bag followed Mike's into the hole.

Ten minutes later, after 5 hole-outs by Action Jackson, the game was over by a score of 21-9.

"I love a challenge," Lee said as he shook the hands of Gary and Mike. "Too bad you guys didn't give us one."

"Who's next to get their asses kicked?" asked A.J.

"Richie Freeman and I," said Steve Morris, "and I want Ron Lee's end."

"God, help me," Ron mumbled.

CHAPTER 18
Confliction

July 5, 2018

"That was a good cookout that Rick had yesterday. Wouldn't you agree, Ron?"

"I'd agree with that assessment, except for having Stevie as my opponent in cornhole. I thought he would never stop talking. And guess what? I was right!"

Chuckling, Tim asked, "Where do you want to canvas? North, middle, or south?"

"I'll tell you what I'm thinking, partner."

"I'm listening."

"I'm conflicted by these two murders. They are the same, but so different."

"Explain yourself," said Tim as he poured a cup of coffee.

"Two things. He waited for someone to cut the green before placing Sara's head at the base of the flagstick. Why? Why have a bunch of golfers discover the head? What was the point of that?"

"You said it yourself, Ron."

"What did I say?"

"He's announcing his arrival in our world."

"Yeah, I said that, didn't I? Well, now, I'm thinking there's more to it."

"What are your thoughts on the second head?"

"Here's where I find conflict. Why did he stick the second victim's head at the base of the flagstick in the middle of the night, knowing the guy mowing the green would most likely find it?"

"Maybe he didn't want to take a chance in the morning light. He probably thought a passing car might spot him."

"Okay, that makes perfect sense, but why pick that hole?"

"Maybe its location gave him the easiest and safest access to a hole."

"I can think of a few holes where access would have been easier and just as safe, maybe even more so. Numbers nine and ten come to mind."

"I can't argue with you there. Anything else troubling you?"

"This frostbite thing has me bugged."

"The second girl had no frostbite."

"Exactly and that's what has me conflicted."

"How so, Ron?"

"I understand why Sara's head had frostbite. He had to keep it on ice all night because he wasn't putting it out for display until the following morning, but why was the second woman's head barely even cool?"

"That's easy. He more than likely placed her head on the green soon after he murdered her."

"Exactly! But why did he even bother to put it on ice?"

"Maybe he planned to wait until morning but changed his mind when he realized the chance of being spotted."

"Possible, but not probable."

"So tell me your thoughts."

"Let's think about this guy's M.O.," suggested Ron.

"Okay, I'll start," Tim said. "First thing he does is pick up his victim."

"I can assure you they will all be women."

"That's the scenario. His next step," Tim continued, "is to kill them by snapping their necks."

"Where does he do that? Don't answer. That was a rhetorical question. I'm guessing that this guy is methodical. He plans out every step well in advance. No doubt he has a kill zone where he feels reasonably safe. A place at night where there is little chance of being seen."

"Okay, Ron, so he takes them to this place and kills them. Then what?"

"If you were chopping off your victims' heads, which would you do first: Chop off the head, take it to the golf course, and then get rid of the body, or vice versa?"

"Well, I wouldn't want a headless body rolling around in my trunk, belching blood. I'd get rid of the body first, then take the head to the golf course."

"As would I. Now, I doubt his kill zone is also where he disposes of the body."

"Why not?"

"Let's say you pick up a woman and drive her into the woods. What do you think might happen?"

"She'd be freaking out would be my guess."

"Most likely, and then you would experience some unwanted resistance. I'm sure the killing spot is somewhere where the victim feels secure. It must be a place that is public, so the victim feels at ease, yet quiet, so the killer feels confident he can do his killing without being detected."

"Good point. Where do you think he disposes of the bodies?"

"I have no clue, but let's look at Sara first. Since her hotel was near the boardwalk, let's assume, someone killed her somewhere in that vicinity."

"No doubt a safe assumption," commented Tim, "but still in no way a lock."

"I think he kills her, takes her body to his disposal site, mutilates it, buries the body, and then drives home."

"Drives home?"

"He didn't put the head on the green until around seven o'clock that morning. With her head on ice, he could have gone home, slept for a few hours, gotten up, showered, and had breakfast before driving to the

Tradition. Hell, who knows? He might live just minutes from the damn green."

"If what you're saying is right, then her head could have been on ice for... eight or nine hours."

"Plenty of time for frostbite."

Tim concurred by nodding his head.

"Okay, now we have this new girl on ice, but no frostbite. What does that tell you?"

Tim pondered for a moment before saying, "He killed her late. More than likely long after midnight."

"I'd say you're mighty close on that one, partner. He kills her. Does he take off her head right there and put it in a cooler?"

"Definitely not," exhorted Tim. "He would still have to deal with a headless body gushing blood."

"Precisely. So, he takes her to his disposal spot, which I'm sure is the same for each kill."

"They found both heads on the south end of the Strand. Might that be where he disposes of the bodies?"

"That's possible, Tim, but I'm thinking it is not."

"What are the reasons behind your thinking?"

"I'll get to those in a minute. So, he gets to the disposal site, and he chops her up..."

"What makes you think he chops her up?" interrupted Tim.

"Because he's a sick son-of-a-bitch! He's using a damn axe to cut off the heads! What? Do you think he doesn't go hog wild on the rest of the body? I'll garner a guess he feels like he's chopping up nothing more than a chord of wood."

"You're undoubtedly right. If he's chopping off heads, why not keep going?"

"Damn right, I'm right!" said Ron, unexpectedly caught up in his own rage.

After taking a moment to calm down, he continued with his theory.

"Then he disposes of the mutilated body, puts her head in a cooler, and drives to Indian Wells. How far from the state line to Indian Wells?"

"The state line? Why the state line?"

"Humor me for a minute. Just tell me how far."

"I'm guessing 35 miles but let me check."

"That's a good guess, Tim, but verify it, if you would."

Moments later, Tim proudly announces, "It's 34.8 miles to Little River. It would take 46 minutes if you took 31, and an hour if you took 17, although it is shorter by two miles."

"That's assuming his disposal spot is that far away. It might just be in North Myrtle."

"More wooded areas up in Little River near the state line."

"True."

"So, where are we?"

"Well, if he kills her at midnight somewhere in the middle of Myrtle Beach, drives to Little River via 17, that's 45 minutes. He chops her up and disposes of the body. What would you guess that would take?"

"Damn, I can't imagine such a thing, Ron, much less try to guess how long it would take. An hour, maybe?"

"I was thinking two hours, but let's split the difference and say 90 minutes."

"Then an hour back to Indian Wells," added Pond.

"Yeah, so if he doesn't put her head on ice until after he finishes chopping her up, then she's only on ice for less than two hours. If he chops off her head first, which I think would be a safe assumption, then her head is on ice for less than three hours."

"I wonder what he does with the body?"

"He likely has a prepared grave," suggested Ron. "He throws the body pieces in and fills it in with dirt. What's that gonna take? A half hour, maybe?"

"Okay then. He chops off the head and puts it on ice. You assume that he cuts the body into pieces. There's an hour and a half. He buries the body. That's another half hour. Then he drives to Indian Wells. That's another hour. So, we have about three total hours... that's if he goes to Little River and if he chops up the body."

"Oh, you can bet he chops up the body. I guarantee he relishes every moment. I'm betting that it's the biggest high he gets from the whole experience."

"You don't think the kill itself is his high moment?"

"Naw. Breaking a neck? No high there," asserted Ron with a slight wave of his hand. "Now, had he stabbed her, that's something else again. Even strangling would be a high, but, breaking a neck? No way. Too mundane."

Ron would have been right, but he didn't know about the killer's method of disposal. The feelings Ichabod experienced from feeding the bodies to the gators had been unlike anything else he had ever felt. It was simultaneous orgasms, but, lasting significantly longer with far more intensity.

"Okay, so the second head is on ice long enough to get cool, but not long enough to get frostbite. Now, I see why you think his disposal area may not be on the south end," said Tim, nodding his head in agreement.

"Yeah, if it were on the south end, he wouldn't need to ice the second victim's head. That would eliminate two hours of driving time, leaving only an hour for the head to be on ice. If it were on ice for that brief amount of time, the cold would dissipate after lying on the ground for five to six hours on a warm summer night. I'm convinced, Tim, that our boy does his butchering and his disposal somewhere up at the north end."

"All this doesn't tell us where or how he selected these women, although it is safe to say, he picked Sara up on the boardwalk. We don't, however, have a clue where the second victim could have engaged the killer."

"That's true, Tim. Our theoretical timeline begins at an assumed kill spot right in the center of the Grand Strand. We don't know if he gets there from the north or the south or right from the heart of the city."

"So, as I asked about an hour ago, where do you want to start the canvassing: up north, down south, or somewhere in the middle?"

"How many prospective establishments do you have on your list according to the compass?"

"I have 14 in the north from Barefoot Landing all the way to the state line. Then I have 22 from Barefoot south to Market Commons. I also have 17 from Market Commons to Pawleys Island."

"Is it too late for breakfast?"

"No. It's only 8:30. Why?"

"Then let's go south. I feel like pancakes."

"What?" Tim said with more than a hint of outrage. "When I felt like pancakes last week, you wanted nothing to do with pancakes."

"That is a true statement, no doubt."

"Now, however, because you're hungry, you want pancakes!"

"Yep. You know why?"

"No. Do tell."

"Rank has its privileges, Tim-o-thy."

"Geez, what a dick you are."

"I'm thinking that wasn't complimentary, partner."

"Boy, nothing gets past you."

CHAPTER 19
Ichabod

July 5, 2018

As he read the newspaper's account of the latest bodyless victim, the killer smiled widely, but it was a smile short-lived. It quickly evaporated when he read the fourth paragraph:

Special Agent Ron Lee of the FBI would not disclose any details of the murder scene other than to say the killer left the victim's head on Indian Wells' 15th green around two o'clock on Tuesday morning. Lee said, "Ichabod parked in the Health Care facility about a hundred yards from here and made his way up to the green to dispose of the victim's head."

When asked where the name Ichabod came from, Lee responded, "It came to mind the other morning as we were doing our investigation. It seems appropriate."

"Ichabod!" screamed the man who had beheaded two women in the past week. "How dare that…"

"What's the matter, Dad? Why did you scream?"

"Sorry, Doug. I got overly emotional about something. I'll be fine. You better get yourself ready for the beach. Your mom is just about ready to leave."

"What about you, Dad? Aren't you coming?"

"No, daddy has something he must take care of at work. I'll see you tonight."

"What time should I expect you, dear?"

Standing in the living room doorway wearing a provocative two-piece bathing suit was Deni, his wife of ten years.

"I'm not sure, hon. I'll try to get everything put to bed as early as I can, but you better not wait on dinner for me."

"I'm making a turkey breast with mashed potatoes and gravy."

"That sounds delicious. I'll call you if I can get away, otherwise, just put it away for me. I'll eat when I get home."

"Okay, dear, but I hope this project gets over soon, so you can be home with us more often."

"I'm afraid it may take the better part of the summer, but I will try to accelerate the process. Maybe we can get away in August."

"Oh, that sounds marvelous! Spending August together would be great. You take as many nights as you need to get it done this month. I won't complain. Promise."

"I'll do my best, but there are still about seven more steps to complete. I don't want to rush them as I can't afford to make a fatal mistake."

"Fatal?"

"Well, not in the truest sense of the word, but something akin to it."

"Okay, dear. Well, I'm meeting Margie at 9:00. We expect to spend most of the day at the beach."

"Be careful of the sun," he warned her. "Too much can cause some severe problems."

"Okay, dear. Bye-bye."

"Goodbye, Deni. See you tonight."

He watched as she drove out of the driveway and headed toward the beach.

"So, Mr. Ron Lee, you've hung a moniker on me. You'll come to regret it, I'm afraid."

Marching to his bedroom, he dressed for the day all the while thinking about the name, Ichabod, a name he knew meant "without glory."

Incensed, he spoke to the reflection in the bathroom mirror.

"I'll have all the glory when this is over, Mr. Lee, and you, well, you'll be just another dumbass, much like all the other so-called law enforcement agents I've left scratching their heads. The great Air Force detective, foiled by... Ichabod."

Laughing like the madman he truly was, he grabbed his car keys, locked the door, and made his way to his dark blue Chrysler sedan.

As he entered the car, he said aloud, "I will leave you another clue tonight, Mr. Lee, but you're too dumb to even have a hint of what it will mean."

CHAPTER 20
Pawleys Island

July 5, 2018

"How do you know all these establishments?" asked Ron as he scanned the photo of the second victim, sent, as promised, by forensic guru Charlie Spencer.

"Hey, I'm an FBI agent. It's my job to know things."

"So, bars are your area of expertise?"

"You might say that," responded Tim proudly.

They had begun their canvassing on Pawleys Island, but not before having a huge breakfast at the Applewood Pancake House.

Their first stop was the Rustic Table, a restaurant and bar that sat just off the road on 17.

"Might it be too early for these bars to be open, Tim?"

"Yeah, we likely should have waited till lunch, but we'll catch most."

The Rustic Table welcomed their entrance with two pleasant scents: fried bacon and cherry. The bacon smell came from the kitchen while the cherry aroma emulated from a pipe being smoked by an older man in a baseball cap. The man, deep into his 70s, occupied a stool behind something that reminded Tim of a lectern.

A half-dozen tables scattered around the room comprised the immediate dining area, while an L-shaped bar occupied the right rear wall. Straight ahead, a hallway led to a back room dining area. Four dining tables that could accommodate two people hugged the hallway's left wall.

"Morning, men," greeted the old man. "Would you like breakfast?"

"No, sir," answered Tim. Then, holding up a photo, he said, "We were wondering if you've ever seen this woman in here."

Reaching up to his head, the man lifted a pair of glasses, whose lenses appeared to be an inch thick, off the brim of the hat. He stopped short of placing them on his head by holding them an inch short of his eyes.

"Can't stand wearing glasses, if you be wonderin' what the hell I was doing."

Neither Ron nor Tim offered a reply.

Taking the picture, he drew it up near the lenses. After closely studying the photo for at least a minute, he announced, "Can't say I have, men. What's she done?"

"She has done nothing, sir. Is there anyone else we could ask?"

"Yeah, Ann is in the back. Let me fetch her for ya."

Thinking the old man would step off his stool and walk to the back, Tim momentarily turned his attention to the new outside eating area. Seconds later, he grabbed his left ear when the old fella cupped his hands to his mouth and screamed, "ANN! COME ON OUT HERE!"

None of the customers, sitting at various tables, bothered to even flinch.

"That should get her here mighty quick."

"It surely should," quipped Ron, adding, "and maybe a few dead people too."

"Thank you, sir," Tim said, while wiggling his finger in his left ear that had been in a direct line of the man's unexpected bellow.

Moments later, a spry looking older woman appeared, saying, "Otis, why are you screamin' like that? We got paid customers trying to enjoy their morning breakfast and you're brayin' like a wild donkey."

Morning breakfast? thought Ron. *Versus?*

"These fellas got them a picture to show ya, Ann."

"That ain't no reason for you to be screechin' like a grade-school girl, Otis."

"I was just tryin' to get your attention, is all."

Ignoring Otis's excuse, Ann turned to the two men, saying, "Who be you fellas?"

"We're with the FBI, ma'am," explained Ron, showing his credentials.

"FBI! Oh, my. I ain't never seen a real FBI agent before... except on television. I don't think those are real FBI folks, though, like you appear to be."

"Have you ever seen this woman in here, ma'am?" said Tim, holding up the photo.

"Hmm, she sure as heck wouldn't be hanging around in here. This is a family restaurant."

"What makes you say that, ma'am?" Ron asked.

"She's just got that white trash look about her. Don't she? If I was guessin,' you'd most likely find someone like her down in Murrells Inlet. Those be the bars someone with a face lookin' like hers would favor."

"Why do you say that, ma'am?"

"Just do, is all. Look in the Dead Dog Saloon or the Beaver Bar. Maybe even The Half Shell."

"Are those places on your list, Tim?"

"Yeah."

"Okay, ma'am. Thank you for your help."

"You're surely welcome, officers. Pleased to meet two fellas from the FBI."

"See ya, Otis," said Ron as they walked out the door. "Get those vocal cords checked Otis. I doubt if anyone in Georgetown heard you."

"Georgetown! Why, that's ten miles down the road! What a dumbass for an FBI agent."

"I'll second that," snickered Tim as they headed toward the car.

CHAPTER 21
Chelsea

July 5, 2018

They canvassed a few other places in Pawleys before deciding that if the shallow profile of the victim was even close, then Pawleys Island bars were way above her pay scale.

As it approached 1:00, Tim suggested they head to Murrells Inlet.

"What do you think is our best bet, Tim, the Dead Dog Saloon or The Half Shell?"

"The Dead Dog is a beach place with lots of tourists. According to Ann's evaluation of our girl, I don't think it fits her profile," answered Tim with a chuckle.

"Then it's The Half Shell?"

"It has the perfect profile. Small, neighborly, good food, cheap drinks, country music, chicken wings, and ball scratchin'."

"You know, Tim, if this turns out to be right, the FBI may need to hire Ann as a profiler," said Ron with a chuckle.

"Yeah, and that Otis fella could be a lookout at the pentagon."

"Let's give The Half Shell a try. Besides, I could eat lunch and this time you're buying."

"You're hungry? Damn, Ron, you ate a foot-tall stack of flapjacks, along with home fries and sausage just a few hours ago. It's no wonder you can't see your weenie."

"Yeah, well, my weenie's been at half-mast for quite some time now. You might say, it's retired."

"I sure hope it has life insurance."

"When it dies, I'll call you, so you can rush on over and provide resuscitation."

"I'm afraid, partner, that due to my poor eyesight, I wouldn't be able to find something that small in time."

"Get in the damn car," said Ron with a big grin.

Twenty minutes later they pulled into the parking lot that fronted a small, greenish-blue building that appeared to be nothing more than an old 1950s ranch house, but not as appealing.

As they approached the entrance, Ron quipped, "Damn, Tim, this place even looks right from out here."

"Yeah, well, let's step inside, and then tell me how it feels."

Once inside, Ron knew they had come to the right place. Everything fit: country music, comfort food, non-matching chairs and tables, a pool table and a bar that looked like it had been around since the turn of the century. The only reason the bartender wasn't scratching his balls was because he was actually a woman.

A moment later they had seated themselves at the bar. The young and pleasant looking barmaid, who was obviously pregnant, greeted them.

"What will you have, fellas?"

"What's your name, darling?"

"Chelsea."

"Well, Chelsea, I'd like a plate of information," Ron stated.

"Huh?"

Tim pulled the photo from his jacket and showing it to the barmaid, asked, "Have you ever seen this woman?"

Without a moment of pause, Chelsea answered, "Oh sure, that's Laura Cantor. She looks like she's in a trance in that photo, though."

"When's the last time you saw Laura?"

"Hmm, I'm relatively sure it was Monday. Yeah, it was Monday."

"What makes you so sure?"

"Because… I served her a lot of drinks and food right over there at that table," she said, pointing toward a table not over 15 feet away.

"What kind of food?"

"Chicken wings, mussels… she always has mussels when she comes in here… hey, wait a minute! Who are you and why the questions about Laura?"

"Sorry, Chelsea. We should have introduced ourselves. I'm Special Agent Ron Lee and this is my partner…"

"Agent Tim Pond," Tim said, extending his hand.

"We're with the FBI," added Ron.

"FBI? What the heck has Laura done that the FBI would ask questions? Is she a spy or something?"

"No, she's not a spy," answered Tim.

"What else did she eat?"

Scrunching her face at Ron's question, she pondered a moment and then listed, "Cheese bread, shrimp, and what I already told you."

"Was she alone?"

"Oh, no. She was with John."

"John? You know this… John?"

"No. I heard her say his name when I delivered the food."

"Had he ever been in here previously?"

"Not that I recall."

"Can you describe John?"

"Big guy. I'd say well over six foot. Well built. Weighed around 210 or 220, but he was in good shape. No belly like most guys. He had on jeans and a dark T-shirt."

"What about facial features?" asked Tim, hoping the barmaid could give them a detailed description.

"Can't help too much in that area. He had a baseball cap pulled down in front, and he had on a pair of dark sunglasses. I could see gray hair under his cap. It matched his gray mustache."

"Did Laura know him?" asked Ron.

"I don't think so. He had been sitting at the bar... in fact, you're sitting on the same stool," she said, nodding at Ron. "I remember Laura arriving and walking toward the end of the bar. That's where she always sat, until..."

"Until what?" Tim asked.

"Well, Laura liked... men, if you know what I mean. Being a divorcee for a while, well, she may have been looking for comfort."

"You mentioned she was heading toward the end of the bar," voiced Ron. "What happened then?"

"Can't rightly say for sure. Apparently, this guy said something to her because when I next noticed, they were talking and smiling like long-lost friends."

"You hinted that you didn't think she knew him."

"Yeah, the reason is, he bought her a drink and when he ordered it, he called, saying, 'Chelsea, a Jack and ginger for...' then he stopped and turned to Laura for a moment. I saw Laura tell him her name. Then he finished by saying, '... for Laura'."

"I guess that was her first encounter with him, then?" asked Tim.

"As far as I know, it was. They hit it off rather well, though. They sat at that table until roughly 10:00, eating and drinking before leaving together."

"Did you see which car they took?" Ron asked.

"Laura didn't drive here. She only lives a block away."

"Is that where she goes to...?"

"Get laid? No. Definitely not! She told me she never wanted a guy to know where she lived. They always went to the guy's pad. She made them bring her back here before we closed."

"What time would that be?"

"Around 2:00."

"Did you see his car?"

"No, sorry. I didn't."

"What's this all about, anyway? Is Laura all right?"

"No, she isn't," answered Ron. "She's dead. Murdered."

"Oh, my God!"

"I have a few more questions, Chelsea," said Ron.

Shaken, the young barmaid responded, "Like what?"

"Do you recall how long this John guy had been sitting here before Laura came into the bar?"

"One drink."

"One drink?"

"Yeah, I served him a ginger ale about 10 minutes before Laura showed her face."

"A ginger ale?"

"Yeah, with no ice. He didn't want ice in his drinks."

"He had more?"

"Oh, yeah. While Laura was throwin' down Jack and gingers, he kept drinking ginger ales."

"Was Laura aware of what he had been drinking?"

"You know, now that you ask, I don't think so, because whenever I took a drink order, he held up his glass and said, 'The same'."

"Okay, Chelsea, just a few more questions," stated Ron. "You said to the best of your knowledge he had never been in here previously."

"That's correct."

"Did you introduce yourself to him when he came in on Monday?"

"No."

"You're not wearing a name tag. Were you wearing one on Monday?"

"No. We don't wear name tags."

"Did you have any conversation with him?"

"Nothing more than asking for his drink order."

"That, was it? No polite chatter?"

"Not a word."

"You said when he ordered a drink for Laura that he called you by name. Is that correct?"

"Yes, he did."

"How did he know your name?"

She stood there with a blank look on her face before replying, "I don't have a clue. Maybe he overheard someone else say it."

"I suppose that's a viable possibility. How many people were sitting at the bar while he was here?"

"Just a couple guys sitting down there on the right turn, as we like to call it. You're sitting on the left turn."

The bar was half of a rectangle with two right angles. The long edge of the bar accommodated approximately twelve bar stools. The left turn side, where Ron was sitting, was about four feet longer than that on the right side. A four-foot opening at the end of the right side allowed waitresses access to the kitchen. Ron counted five stools on his side, which included his seat. He guessed there would only be room for three stools on the opposite side, due to the kitchen access.

"So, he was basically the length of the bar apart from them?"

"Yeah, he was."

"Do you recall if they called you by name during that time?"

"Sorry, but I can't swear that they did or didn't."

"Understandable. Last question, but I already know the answer."

"What's that?"

"I'm assuming he picked up the check."

"He did."

"Cash or credit?"

"Cash."

"Yeah, well, that's not a big surprise."

"Do you think this John guy killed Laura?" asked Chelsea, her question directed at Ron.

"Do I think it? Yes. Do I know it? No."

"Geez, he seemed like a pleasant guy," said Chelsea. "He left me a big tip."

"Yeah, well, looks can be deceptive," remarked Tim. "Take my partner for example. He looks intelligent."

Chelsea, apparently having recovered over the shock of a customer's death, chuckled.

"Okay, Chelsea, let's see a menu. We may as well eat while we're here."

"Damn! I had hoped you had forgotten about lunch," moaned Tim.

"Forget! Ha! Not a chance, partner. Not when I know that you're buying."

They had lunch, and leaving Chelsea their card, instructed her to call if "John" should ever return, even though they knew the chances were slim.

They were heading back to FBI headquarters when Tim asked, "What was that all about there at the end?"

"She had said something earlier that just set off an alarm in my head."

"What was that?"

"Let me ask you, Tim. If you were sitting at a bar for the first time, and you needed to get the bartender's attention, whose name you didn't know, how would you go about doing it?"

"I'd might say, 'Hey, barkeep, give me another'."

"Yeah, me too, but he didn't. He called her by name."

"That means he had to have been there previously!"

"Yeah, that was my thought, but Chelsea couldn't recall ever seeing him previously."

"He knew her, but she didn't know him."

"Yep. That means that our man, besides being a head chopping murderous psychopath, is also a person of disguises."

CHAPTER 22
Pepperoni, Sausage, and Peppers

July 5, 2018

It was approaching 8:00 when he left his office. Having predetermined his next target, he headed to Chris's Pizza and Pub restaurant in Little River.

Tonight's kill would be one of rage. Although the victim would pay the ultimate price, Ron Lee, the man who had mocked him, in public no less, by labeling him with the moniker, Ichabod, would be the true target of his wrath.

Turning left off Route 9 into the strip mall, he parked some distance from the pub's entrance. Leaving the car, Ichabod sauntered toward the pub observing all movements around him.

Tonight, he wore a pair of white Bermuda shorts, a dark blue golf shirt, and sandals, while disguising himself with a wig of dark hair, blue contacts, a small but impressive looking goatee, and, on his right arm, a temporary tattoo, which displayed the date, 12-28-46.

A smug smile crossed his face as he entered the restaurant. Just as he had expected; only a single customer, the man called, Doc, occupied the restaurant. Ichabod took a seat two stools from Doc's left.

"Good evening."

"Hey," Doc responded in traditional southern fashion.

"Hello," said a smiling barkeep whose name tag read, Betsy. "What can I get you?"

"I'll have a ginger ale, and can I get two slices?"

"Sure, but I think we're limited to pepperoni or sausage. Will one of those be okay?"

"Perfect. In fact, I'll have one of each."

"No, problem. I'll have them out here in a jiffy."

As he awaited his order, he heard Doc, say, "Hey, I couldn't help but notice your tattoo. Is that your birthday?"

"No, but, it's the birthday of a friend."

"A friend? Ain't it a tad strange to have a friend's birthday tattooed on one's arm?"

"Well, he's a guy who has inspired me."

"I see," replied Doc with a confused look. "Funny thing is my wife's birthday is 12-29-46. That's why I noticed it."

"What a coincidence," Ichabod said with a big grin. *This may work out even better than I thought.*

A moment later Betsy brought out two huge slices of pizza, one with sausage, the other with pepperoni. Placing them in front of him, she said, "Now, your drink was a ginger ale. Correct?"

"Yep," he answered. Then, upon noticing the content of the plate, he exclaimed, "These are generous slices!"

"Yeah, well, Chris wants to get rid of the pizza he's made, and we aren't far from closing at 9:00. It's your lucky day, fella!"

"Is Chris your boss?"

"Yeah. He's the owner. I get off at nine, but he's here until midnight cleaning up and counting receipts."

"How much do I owe you, Betsy?"

She was only about five-foot tall and couldn't weigh much over 100 pounds soaking wet. He guessed she was in her late forties. She was no beauty, but she had a pleasant face and a well-kept body. Seeing no rings on her fingers, he correctly assumed that she was single.

"Five bucks should cover it."

"Here's ten. Keep the change."

"Thanks, mister. That's especially generous of you."

"I'll say it was," sighed Doc. "You're making me look bad," he added with a smile.

"Hey, Doc, don't worry about it," said Betsy. "You've never been a good tipper. Why start now?"

"Oh, Betsy, you know I'd leave bigger tips, if I could."

"I know. I'm just pulling your leg, Doc."

Turning toward Ichabod, she said, "Doc's in here every single night, rain, or shine. He babies that beer he's drinking for about two hours while he watches sports on the big screen television."

I had been counting on that, Ichabod's inner voice whispered.

"Where do you live, stranger?"

"Oh, I live in Myrtle. Near the airport."

"Did you play golf today?"

"Yes. How can you tell?"

"Two things: Your left hand isn't as tan as your right because you wear a glove when you're playing. Then there's your clothing. Typical golfing clothes, although blue and white seems to favor you."

Looking at his two hands, Ichabod remarked, "You're a regular Columbo, ma'am. As for my clothes, I rarely get compliments, so thank you."

He knew Betsy liked to flirt with guys, as most barmaids do, with their intent being to entice the customer to buy another drink. Hoping she would stay with the script; she didn't disappoint him.

"Hey, I've been wondering if you knew a place nearby that had a bar and served oysters. I've had a hankering for oysters all day."

"Well, not being an oyster eater myself," she explained, "I do, however, know Crab Catcher's down on the Little River waterfront serves oysters. It's just a ten-minute drive from here."

"Crab Catcher's? Can't say I know of it. Do you go there often?"

"I normally stop a couple times a week and have a beer or two with some of their fried corn. Have you ever had fried corn, mister?"

"Can't say I have."

"Well, it's to die for. Why don't you stop at Crab Catcher's and have some with your oysters?"

"You make it sound mighty tempting, ma'am. I think I just may do that. If you stop by, I'll be more than happy to buy you a beer."

"A free beer sounds good, and please, call me Betsy."

"Yes, I see that on your name tag. I'm Mike. You know, since I'll be eating oysters and fried corn, I really don't need two slices of pizza." Turning to Doc, he asked, "Say, Doc, would you take this sausage slice off my hands?"

"Why, thanks, fella! I'll be more than happy to relieve you of your burden," replied Doc with a wide grin.

"Might you be going straight to Crab Catcher's after you close up, Betsy?"

"Yeah, I guess I will if you're buying me a beer."

"Since I'm not exactly sure where it is, do you mind if I follow you over there?"

"No problem. I drive a white Toyota. It's parked out back. Wait for me by the Route 9 exit. We'll be closing up in about five minutes."

"Well, that's my signal to get the hell out of here," announced Doc. "Thanks for the pizza, mister," he added as he headed toward the door. "See ya tomorrow, Betsy."

"Good night, Doc."

"I better get along then too."

"I'll be just a few minutes, Mike."

"Okay, I'll wait for you by the exit," he replied as he headed toward the front door.

He waited until Doc had driven off before he left the pizzeria and proceeded to his vehicle. There was no reason to give Doc any suspicions why he had parked such a distance away from the pizzeria when there were plenty of spots available in front of the restaurant.

Once in his car, he drove not toward the exit, but instead turned left and made his way to where the employees parked behind their respective store. Reaching the rear of the pizzeria, he saw two cars, one of which was Betsy's white Toyota. Parking just a few feet away, he popped open his trunk.

Knowing a fully opened trunk might scare his quarry away, he moved to the rear of his vehicle and pushed the trunk lid down to where it remained open by just a crack. He then moved behind the Toyota and assumed a kneeling position. It was dark and although there were at least another half-dozen employee cars parked behind the nearby shops, there was no one in sight.

Only two minutes passed before he heard a door open and then slam shut. It had to be Betsy. He didn't look. He waited.

Seconds later he heard the Toyota's locks being remotely opened. Hearing her approaching the car, he peeked ever so carefully over the car's trunk, and seeing she was about to open the door, he sprung from his kneeling position.

Betsy's last breath was only moments away.

Her door now wide open, she was about to slide into her driver's seat. She never made it.

Grabbing her around the shoulders with his left arm, he covered her mouth with his right hand. Tightly clutching her jaw, he twisted it while pulling upward. It was over in a split second. The neck snapped like a dried twig.

Using little effort, he carried her to his car, opened the trunk fully, and tossed her limp body inside as if it were nothing more than a bag of dirty laundry.

Closing the trunk with a thud, he then took a moment to survey the area for any witnesses. There were none.

Driving slowly, he made his way toward the exit. Reaching the exit, and seeing no traffic coming from his left, he turned right onto Route 9 and drove toward Little River. His destination was the River Hills Golf Club, only ten minutes away.

Three miles later he merged north onto Route 17, but that portion of the journey was short-lived. A quarter mile further on he turned left into the entrance of the River Hills Golf Club. Following the entrance road, he eventually turned onto Cedar Creek Run. Turning off his headlights, he followed the road until finding himself in the golf course's parking lot. Pulling to within ten feet of the bag drop, he stopped and popped open his trunk.

Lifting Betsy from the trunk, he dropped her body on the ground between his car and the bag drop. There would be no plastic sheets tonight. After stripping her of her clothing, and placing them on the bag drop, he changed into his "work" clothes. Then he grabbed his axe and went to work.

Oh, did he ever.

The newly found hatred for Ron Lee, obvious in every savage swing of the axe, had consumed him. Blood burst from Betsy's body and splattered everywhere, with some large drops splashing his car doors and trickling down the paint before slowly dripping to the ground. He paid no mind to the helter-skelter splashing of blood as he continued hacking with uncontrolled abandon.

Immediately after decapitating the head, he placed it in his cooler and set it inside the car. Chopping off another specific piece, he picked it up and placed it in the cooler with the head.

The destruction of Betsy's demure frame took only 20 minutes, but when completed, it covered the ground in blood-soaked human hamburger. Bagging all the pieces he could, he put them in his trunk along with his blood-soaked scrubs. Closing the trunk, he avoided the puddle of blood beside the driver's door by using the passenger side entrance.

Pulling away from the bag drop, he exited the parking lot in darkness, leaving behind things he shouldn't have left. In his uncontrolled rage, he had been sloppy.

Left behind was a bloody shoe covering and a bloody tire imprint.

He would continue to get even more sloppy as the days of killing continued.

Turning onto Cedar Creek Run he followed it, with his headlights off, until he found himself next to the 17th green.

Exiting the car, he grabbed the cooler and ran toward the green. Reaching the pin placement, he opened the cooler, extracted the head, and placed it near the base of the pin. Reaching again into the cooler he selected the second body part and placed it against Betsy's bloody mouth.

He smiled at the message he had left. Emptying the cooler's small accumulation of blood onto the green, he returned to his car. As he opened the car door, he heard a voice from somewhere in the dark, yelling, "Hey, what's going on out there?"

Calmly, with headlights off, he drove away. His next stop: Alligator Adventure.

He was excited.

CHAPTER 23
Texas Chili

July 6, 2018

The call came at 6:43 in the morning. Ron, seeing the time, knew something had happened. The phone rang for a fourth time before he answered, "Hello."

"This is Tim. I'm on my way to River Hills. They have another head."

"River Hills? Way the hell up there?"

"Yeah, Ron, way the hell up there. Geez, you make it sound like it's the damn North Pole. They said for us to get there pronto. There's blood everywhere."

"What's that supposed to mean?"

"I don't know, Ron, but I'm guessing it means... there's blood everywhere. Meet me at the clubhouse."

"Clubhouse? Why there, wiseass?"

"I'm guessing that since there's blood everywhere, there must be some at the clubhouse!"

"Okay, dickhead, I'll be there in about 45 minutes."

"Forty-five minutes? Oh, I get it. You're finally setting aside 30 minutes to trim your nose hairs."

"Bite me, Pond."

It was 7:40 when Ron pulled into the River Hills parking lot. State Police cars were everywhere. He parked as far away as possible and made his way toward where the biggest crowd had congregated. Pond stood in the middle.

"Let me through, gentlemen," Ron repeated over and over until he stood just a few feet away from a fly-infested puddle of blood and flesh.

"Good God! What the hell is this!"

"Morning, Ron. Glad to see you could make it," said his smirking partner.

"Damn, it looks like someone spilled a barrel of Texas chili on the ground."

"Thanks for that analogy. I used to love chili," mumbled Pond.

"Tell me what you got, so far."

"The maintenance guys found this at around 6:15 this morning. About 20 minutes later, a greenskeeper found the head out on the 17th green."

"This is all wrong, Tim. Something is not right here, other than the obvious carnage. My first thought was we have us a copycat."

"I don't think so. C'mon, there's a cart ready to take us out to the green. I'm told that we need to see something out of the ordinary."

"Out of the ordinary?" replied Ron. "Everything about this damn case has been out of the ordinary."

Minutes later the cart stopped alongside the 17th green and the two FBI agents made their way toward the pin. They could see the back of the head as soon as they stepped from the cart.

"Same as the other two," whispered Ron.

"Yeah, so it appears."

"Okay, what's the surprise, guys?"

A state police officer stepped forward, saying, "Colonel, I'm Sergeant Lewis. I'm familiar with the past two crime scenes, and although this one is similar, the previous two had nothing like this."

"And what would that be, Sergeant?"

"This, sir," the sergeant declared, pointing down toward the front of the head.

Being out of position, Ron had to move around to the front to see the targeted object.

Propped against the victim's lips was one of the middle fingers of the victim. It appeared as if she was saying, "Shh."

"What the hell!" said Tim.

104

"It's a double message."

"Double?"

"Yeah, this thing just became somewhat personal between him and us."

"Us? Well, if that's the case, I'm guessing we may have hit a nerve someplace."

"No doubt that's the case, partner. He's definitely telling us to watch what we say, and in addition, he's saying, 'Up yours'."

"Any idea who the victim is, Sergeant?"

"Not yet, sir, but there was a call that came in last night around midnight from the guy who owns Chris's pizza out on Route 9."

"Yeah, I know it well. The guy makes a good pizza. Tell me about the call."

"Guy claims his waitress's car was still in the parking lot when he left last night at midnight. He said she left shortly after 9:00. Her name is Betsy Parker."

"What's this on the ground, Sergeant?" asked Tim.

"It appears to be a smattering of blood, sir."

"What's it doing ten feet from the head?"

"My guess is that's where he emptied the cooler," answered Ron. "I'll bet there wasn't any ice in that cooler though."

"Why do you say that?"

"I'm guessing the missing woman is our victim. He snatched her at the pizzeria. Then drove over to the River Hills parking lot to dismember her. He put her head and the finger in a cooler, then took the two-minute drive over here to drop the head off."

"Yeah, why not? It's plausible," agreed Tim.

"Let's go back to the clubhouse."

Minutes later they were standing at the bag drop.

"This guy lost it. He was way out of control when he did this. Did you notice the woman's head, Tim?"

"You mean the chops on the skull?"

"Yeah. He was in a state of rage when he killed this woman. Something has our boy mighty pissed."

"Killed her early too."

"What do you mean, Tim?"

"Today's Friday. He's a Monday-Tuesday killer."

"I don't think we have established enough of a pattern, to make a definitive statement like that. If you're right though, then he blew his pattern all to hell."

"He made mistakes, though, Ron."

"Like what?"

"We found a blue scrub shoe covering. It was an extra-large size."

"So, maybe our boy has big feet."

"Yeah, but based on Chelsea's description, we could have assumed that to be the case."

"Not entirely true, Tim. Just because a guy is big, doesn't mean he's big everywhere."

"I guess you'd know about that better than me."

Ron, giving his partner his patented formidable look over the top of his glasses, brought a smile to Pond's face.

Having trouble holding back his false bravado, Lee also smiled.

"What else is there?"

"Tire tracks."

"Oh? Now that might be something that's useful."

A state trooper interrupted their conversation.

"Agent Lee. Sergeant Lewis says they have found a Mr. Roger Bartlett who claims he saw something last night."

"Where is he?"

"He'll be here shortly."

Bartlett appeared minutes later.

"Mr. Bartlett, I'm Special Agent Ron Lee and this is my partner, Agent Tim Pond. I'm told you saw something last night, sir."

"Yes, I did," replied Bartlett, a man short in stature, and who couldn't have weighed much more than 125. He wore large, rounded glasses that made him look like an old television character, Mr. Peepers, played by long-dead actor Wally Cox.

"Tell us what you saw, sir."

"I had been sitting out on my rear patio when I heard a car stop on the road."

"How far away is the road from your patio, sir?"

"I'd say only 70-80 yards. I heard the car, but I didn't see it. Its headlights were off. A few seconds after it stopped I heard a door open and close, followed by another door opening and closing."

"I'm guessing that's when he grabbed the cooler from the back seat," quoted Ron to no one in particular.

Bartlett continued, saying, "Then I saw a figure, just a shadow, running toward the green. As he got closer he became clearer, but not to where I could give you a definite description, mind you. All I can tell you, is that he was tall, well-built, and wearing a baseball cap."

"You could tell he was wearing a baseball cap with those glasses?" chortled Pond.

"You'll be surprised to know, sir, that I wear them, so I can see," answered a bullish Bartlett.

"What did you see then, Mr. Bartlett?" asked Ron while giving Pond a snickering look.

"Well, sir, I saw he carried something, which, according to you, was a cooler. As he approached the flagstick, he bent down, opened the cooler, and removed something from it. Whatever it was he removed, he laid it beside the pin. Then he removed something else from the cooler and placed it near the flagstick. He stood up, stepped away, and as he did, he turned the cooler upside down. After that, he stood there for a moment, then he returned to his car. I shouted at him, but he ignored me. He casually got in his vehicle and calmly drove off... with no headlights."

"Did you go out to the green after he left, Mr. Bartlett?" asked Tim.

"No," replied Bartlett, his eyes falling toward the ground in what they all perceived as shame or cowardice.

"Well, thank you, Mr. Bartlett. Give the officer your address and phone number in case we need to talk to you again," instructed Ron.

Turning to Tim, Ron said, "We're done here. Let the lab guys do their work. We'll get the results later. Besides, I'm somewhat eager to talk to the pizza guy."

"It's only 8:30 in the morning, sir," offered an officer standing nearby. "He won't open until 11:00."

"Do you have an address for him?"

"Yes, sir. His name is Chris Aycock and his address is 17 Pine Cone Lane."

"Where is that?"

"You turn off Route 9 just as if you were going to Chris's, but instead just go straight on Cloverleaf Drive. When you reach the end, turn right, and Pine Cone will be the first left."

"Officer, please call Mr. Aycock, and let him know we'll be at his home at... let's say... 10:00."

"Will do, Agent Lee."

"Thank you."

"Why so late, Ron?"

"Had breakfast yet, Tim?"

"No, I haven't, but I could eat something."

"Ever been to the Little River Deli?"

"Can't say I have."

"Let's have breakfast before talking with Aycock."

"Sounds good. Are you buying?"

"Negatory, Tim-o-thy."

"Cheap bastard, aren't you?"

"Mama once told me, 'Son, you can't win an argument against the truth, so don't try.' Mama was a smart woman."

"Yeah, she was. Too bad it wasn't hereditary."

CHAPTER 24
Now It's Personal

July 6, 2018 –

"That was a helluva breakfast sandwich, Ron. Good choice."

"Try their lunches. The sandwiches are fantastic. I've eaten at the diner dozens of times and never had a bad lunch yet."

"You look like you've eaten at a lot of places dozens of times," said Tim, with a laugh.

"You are nothing but a wiseass, aren't you?"

"I'm thinking it's better than being a dumbass," responded Tim.

"Yeah, well, I think you have them both covered, Tim-o-thy."

"Hey, there's his house!"

Pulling into the driveway, they were both impressed by what was not only a newly built home, but one of some substance.

"The pizza business is surely getting its slice of the pie - no pun intended."

"That was a pun?" said Tim with a shit-eatin' grin.

"You know, every day you're becoming more of a real dick."

"A big one, like you?"

"Big or little, you're still a dick."

"Like looking in a mirror, Mr. Lee?"

Ignoring Tim's last response, Ron said, "Fancy looking house. Boy, look at that, a three-car garage!"

"Never seen one of those before, heh? You need to get out more, big fella."

"Damn, you're obnoxious today."

Minutes later, after introductions, they were sitting in the large expanse of a living room listening to Chris Aycock telling what he knew.

"It was around 8:40 when Betsy comes back to the kitchen and says a guy wants two slices, one with pepperoni and one with sausage."

"By any chance did you see this guy?" asked Ron.

"No, I didn't. I never left the kitchen. After 8:00 things die down, so I clean up and cool down the ovens. We normally close at 9:00."

"So then, Betsy left at 9:00."

"It may have been a few minutes after 9:00. She told me she had plans to meet this guy at Crab Catcher's. That's a seafood restaurant down on the Intracoastal in Little River."

"I know it," said Tim. "Good oysters and fried corn."

"That's the place. Betsy would go there after work, 2-3 times a week. Anyway, I work until midnight, cleaning up and doing the books."

"So, when you leave, you find Betsy's car is still in the lot," noted Tim.

"Yeah. I walk out and there's her car sitting with the driver's door wide open."

"I'm guessing that he must have been hiding and grabbed her when she was about to get into her car," said Ron.

"Wait, a minute!" shouted Chris. "Did something bad happen to Betsy?"

"We don't have an official identification, sir, but can you tell us if this is Betsy?" Tim asked, pulling out his cell phone and showing a picture he had taken of the victim.

Chris, who had been sitting in a chair, fell to his knees upon seeing the photo. Seconds later, with his hand covering his mouth, he stood and ran from the room. There was little doubt he would be sick.

A few minutes later he returned. It was obvious he had been crying.

"I'm sorry, fellas. Betsy was special."

"No apologies necessary, sir," said Tim, "but I'm afraid I will have to ask you to confirm that the photo was that of your employee, Betsy Parker."

"Yes, that's Betsy."

"Tell me, Chris, was anyone else in the restaurant?"

"Oh, I'm sure Doc was there."

"Doc?" said Ron quizzically.

"Yeah, his real name is Jimmy Doctor, but everyone calls him Doc. He's an older fella. Comes in every single night we're open. Orders a beer and a sandwich and watches sports on the big screens. He normally leaves at closing."

"Where does this guy live?"

"He on Goodson Drive. Just follow your way out to Route 9, go straight across to Charter and Goodson is the second right. Let me get his house number for you."

"We would appreciate that, Chris."

Moments later, Chris returned saying, "Doc's house number is 190. Would you like me to call to see if he's home?"

"No, I think it better that you don't. Thank you for your time, Chris, and we are sorry for your loss."

"Thank you. But hey, do us all a favor."

"What would that be, sir?"

"Kill that no-good sonofabitch!"

The FBI agents, saying nothing, nodded in unison.

It took less than five minutes to drive to Jimmy Doctor's house. Seeing a car in the driveway, they approached the door and rang the doorbell. It was only seconds before the door opened.

"Yes?"

"Mr. Doctor?"

"Yes, but most just call me, Doc."

"That's what we hear, sir. We're from the FBI. I'm Special Agent Lee and this is Agent Pond."

"Nothing special about you, Agent Pond?"

"I beg your pardon, sir."

"How come he's special and you're not?"

"Oh, well, that's just rank, sir. My wife thinks I'm special, however."

"Yeah, I bet she does," snickered Doc.

"Hmm, apparently you know my wife, sir."

Laughing at Tim's response, Doc waved them in saying, "Can I get you fellas something to drink?"

"No, thanks, sir," Ron said. "We have a few questions we need to ask."

"How about you, 'nothing special' Agent Pond?"

"No, thank you, Mr. Doctor."

"Let's get something straight before we go any further. If we're talking, you'll address me as, Doc. Got it?"

"Agreed," they both replied.

"What is it we need to talk about?"

Ron asked all the questions while Tim took notes.

"Were you at Chris's Pizza and Pub last night, Doc?"

"Hell, yes, I was there. Left at closing, right before 9:00. I'm there every night. Can't remember any night, except maybe last Christmas Eve, that I haven't been there."

"Were you the last patron to leave?"

"I was… no, wait a second… I stand corrected. There was another fella there… pleasant fella… gave me a piece of his pizza. He said his name was… Mike. Yeah, I remember him saying it was Mike."

"Did Mike engage in conversation with you or the waitress?"

"Yeah, he talked with both of us. In fact, he told Betsy that he would meet her at Crab Catcher's. He mentioned that he had a hankerin' for some oysters, so Betsy suggested they go there. She goes there fairly regular... really enjoys their fried corn. I remember him saying he would follow her because he didn't know its location."

"What did you talk about, Doc?"

"We chatted about sports and stuff."

"Could you describe him for us?"

"Sure, but what's this all about? This guy wanted for something?"

"He's a person of interest, Doc. We need to talk with him."

"Okay. He was tall... I'd say over six-foot by a few inches. Looked in good shape. Weighed in around 220, maybe 225. His hair was dark, and his eyes were brown."

"Did he have a mustache, Doc?"

"He had a small beard on his chin."

"Like a goatee?"

"Yeah. A goatee."

"Can you describe his clothing, Doc?"

"He said he had just finished playing golf. He had on a pair of white shorts and a dark blue or black shirt. He wore sandals, too."

"What about his age, Doc?"

"I'd be guessing, but I'd say around 40, maybe a few years older."

"You're kidding!" said a surprised Tim. "I thought he would be much younger. Didn't you, Ron?"

Ron didn't answer Tim's question, but instead said, "Had you ever seen this guy before, Doc?"

"Can't say I have, Agent Lee. Oops, I forgot, you're the special guy. Sorry about that."

Smiling at Doc's humorous jab, Ron asked, "Have you ever seen anyone in Chris's that might have been similar in height or build to this guy?"

"That's a tough one, fella. I've seen my fair share of folks in that pizza joint over the years."

"Narrow it down to the past few months, Doc. It would definitely be someone sitting alone."

"No one comes to mind. If I remember anything, I'll let you know."

"That would be fine, Doc. Anything else you can tell us about this guy?"

He sat pondering for a few moments before saying, "I don't know if it means anything, but I thought it mighty strange."

"Oh! And what might that be, Doc?"

"A tattoo."

"A tattoo? Where?"

"It was on his right arm. I noticed it because it reminded me of my late wife."

"How's that?"

"It was a date."

"A date?"

"Yeah. It was one day earlier than my wife's birthday."

"You said you thought it was strange. Why?"

"Oh, he said it was a friend's birthday."

"A friend? Hmm, I agree, Doc. That is peculiar."

"Yeah, he said something about the guy inspiring him to more and bigger things."

"What was the date, Doc?"

"It was 12-28-46."

Ron, upon hearing Doc's reply, sat motionless for a moment before asking, "Are you sure that was the date, Doc?"

"Oh, yeah. I'm positive. My wife's birthday is 12-29-46. That's why I'm so sure about the date."

Ron turned to Tim, saying, "Now, it's personal."

"Why's that, Ron?"

"12-28-46."

"Yeah. What about it?"

"That's my birthday."

"What's this all about, anyway?" asked Doc. "You're asking all these questions and I don't know why."

Seeing that Ron was in deep thought, Tim responded by saying, "Have you been following the news reports about women's decapitated heads, Doc?"

"Hell, yes! It's on the news all the time. In fact, they're calling him 'Ichabod' now."

That snapped Ron out of his trance.

"What's that you said?"

"The television news reporters are calling this killer, 'Ichabod'," repeated Doc.

"Mother...!" roared Ron.

"What? What is it?" Tim asked, taken aback by Ron's sudden rage.

"That's why it has become personal! I'm the one who threw out that nickname to the press."

"Sweet Jesus," muttered Tim.

"Hey, you still haven't told me why you're here," said an apprehensive Doc.

"I have bad news, Doc," said Tim. "Last night someone killed Betsy Parker. Probably the person who killed those other two women."

"Dear God, no!" screamed Doc. "That woman was a saint! You're telling me the guy who gave me a slice of pizza did this?"

"We suspect he's the man. Yes."

For the second time in less than an hour, they heard, "You find and kill that son-of-a-bitch! You hear me! Kill that bastard!"

Ron looked the old man straight in the eye and said, with total conviction, "We plan on doing just that, Doc."

CHAPTER 25
Stuck

July 5, 2018

Ichabod pulled into the Alligator Adventure parking lot about 10 minutes after midnight. He was eager for the feeding. Popping open the trunk, he grabbed the two bags he had filled with the remains of Betsy Parker, and he headed toward the office.

Five minutes after turning off the alarm system and opening the main gate, he stood on the platform ready to feed the beasts. *The beast, feeding the beasts*, he thought with a smile.

This feeding would differ from the previous two. The contents of the two bags were not as full as they were at previous feedings. There were no intact legs or arms. The bag, in fact, held less than 70 pounds of the slaughtered waitress. Betsy's other remains, minus a head and a finger, were puddling in the River Hills parking lot.

Opening the first bag, he reached in and pulled out Betsy's right foot. She had painted her toenails a dark red. Standing at the railing, he held the foot out over the water and waited. It didn't take long. A 12-foot alligator sprang from the water, rising to within four feet of the outstretched arm holding the small, delicate foot. Its jaws were ready to accept the offering. Ichabod dropped the foot and seeing the animal clasp it, he giggled with delight.

Searching the bag for another piece of something substantial, he found nothing. Lifting the bag, he took it to the railing and poured out the contents. The thrashing that occurred moments later was something to behold. His laughter, the laughter of a true madman, rang out across the park.

Watching the waters finally calming, he picked up the second bag and held it in a tipping position far out over the railing. Tilting it, pieces of Betsy Parker slipped slowly from the bag and down into the dark waters.

What happened next would have scared the devil himself. Four, possibly five gators, in chorus, sprang upward from the water toward the leaking bag.

So shocked was he that he dropped the entire bag! It hit one of the rising reptiles splattering the bag's contents in every conceivable direction. In the waters below, blood, bones, and flesh, were being devoured by a horde of cold-blooded monsters.

As the bag fell and its contents attacked in midair by a contingent of voracious reptiles, Betsy's left foot, avoiding a snapping jaw, ricocheted upward, and wedged itself in the deck crossbeams much like an errant basketball shot occasionally becomes stuck between the backboard and the rim.

Betsy Parker's left foot would remain lodged for five hot and muggy July days, before being discovered.

When found, it would give putrid a new meaning.

CHAPTER 26
"The Shooter"

"**If he returns to his previous pattern, then he'll be out hunting tonight.**"

"Yeah, I know, Tim. Just can't get that finger out of my mind. He's telling me, not you, not the press, just me, to keep my damn mouth shut. He's embarrassed, and I'm the guy responsible. I pissed him off, and he went out and killed, no wait, make that - slaughtered - a waitress who worked in a pizza parlor. All because I labeled the son-of-a-bitch with the name Ichabod."

"Don't be too hard on yourself, Ron. He had her targeted. He'd been there previously. We know that because he knew Doc. He set up that whole scenario that night so that Doc could tell us about the tattoo. He wants you to know…"

"… Betsy Parker's death is on my hands."

"No! He's just taunting you. He knows we're struggling."

"I told you on the first day, guys like him love to leave messages."

"So what are they?"

"They're right there in front of our eyes, but we're too stupid to see them."

"Is it the way he positions the heads? Is it the holes? The color of the flags? Is it the golf courses? Is it the victims? Where's the damn message, Ron?"

"I don't know, but I guarantee you it's there."

A knock at the door interrupted their conversation. One of the staff secretaries entered and handed Ron an envelope.

"This just came in from forensics, sir."

"Thank you."

"What is it?" asked Tim, as he watched Ron tear open the envelope and extract two pieces of paper.

"This one is a report on the shoe scrub. They found some dead skin. They will do a DNA analysis, but we won't get it for about two weeks."

"What about the other one?"

"It's the analysis of the tire tracks."

"Well, finally a clue! We've been working 'tirelessly' before this."

Ron didn't acknowledge Tim's attempt at humor, although he had an internal smile.

"It was a Michelin 235/55R19 Primacy MXM4 All Season tire. Found on most luxury coupes and sedans."

"Aren't most cars that are bigger than a breadbox considered luxury?"

"Good point, Tim. Here's something that might trim the field somewhat. This tire had 99% of its tread remaining which indicates it has only been on the road for less than a thousand miles. Ichabod, based solely on his tires, may be well-off. They run about $200 each."

"Yeah, well, that's about $120 more than I like to pay for my Firestone 500s."

"Are they still making those crappy tires?"

"I think they call them All Season tires now," answered Tim.

"Yeah, and I bet when you're driving down the road, they make this 'cheap, cheap, cheap' sound," snorted Ron.

"Give me a raise and I'll upgrade my tires."

"I'll give that some thought," answered Ron with a non-humorous chuckle.

"We could go to local Michelin dealers and get a list of those who have purchased that tire in the last… what would you say… two months?"

"We could. We should. But… we… won't."

"No. Why not? Are… we… too 'tired'?"

"Ha-ha. That was bad, Tim. You and I have more important things to do. Have the staff run that down for us."

"What will we be doing?"

"See that big white board in the conference room?"

"Yeah. What about it?"

"We will make charts of everything we know. Maybe seeing it up there, on that damn white wall, will wake us up to what he wants us to see."

"How come when I hear you say, 'we will make charts' it sounds more like 'Tim will make charts'?"

"Rank has its privileges, Tim-o-thy."

One hour later they had a board that had four lists.

"Oh, yeah! Now everything is as clear as a bell," Tim said with a strong hint of sarcasm.

"Let's sit and stare at it for a few minutes, Tim. Maybe something will pop."

"While we're staring, Ron, tell me something."

"What?"

"Why did they call you 'The Shooter' when you were with OSI?"

"I picked that up in the late stages of my career."

"How come?"

"I know that you're aware of the command, 'Stop! Or I'll shoot'!"

"Obviously."

"Well, it wasn't so obvious to a few guys I tried to arrest."

"I see. You said, 'stop,' but they didn't."

"That's right. So, I did."

"You shot them?"

"Damn right I did! They had two choices. Stop and I don't shoot. Don't stop, I shoot. Fairly easy to figure out, I thought."

"How many suspects who fled, did you shoot?"

"Six."

"Kills?"

"Two. Both had weapons, though!" Ron stated with emphasis.

"Were you a good shot?"

"I qualified as an expert in all Air Force weapons. I carry today, what I carried then. A Beretta M9."

"Why didn't you give chase?"

"Look at me. How far do you think I could run?"

"I see your point," agreed a grinning Tim.

Ron weighed in at 275 and that may have been with only one foot on the scale.

"How did you pass physicals?"

"They overlooked my two main discretions, shooting people and eating, because of my solve rate."

"Which was?"

"I had exactly 175 cases dumped in my lap in my 35 years. Most were homicide, spying, or high-level stealing. I solved all but 12."

"That's fantastic!" said Tim, while grabbing a calculator.

"Thanks."

"Damn! That's ninety-three percent. That's unheard-of, Ron!"

"So they tell me."

"Why weren't you reprimanded for shooting those suspects?"

"Who said I wasn't? I had a pussy for a boss. He wouldn't back his men up, no matter what. We all hated the bastard," he added with a smile.

"What's that grin about, Ron?"

"Well, come to find out, the bastard killed prostitutes in Denver. He's serving a life sentence. I need to go out there and say hi."

"I'm sure he would appreciate that."

"Okay, enough about me. Let's concentrate on the board."

"See anything, Ron, which gives you any ideas?"

"To be honest, not a damn thing."

Just then, Jim Braddock, the Supervisory Special Agent, and the man to whom Ron and Tim both reported, entered the conference room.

"What are you guys up to, Ron?"

"Oh, we're just trying to put this in a different light, hoping that something will jump out and bite us."

"Anything jumping?"

"Hell, no."

"Look. I know this case is difficult, but the mayor has been getting to be a real pain in the ass. He's afraid that tourists may stay away."

"If I were a female, I'd stay the hell away," Tim said, only half kidding.

"He made mistakes with this last one, Jim," stated Ron. "It's obvious that being called Ichabod got under his skin. Unfortunately, his mistakes haven't been that damning yet."

"Well, keep me informed. I'm afraid this guy will do much more harm before we nail him."

"You may be right, Jim."

"Catch you later, men."

A few minutes after Jim left, Tim had an epiphany.

"I think we could put together a sketch of this guy, in color, Ron."

HEADS FOUND AT:
Tradition - Sara Carson - Hole #7
Indian Wells - Laura Cantor - Hole #15
River Hills - Betsy Parker - Hole #16

Suspect Vehicle
Dark blue or black sedan
Recent model
Michelin Tires 235/55R19 Primacy MXM4 All Season

Picked up Sara - on boardwalk?
Picked up Laura at The Half Shell
Picked up Betsy at Chris's Pizza and Pub

State of Heads - all chopped off with an axe
Sara - frostbite - found within 9 hours of killing
Laura - slightly cool - found within 6 hours of killing
Betsy - no signs of ice - found within 8 hours of killing

Suspect
6'2" to 6'4"
Weight: 210 - 230
Wears white Aussie Hat
Big Head - Large feet
Psychopath
Thought to have a single kill site
Thought to have a single disposal site
Man of disguises - different hair, eyes, clothes

"Oh? How do we do that?"

"We have two eyewitnesses of this guy. Between the two, I bet we can get close."

"You said color. Why color?"

"There are only three main eye colors. Brown, blue, and green."

"Yeah, so?"

"I'm guessing that when he's disguised, he also wears colored contacts. Doc said his eyes were brown. He also described him as having dark hair. I'm thinking he may be bald, and his eyes are blue or green."

"Why do you think he's bald or balding?"

"Nothing you could put money on, but how many guys know how to put on a wig? I'll answer that. Few. And besides that, he's always wearing a hat. We need to call Chelsea and Doc and have them sit with a sketch artist."

"Okay, so once we get this sketch, then what?"

"We put it in the paper and wait."

"Wait? No, no, you wait! Think, Tim!" screamed Ron. "You saw what he did after being called Ichabod. What do you think his reaction might be to an ugly sketch? Huh? No, Tim. We won't be putting it in the paper."

"Okay, but you'll agree to having a sketch made?"

"Yes, I agree. Let's get Chelsea and Doc in here."

"Once we get a sketch, we'll feed it to a computer and it can color the eyes."

"I'll get someone to bring them in tomorrow."

"Hey, are you playing golf tomorrow?"

"Yeah, I am. Where are we playing?"

"Eagles Nest."

"Damn! That's right next door to River Hills."

CHAPTER 27
Hunting

July 9, 2018

Ichabod, having scolded himself for having lost his temper and killing the waitress, was, nonetheless, out on the hunt just three days later. It was Monday and solving a mystery filled his troubled mind.

He arrived at the House of Blues at precisely 6:45 as suggested when he had made the reservation. He also requested a table close to the stage. It was Murder Mystery Night and the play would begin promptly at 7:00.

Tonight, he wore an open-collared shirt, a blue blazer, and gray slacks. Instead of a hat, he wore an expensive light gray wig to match that of his fake mustache. His eyes were green for this occasion.

Glancing around the room, he saw that it was a full house and that his table, which he had reserved for two, had the only empty seats.

He had told the greeter that his date couldn't make it and if anyone were to come in without a seat, they could share his table.

"Especially if it's a beautiful woman," he said with a wink.

As luck, both good and bad, would have it, just moments before the play was to begin, the hostess seated a middle-aged woman at his table.

She was thin with dark hair and blue eyes. Her blue dress was fashionable but not to the extent of being ostentatious. She wore a minimum amount of jewelry and had no wedding band. Makeup was limited to lipstick, eye shadow, and a light covering of face powder. Her nails were long and painted a light shade of blue and her hands had liver spots, putting her age, in his estimation, in the mid-fifties.

"Thank you for allowing me to share your table."

"Oh, you're welcome," he replied. "Please, just call me Rick."

"I'm Julia. It's a pleasure to meet you, Rick."

A waiter stopped and asked what their drink preference would be. Julia ordered a Manhattan while Rick ordered a vodka tonic he had no intentions of drinking.

There was no food ordered as the theatre had already established the menu. It would be salad, chicken breast with rice, and a vegetable. Key lime pie would be the dessert offering.

Moments after they received their drinks, the house lights dimmed, and the play began. Somewhere during the play, a murder would occur and everyone in the audience would be both a suspect and a detective. If you were to solve the case, you would receive an unspecified reward.

The meal, served quietly, came twenty minutes after the play had begun. Ichabod, his insides quivering with excitement, barely touched his food.

"Would you like another Manhattan, Julia? My treat."

"I would," she whispered with a smile. "Thank you."

During the remaining portion of the play, they whispered back and forth their thoughts about the who-done-it. She giggled at his saying, "I truly believe I'm the murderer."

The play would last an hour and fifteen minutes.

The small pill Rick would drop, unseen, into Julia's second drink during the closing of the play would take effect in ten minutes. Rick, ever being a gentleman, would be there to assist her, but not to her car, but to his.

Onlookers, who witnessed him helping her, heard him explain, "I'm afraid she had one too many Manhattans."

The plan went off without a hitch, and Julia, totally knocked out, was on her way to the rear of the Kitchen Table, less than a quarter mile away.

His modus operandi had changed. He didn't drive to the Air Park.

"Too far to go," he told the unconscious woman, then adding, "and obviously unnecessary."

He was less than a hundred yards from the turn onto 46th Avenue South when he glanced into his rear-view mirror to see flashing blue lights. Pulling over, he stopped in front of the Kitchen Table Restaurant which had been closed since 4:00pm.

Reaching across to the glove box, he removed his registration and insurance information. He knew the officer would report the plate number as the cruiser pulled in behind his vehicle. As he waited, he slid his license from a pocket in his wallet.

He was checking on the unconscious Julia when the tap came on his driver's window. Lowering the window, he said, "Good evening, officer. What seems to be the problem? I'm sure I wasn't speeding."

"No, sir, nothing like that. You do, however, have a taillight that appears not to be working."

"Really! I've had this car for only two months. Which one?"

"The left one, sir."

"Well, thank you for letting me know. I'll stop at the dealership in the morning and have it replaced."

"Is there a problem with your lady friend, sir?"

"Oh, we left The House of Blues where we took part in the Murder Mystery play. Do you know of it, Officer... Moore? Is that the name I'm reading on the name tag? It's just a smidgen too dark to be sure."

"Yes, I'm Officer Chris Moore, sir. To answer your question, yes, I know of the theater, but I've never been there. I've seen it advertised in the paper frequently. What's the story with your companion? She appears to be unconscious."

"She has had one too many Manhattans. She conked out once we sat in the car."

"Have you been drinking, sir?"

"Oh, no, Officer Moore. I never touch the stuff."

"I must admit, I cannot smell anything on your breath."

"Never touched a drop in my life!"

"May I see your license, registration, and proof of insurance."

"Here you go. I knew you would need to see them."

The officer looked over the documents and returned them to Ichabod, saying, "I guess you'd better get her home and let her get some sleep."

"Oh, there's little doubt that soon she'll be sleeping like the dead."

"Okay, sir. Drive carefully."

"Thank you, officer. Good night."

Seeing the cop return to his cruiser, he waited for a moment to see if he would pull out first. He didn't.

"He's waiting for me to leave. Okay, Julia we need to do some unnecessary driving, but we'll be coming right back to the Kitchen Table."

Pulling away, he made it through the light before it changed to red. The police cruiser wasn't as fortunate. Driving north until he could no longer see the cruiser, he made a right turn on 41st South. He drove two blocks, then made a right onto Poinsett Street, and followed Poinsett until it reached 46th. Stopping at the corner, he could see the Kitchen Table's rear parking spot to his right, just a few yards away.

Scouring the area carefully, he turned right onto 46th and then turning off his lights, pulled into the Kitchen Table's lot and parked in his normal spot.

Glancing over at the unconscious woman, he gave thought to not snapping her neck.

It might be worth a try.

Exiting the car, he prepared the chopping zone and afterward removed the unconscious woman from the car. Removing her clothes, he placed her on the plastic and grabbed his axe. He was within a second of chopping off her head when a car pulled into the lot.

Hidden by the bushes and the dumpster, Ichabod watched as a police cruiser turned right and headed toward the front of the restaurant.

"He has to come back," he whispered to himself. "This is the only way in or out of the lot."

Moving to his open trunk, he reached under the spare tire and extracted a gun. He hadn't used the gun since the woman in Coquitlam, British Columbia had fought him off and made a run for it. She only made it about 30 yards before he shot her in the back of the head.

Thirty seconds later the patrol car exited the lot and headed west on 46th. The cop's moving on, spared Ichabod from being labeled a cop killer.

Turning to the job at hand, he went into momentary shock when he saw Julia in a sitting position. She said something incoherent. Whatever she said were her last words as Ichabod swung the axe and took her entire head off with just one swing.

Wow, that's a first, he thought.

He had Julia bagged, and the area cleaned up, inside thirty minutes. Glancing at his watch, he saw it was only 10:30. It would be another 90 minutes before Ernie went home.

Not wanting to linger in the lot, he made his way to Jersey Mike's on 41st Avenue. Having completed the kill, he was now famished. He ordered a meatball sub and a ginger ale.

"Will this be a takeout, sir?"

"No, I'll be eating it here," he responded.

Minutes later, the server placed a tray containing his order on the counter. As he was about to take it away, the young girl said, "Excuse me, sir, but it looks like a drop of blood on your forehead. You may have a cut. Why don't you use the restroom to check it out?"

Startled by her comment, he panicked. He rushed from the restaurant as if it were on fire, leaving his food order on the counter, right where the girl had placed it.

"Hey, mister! What about your food?"

Backing out of the lot so that no one could see his license plate, he headed down 41st and turned right onto 17 Bypass.

Seeing he had well over an hour before he could gain access to the alligator park, he put the time to good use by laying Julia's head to rest.

He headed north toward Little River, with his destination being the Eagle's Nest Golf Club.

"This will be your fourth clue Mr. FBI man, and you still don't have an inkling," chuckled the demented killer, whose forehead still held Julia's drop of dried blood.

CHAPTER 28
Job Dedication

July 10, 2018

Ernie, having left promptly at midnight, was driving past Coastal Grand Mall when he had doubts about whether he had turned on the alarm system.

"Damn. I'd better go back and check. If they find the alarm system off in the morning, I'll be out of a job."

He made the first available U-turn and headed back to the gator park. It was 12:23am.

****

Returning from Little River, he caught the 46th Avenue signal light, which allowed him to witness Ernie's Malibu turning south onto 17.

"Have a good night at the Sundown, my friend," said Ichabod as he watched Ernie's taillights disappear into the distance.

Turning right, he stopped in front of the parking lot entrance, unlocked the gate, returned to his car, and drove through the opening. Once in, he returned to close the gate, but, as was normal, he didn't lock it. Returning to his car, he drove it to the darkest parking spot on the far-right side of the building. Surveying the area and seeing no one, he once again exited his car and popping open the trunk, gathered the two garbage bags of Julia's remains.

Dropping the bags at the entrance of the office, he unlocked the door and entered.

Opening the panel box, he found the alarm switch to be in the off position. For a moment he wondered if someone were still on the property, but, seeing the office was dark, he reckoned that Ernie had forgotten to set the alarms.

"Bad boy, Ernie. You would be in trouble if someone else had discovered you were derelict in your duties. Not to worry though, I'll cover for you tonight."

Leaving the office, he grabbed the two bags, made his way to the main entrance, unlocked it, stepped inside, and closed the gate behind him. Then, in total darkness, he carried the bags to the feeding dock. Looking upward, Ichabod gazed at the thousands of stars filling the night sky. Fascinated by the heavens, he almost forgot why he was there. Twenty deadly minutes passed before he began the feeding.

At the same moment that Ernie had turned to make his way back, Ichabod had been teasing the gators with Julia's lower left arm. He held it much higher than any of them could vault. Finally, he dropped it into the water and listened to the beasts' thrashings in their attempts to grab the morsel.

After emptying the first bag, he glanced at his watch. It read 12:40.

I'm taking way too much time, he told himself.

It would prove to be both a true and an unfortunate admission.

****

It was 12:46 when Ernie exited his car and made his way toward the parking lot gate. As he reached for the gate's lock, his body went rigid. The lock was open.

He couldn't believe it. He had forgotten to lock the gate!

No! His mind silently told him. *I locked this damn gate. I know I did! I remember leaving my car! What the hell is going on?*

Swinging the gate open, he returned to his car and drove in, parking in front of the office. Had his mind been clearer, he would have seen Ichabod's car parked near the rear of the building.

Approaching the office door, he found it unlocked.

"Have I lost my mind!" he shouted.

Entering the office, he checked the alarm system.

"Good God!" he proclaimed, "The damn alarm is inactive!"

His heart was pounding as he rushed to the main entrance and found, not to his surprise, it too was unlocked.

"What the hell," he whispered as he entered the park.

Silently making his way down the walkway, Ernie stopped in his tracks when he caught movement out of the corner of his eye.

Standing on the feeding deck, he saw a man tossing something into the water. Ernie, moving cautiously toward the deck, yelled, "Hey! What the hell are you doing up there?"

His blood ran cold when he heard, "Ernie! Is that you?"

"Yeah. Who are you?" replied Ernie as he made his way up the walkway and onto the deck.

"You forgot to set the alarms. Tsk, tsk."

"I thought so. That's why I came back."

"Your dedication to your work is admirable."

"Do I know you?"

"Yeah, we shared a beer and a sandwich at the Sundown a couple months back. Don't you remember?"

"Yeah. Yeah, I remember now."

"How's your head, Ernie?"

"My head?"

"Yeah, I hit you rather hard with my blackjack."

"That was you! You bastard! You could'a killed me!"

"I needed your keys, my friend. Besides, if I wanted you dead, you would be dead."

Ernie, his eyes bulging with sudden fear, asked, "What do you have in that bag?"

"Oh, this? Why this is the remains of someone named Julia," answered Ichabod as he reached into the bag and extracted a body part.

"You have got to be kidding," Ernie said in a whisper.

"Oh, look! A lower leg. These guys love lower legs," said Ichabod as he tossed the extremity over the railing and down into the water.

The sounds of a dozen gators had muted Ernie's next remark.

"I'm sorry, Ernie. What was it you said?" asked Ichabod, having deceptively moved to within six feet of the security guard, who now stood paralyzed by the horror he was witnessing.

"I'm calling the... pol... pol... police," Ernie finally said.

"Are you now?"

"You're crazy. You're a monster!"

"Now, now, Ernie, that title may be too extreme. You didn't think I was a monster that night in the Sundown."

"You're the guy they call... Ichabod!"

Dropping the half-empty bag, Ichabod grabbed Ernie by the throat with one hand and lifted him off the ground.

"Big mistake, Ernie. Big, big mistake. I don't like that name. Don't like it one bit!"

Ernie, choking, tried to remove the vice-like grip of Ichabod's hand from his throat, but to no avail. Raised into the air, his legs kicking madly, he saw the hate in the man's eyes, and he knew he was about to die.

What he didn't know, however, was how gruesome his death would be.

Carrying Ernie like he was nothing more than a rag doll, Ichabod moved to the railing, and with a repulsive smile, said, "I guess job dedication doesn't always pay. Sorry about this, buddy."

Lifting Ernie over the railing, he dangled him above the water, while saying, with irrational joy, "Let's see, little buddy, just how high these creatures can jump."

There was little doubt that Ernie's gurgles could only be screams of "Nooooo!!!!"

As if shot from a cannon, a monster gator leaped from the darkness and locked his jaws onto one of Ernie's flailing legs which easily pulled the man from Ichabod's grip. As he fell back into the water with a tremendous splash, hungry others inundated the huge reptile. The sound of the roiling waters was thunderous. They did not, however, drown out the distinct sounds of Ernie's short-lived, but horrendous screams, as the beasts tore his body to shreds.

After watching Ernie's horrific demise with sickening glee, Ichabod picked up the bag and dumped what remained of Julia into the water. The battering noises increased tenfold. He watched for ten minutes or more.

When the thrashing sounds finally abated, he walked off the deck and down onto the walkway leading to the front entrance.

"Apparently everyone has had their fair share tonight."

Returning to the office, he turned on the alarm system... *I promised Ernie I would...* locked the office door and left.

He approached his car carrying the two garbage bags that Julia's remains had formerly occupied. As he approached the trunk, he realized that he hadn't locked the park's entrance gate. Dropping the bags, he returned to the gate and secured it. Proud of what he had accomplished, he returned to his car and seeing the parking gate wide open, he thought, *Damn! Ernie must have left it open when he arrived.*

Jumping into his car, he exited the lot, then stopped, and closed and locked the gate. Satisfied with the results, he drove off toward home.

He no longer had control of his faculties, because if he did, he would not have forgotten the two bags he had dropped before rushing off to lock the main gate. Any control he may have had, became extinct the moment he killed Betsy Parker.

As he casually drove home, his thoughts cold-heartily pivoted to the meatball sub he had to leave behind at Jersey Mike's.

He had become far more than a monster. He was now the devil incarnate.

CHAPTER 29
Eagle's Nest

July 10, 2018

It was 7:00am when the first of the Hagan Hackers group arrived. There would be 32 golfers today with the first foursome teeing it up at 7:30.

Fifteen minutes later, the bag drop area was a beehive of activity as over twenty members of the group had already arrived.

"Who's in the first foursome, John?" asked Cliff Dittrich.

"That would be Carl Leslie, Ken Hall, Artie Albertson, and myself. You're in the third group, Cliff."

Moments later, Tim's car pulled up next to the bag drop with Ron sitting in the passenger seat.

Ron, opening the window, yelled to Hagan, "Hey, John, thanks for putting Stevie in my group."

"No thanks are necessary, Colonel. You better get a move on, you're in the second group."

"Who's my 'A' player."

"Good news! You are!"

"The hell you say! How did I get to be an 'A' player? I was a solid 'B' last week, and we didn't play!"

"Lack of participation. Haase, Al Lowe, Gary Wendt, all 'A' players, couldn't play this week."

Resigned to his fate, distant shouts prevented Ron's salty reply.

Running across the 18th green toward the clubhouse was a Mexican worker, screaming "¡Hay una cabeza! ¡Hay una cabeza!"

"What's that all about, I wonder?"

A bag drop worker named Joe, replied, "That's Juan. He cuts the greens. I don't know what he's saying, but he looks like he saw a ghost."

Ron turned to Tim, saying, "It can't be! Can it?"

"I hate to admit it, Ron, but it was my first thought."

A moment later Juan was at the bag drop, saying, "¡Fuera en el número 17! ¡Hay una cabeza!"

"I understood that. It's on the 17th green. Call the office, Tim, and have them send a team out here. Let's go!"

Leaving their car parked at the bag drop, Ron identified himself as the FBI and ordered someone with a cell phone to call the State Police.

"We're taking a golf cart, Joe."

"Yes, sir. No problem."

Moments later, Ron and Tim were driving down the cart path toward the 17th green.

"How did he know where we were playing, Tim?"

"Good question. I doubt that he calls every golf course on the Strand to determine where our group might be playing."

"Maybe he's a neighbor of one of our guys?"

"Could be."

"Then again, maybe he's one of our guys."

"Damn, Ron, that's crazy. We've known these guys for a long time. No one appears to be anything like a serial killer."

"Yeah, you're right. But how the hell does he know?"

They were within 80 yards of the green when Tim said, "I can see the head from here."

"Yeah, so can I."

A minute later they were walking up onto the green. Parked on the far side of the green and still running, sat the Mexican's mower. It appears he had made one cut, then turning to come back, saw the head, panicked, jumped off the mower, and ran toward the clubhouse.

"It's a woman," confirmed Tim.

"God, look at that cut!" exclaimed Ron. "It differs extensively from the cuts on the first two."

"Same M.O., though. Head laid at the base of the pin. The eyes open and staring toward the west. The usual puddle of blood. Nothing substantial that might give us a lead."

"Sadly, partner, I have to agree with you."

Looking up, they saw a caravan of golf carts headed their way.

"The state police have arrived," announced Tim.

"I'll be interested in seeing what Charlie has to say about this cut, Tim," said Ron, still examining the head while in a kneeling position.

"Morning, Ron. Not a good way to begin a day, is it?" said Captain Bill Baxter.

"That, sad to say, is especially so for her."

"We'll keep the area clear until your lab crew arrives."

"I think they'll finish up fairly quickly," replied Ron.

"Should I tell the golf course to stay open?" asked Baxter.

"Yeah, I would. The first group won't get here until 11:00. Our guys will have left by then."

"Got any thoughts?" asked Baxter.

"There's something different about this one."

"Oh? What do you see that's different?"

"The cleanness of the cut."

"Hmm, well, let me know what your lab says, Ron."

"Will do, Bill."

"Captain Baxter!"

A uniformed officer had approached the two men.

"Yes, what is it, Trooper Michaels?"

"Just got a call from the Alligator Adventure outfit. Their night security guard has come up missing."

"Okay, Michaels, you head over there. I'll stop by when I'm finished here."

"Yes, sir."

"I wish all my problems dealt with missing night watchmen, Bill."

"Sometimes, as you well know, Ron, what appears to be nothing, turns out to be something."

"Ain't that the truth, Bill."

"Our lab guys are here," said Tim, interrupting Ron's conversation with Baxter.

"Tell them to get the head to the lab right away, Tim. Then let's go back to the clubhouse. I'd like to speak to someone who knows something about this place."

"You seem to have things under control here," said Baxter. "I'll head over to the alligator park."

"I'll keep you posted."

"Thanks, Ron. Good luck."

Five minutes later, they were talking with owner Rick Elliot, who had just arrived after being called by the golf staff.

"God, I can't believe it!" cried Elliot. "I heard about this happening at other courses, but I had hoped this horror would spare Eagle's Nest."

"I'm sure that the victim longed for the same thing," Tim said sarcastically.

"I'm sorry. I didn't mean to sound insensitive."

"We understand, Mr. Elliot," said Ron, wanting to get on with the questioning. "Tell me, sir. What's the best way to get to the 17th green? That's where they discovered the head."

"Well, there would be two. The trees to the left of the green separate a residential neighborhood from the course. It's swampy in there, but I suppose someone could access the course by that means, or you could do the simple thing."

"What's that, sir?"

"Drive into our parking lot and walk down the cart path."

"Do you have any security cameras that focus on the parking lot, sir?"

"No, I only have two cameras. One in the pro shop, the other in the cart barn. Sorry."

"I need to talk to someone in the pro shop."

"Chuck should be in there."

"Thanks for your help, Mr. Elliot."

Walking into the pro shop, they saw a man standing behind the counter. He was engaged in a phone conversation. They waited until he hung up before they approached.

"Chuck?"

"Yes, I'm Chuck Smith."

"I'm Special Agent Lee with the FBI, and this is my partner Agent Pond. We have a few questions, sir."

"I hope I can help."

"Do you work every day, Chuck?"

"All but Sunday."

"Might you recall getting a phone call asking if the Hagan group might play here on Tuesday?"

"Can't say I have, sir."

"I'm not surprised."

"Where is the security camera located?" asked Tim.

"It's right there," Chuck replied, pointing to a camera on a shelf.

Tim walked over to the camera and after a moment, said, "Say, Ron. Come over here."

"What do you have?"

"Not sure, but this camera may point out that way. Isn't that the direction of the 18th green?"

"Was the camera running last night?" asked Ron.

"It should have been. The cleaning crew has been consistently responsible about turning it on before leaving."

"Let's look at the tape from last night."

"The monitor is in the back."

Two minutes later, they were viewing last night's tape. The camera focused on the counter. Behind the counter was a large picture window that looked out toward the 18th green.

The timer on the screen showed it was 10:30:24.

"Can we fast-forward?" asked Ron.

"Sure can," replied Chuck.

Now the film buzzed along at a quick clip as a minute passed in less than five seconds. It showed 11:24:41 when Ron yelled, "Stop! Back it up about two minutes."

Chuck reversed the tape until 11:22:00 appeared on the screen. Then, hitting the play button, the images proceeded in real time.

At 11:23:05, they saw a blurry image of a large man crossing the 18th green carrying what appeared to be a cooler.

"I guarantee you there's a head in that cooler," remarked Tim.

"No doubt in my mind, partner."

"I can't make out much of anything else though. How about you, Ron?"

"Not much. Maybe his gait."

"He's big, that's for sure."

"Oh, it's him all right."

The image passed from view at 11:23.

"He's walking to 17," remarked Ron. "That will take him five minutes there and five back."

"Plus, a minute on the green," added Tim.

"Fast forward to about 11:34."

Chuck, doing what Ron asked, stopped the film at 11:34:02 and then let it run at normal speed.

The image appeared again at the 11:38:12 mark.

They could derive nothing discernible from the image as he walked toward the camera.

"He's either a slow walker or he likes spending time with the head."

"Tell me, Ron. Does his head look bald to you?"

"Hard to tell, Tim."

"It's just so rounded. I think he's bald."

A moment later he disappeared from the screen.

"Would the camera in the cart barn have a chance of picking up something in the parking lot, Chuck?"

"No. There's not even a window in there."

"We'll need this film, Chuck."

"Do you think our labs could enhance it, Ron?"

"Possibly, but it's doubtful. They focused the camera on the counter, not the outside. I think it's too dark and murky."

"Thanks, Chuck, for your time."

"You're welcome, gentlemen. I hope you kill that sonofabitch."

"That's becoming a familiar sounding phrase," Tim uttered, as they stepped outside and made their way toward the bag drop area.

At 8:10 the last foursome of the Hagan group passed by on their way to the first tee. Rick Geslain, a member of the last group, stopped a moment to ask, "Any luck, Ron?"

"Not much, Rick."

"I heard it was on the 17th green."

"That's correct."

"That's their signature hole," said Joe Saffran. "It's a long par five and tough."

A jolting ring coming from Ron's cell phone interrupted the group's conversation.

"Hello, Bill. What's up at the alligator park?"

Tim, Rick, and Joe saw the expression on Ron's face and knew immediately there was trouble.

"We'll be there as fast as we can, Bill."

"I can tell you have things to do, Ron. I'm sorry you're missing golf again," said Rick as he and Joe drove off toward the tee box.

"What's up?" Tim asked.

"They found two 33-gallon garbage bags at Alligator Adventure."

"So?"

"Blood, hair, and bone fragments covered the insides of both bags."

CHAPTER 30
Alligator Adventure

July 10, 2018

Arriving at the scene at 8:45, a trooper directed them to the office where Captain Baxter waited.

"Thanks for coming over, Ron. We've closed the place down for the day. An office worker found the garbage bags in the parking lot near the rear of the building. They are your standard 33-gallon bags."

"Did you dust them for prints?"

"We did, but at least two employees handled them. The guy who found them and his supervisor who made the call."

"Well, we'll just have to print them and eliminate their prints on the bags as we come across them."

"One of my lab guys says the hair found in the bags is pubic hair."

"Makes sense, Bill. If our guy cuts off the head and puts it on ice, there won't be any head hair in here."

"I'm guessing that if it is human hair than the blood and bone slivers are also human."

"Safe assumption, Captain."

"Do you think this is where he chops them up, Ron?" Tim asked.

"Where did you find the bags, Bill?"

"Right this way."

"Was there any sign of blood?"

"None."

"He could have put down a cover on which to do the chopping," suggested Tim.

"Maybe so," commented Ron, "but why leave the bags and take the covering?"

"Captain, you said the night watchman is missing. Might he have caught the guy in the act? Maybe we're looking at his blood and hair?" asked Tim.

"It could be, but I'm thinking we may connect these bags to your lady's head at Eagle's Nest."

Upon reaching the parking lot, Ron immediately exclaimed, "He did no chopping here. Anyone driving by, especially coming from that direction," pointing toward the Barefoot Resort Bridge Road, "could have seen him."

"Then why were the two bags found here? Is it possible he brought them here to throw us off the trail?" asked Tim.

"Off the trail? Hell, partner, we need to get on the damn trail before being thrown off it, but, your reasoning bears consideration."

"Gee, thanks, Columbo."

"Sorry, but you're mistaken. Look, no raincoat."

"Is that the security guy's car sitting in front of the office, Captain?"

"Yeah, it is. There's something you should know, although I'm not sure if it is connectable or not."

"What is it?"

"We checked on the guy. His name is Ernest Cavanaugh. The people here say he goes by Ernie. A widower, he lives alone in Surfside Beach. Been working here since 2010. Works from 6:00 until midnight. The thing is, back in May, May 13th to be exact, at around 2:00am, someone mugged him in his condo parking lot. The police report stated that earlier that evening he had had a long conversation with a stranger he met at the Sundown Sports Pub. You know the place?"

"Yeah, I've been there a few times in the past. Its previous name was the Sundown Saloon. It's a decent neighborhood sports and family type bar."

"And, I presume, a spot where a guy can pick up women?" Tim asked.

Ron's nod, confirmed Tim's point.

"Anyway, the thief only took about ten bucks. Left him lying there. A woman found him while walking her dog. They took him to the hospital where a doctor diagnosed a serious concussion. According to the doctor's report, a blackjack delivered the blow. The guy stayed out of work for about a week."

"A blackjack? That's not your ordinary knockout weapon unless you're a professional," commented Tim.

"Ten bucks! Nothing else?" asked Ron.

"Not according to the police report."

"Okay, the big question I have then, is why are these bloodied bags here? There's no doubt in my mind that these bags contained the body of either that woman found at Eagle's Nest, or your missing security guard. My money is on the woman."

"Mine too," said Tim.

"I concur with you guys," added the Captain.

"Was this place locked up when the employees arrived this morning?" asked Ron.

"According to the employees, it was."

"Did they call his home?"

"Yes, but they got no answer."

"Have you tried to start the car, Bill?"

"No. Why?"

"Maybe his car wouldn't start, so he called someone, or maybe he took a cab home."

"Or... maybe he's in the trunk," added Tim dryly.

Turning to Trooper Randy Michaels, the Captain asked, "Do you know how to hot wire a car, son?"

"Will I be incriminating myself, Captain, if I answer yes?"

"No, but another smart remark like that, might," answered the Captain with a big smile. "Go do it, and while you're there, check the trunk."

"Funny," said Ron.

"Yeah, smart kid. One of my best."

Two minutes later the trooper returned and reported, "The vehicle started, sir, with no problem. I found nothing suspicious in the trunk."

"Good job, Michaels."

"Was everything on the property locked, Bill?"

"Everything, Ron: the parking gate, the office, and the main entrance. All locked tight."

"I'm sure they have an alarm system."

"They do, and it was active."

"So if anyone got in, the alarm would sound?"

"Correct," answered Baxter.

"Have you been in there yet?"

"No. I waited for you."

"A little presumptuous, Bill, but appreciated."

"I believe what we have, Ron, is a home run."

"Could be a grand slam," stated Tim.

"Is the alarm system active?" asked Ron.

"Yes, it is, sir," answered Tom Biggs, the daytime supervisor who would walk them through the facility.

"Okay, let's try it out. Do you have a key to the main gate?"

"Right here," Tom revealed, removing a chain of keys from his pocket.

"Will the alarm go off if we open the gate?"

"It had better or else we paid a lot of money for nothing!"

It was money well spent. The alarm sounded immediately.

"Good," said Ron. "Have someone turn it off."

A few minutes later they pushed open the gate and entered the park.

Unbeknownst to anyone at that moment, they had entered through the gates of revelations.

CHAPTER 31
Ernie's Pants

July 10, 2018

Tom Biggs was leading the contingent of lawmen around the pathways of the park, when Ron, his head on a swivel in his need to see everything, accidentally tripped and fell to his hands and knees.

After regaining his balance, he looked up to be staring at something bordering on unbelievable.

"Jesus! What the hell?" yelled Ron.

"That, sir, is Utan, the largest crocodile in captivity," answered Tom Biggs.

"Hot damn! That is the biggest damn beast I have ever seen!"

"Can I assume you have no mirrors in your house, partner?"

"Pond, my boy, you're a Rodney Dangerfield, wannabe, aren't you?"

Grinning, Tim asked, "How much does it eat, Tom?"

"He's fed on Mondays, but it is a hefty meal."

"Hefty meal, you say," said Tim. "Sounds like you could be a candidate, Ron."

"I know this will not sound professional, gentlemen, so I'd like to apologize beforehand, but, here goes... fuck you, Agent Pond."

"You were spot-on again," said Tim. "That did not sound professional."

They spent the next 30 minutes patrolling the park, including some inside exhibits. Finding nothing suspicious, they headed back toward the entrance gate.

As they walked, Tim pointed to a deck across a pond, and asked, "What's that, Tom?"

"That's the feeding deck. The animal handlers dangle food over the railing and the gators leap out of the water to grab it."

"How high can they leap?" asked Captain Baxter.

"Anywhere from 4 to 6 feet, depending on the size of the animal."

"What do they eat?" Ron asked.

"Mostly chicken and fish. Occasionally they get a treat of beef or pork."

"Can we get closer, Tom?" Tim asked.

"Sure. Just make a right turn at the next intersection. That's the walkway to that deck."

Moments later they were standing on the feeding deck, peering down at the water where they saw a dozen or more motionless reptilian bodies.

"Some of those things are huge," remarked Captain Baxter.

"I believe the biggest one in this feeding pond is about 15 feet. The smaller ones you see are the females."

"Tom, didn't you say they could jump about six feet?" asked Ron.

"Some can. Yes."

"Well, this damn railing can't be much more than that from the water, can it?"

"It's seven feet from the railing to the water."

"Any of those handlers ever get their arms torn off by a critter that may have gotten higher than expected?"

"No," answered Tom, with a smirk.

"Hey, Tom! What's that lying on the far bank?"

Straining to see what Tim had been alluding to, Tom answered, "It looks like clothing. There is, however, a gator lying close by."

"How did someone's clothes get in there?"

"I can't say, sir."

"Michaels!" yelled Captain Baxter.

"Yes, Captain?"

"Go get a pair of binoculars from a cruiser. On the double, trooper!"

"Yes, sir," said Michaels as he ran off toward the main gate.

The trooper, with binoculars in hand, returned in two minutes.

"Let's see what we have here," said Captain Baxter, while raising the binoculars to his eyes.

After adjusting the focus, he scanned the object for the better part of a minute before announcing, "It appears to be a half a pair of green khaki pants. There is a belt with an attached key valet. And you're right, Mr. Biggs. There is a fair-sized gator lying right next to it."

"Oh, no!" cried out Tom Biggs.

"What is it?" said the captain.

"Ernie."

"What about Ernie?" asked Ron.

"He had a key valet attached to his pants. Our work uniform for the security guards is green khakis."

"He couldn't have fallen into the pond. Could he?"

"No," replied Ron, convincingly. "Someone fed Ernie to the gators."

"Fed to the gators! How do you come up with that unfounded revelation?" asked Baxter.

"You said someone locked the park's gates and activated the alarm system. Is that correct, Tom?"

"Yes, sir."

"If we are to assume that those are Ernie's pants and those are Ernie's keys, then it is a given that someone else has a set of keys. Ernie could neither activate the alarm nor could he lock the park gates. Agreed?"

Everyone nodded their heads slowly as they digested Ron's words.

"Okay then. If someone had keys to turn the system back on, then they had keys to deactivate the alarm and unlock gates. If the alarm system had been on, then Ernie would have set off the alarms when he entered the park. Does that make sense?"

"Yeah, it does," admitted Baxter.

"Therefore, Ernie returns to the park for whatever reason. Maybe he forgot his thermos or maybe he thought he forgot to do something. Whatever it was, it no longer matters. Finding something askew, he enters the park. He catches a trespasser who overpowers him, and he gets tossed to the gators."

Somewhat wary of Ron's deduction, Bill asked, "How did this trespasser get a set of keys, Ron?"

"Good question."

"You have an answer?"

"Yeah, I do. The guy with the keys is the same guy who mugged Ernie back in... May, was it?"

"Yeah, May 13th."

"It wasn't Ernie's money he was after that night, Bill. He wanted his keys."

"But Ernie had his keys on him when he arrived at the hospital!"

"Ernie's attacker didn't take the keys, Bill. He made impressions and then had duplicate keys made."

Giving thought to Ron diagnosis, Bill shook his head while mouthing a quiet, "Damn!"

"He wanted the keys to get in here and dispose of the bodies. Ain't that right, Ron?"

"That is correct, Tim-o-thy!"

"You're saying that he's been feeding these headless women to these animals?"

"I'd bet money on it, Captain."

Turning to Tom Biggs, Ron asked, "Can we get someone here who can gut one of these guys?"

"You want us to kill one of our animals!" shrieked Biggs.

"That's correct, Tom. We could get a warrant if need be, but one of these critters needs to,"... he paused before saying with a mild smirk... "spill his guts."

Biggs, his astonishment at Lee's initial question wavering, fully realized what needed doing.

Nodding his head, he said, "I'll contact the zookeepers. It will take time to get these animals herded to another pond."

"Will they be able to determine which gator to cull from the group?" asked Tim.

"I guess so. They're all expert reptile handlers."

"Is there anyone here who could get down in there and retrieve that pair of pants?"

"Now!" exclaimed Biggs. "With all those crocs and gators in there? It won't be me, Agent Pond, that's for damn sure."

"I'll do it," volunteered Trooper Randy Michaels.

"You sure about that?"

"Yes, sir. I grew up in the Louisiana bayou, Captain. I've been around gators all my life. I can assure you, they're more afraid of you than you should be of them."

"I don't know all that much about gators," said Biggs, "but what the trooper says is true. Gators are afraid of humans."

"I can hop over the railing on the other side, Captain. I'll make my way through the tall weeds to the edge of the bank and retrieve the article."

"Be careful going through the weeds, trooper. Might be a gator in there. If you spook them, they may attack," warned Biggs.

"Thank you, sir, for your concern. I'll be careful."

They all watched as the trooper walked down the walkway and made a left. A moment later he appeared approximately 40 yards opposite from where they all stood.

"I can't see the article from where I'm standing," Michaels yelled. "Tell me when I'm in line with it."

"Will do," answered Baxter. "Move about fifteen feet to your right."

"How's this?"

"That's dead on, trooper."

A moment later, Michaels climbed over the railing and jumped down into the tall grass. Only the top of his trooper hat was visible as he made his way.

When he exited the tall grass, there, a few feet away, lay the 12-foot gator. Less than ten feet of ground separated the gator from the partial pair of pants. Having never been in danger while confined to the park, the gator's alarm system was turned off. Napping soundly, it was oblivious to the man's presence.

Michaels, showing caution, slowly approached the slumbering gator and while vigorously slapping his hands, barked, "Go away!"

Startled, the gator erupted into the water and disappeared for a moment before floating to the surface some 40 feet away. He watched but made no movement toward the intruder who had disturbed his morning nap.

All eyes shifted to Michaels, who had already retrieved the article. The onlookers, puzzled by his inattention to what he held in his hand, instead saw his eyes trained on something in their vicinity.

"Trooper!" yelled Baxter. "You should get out of there. Now!"

"Sir! There's a foot wedged between two beams just below where you stand."

"It must be that guy's foot."

"Not unless he painted his toenails, sir."

CHAPTER 32
The Park is Closed

July 10, 2018

Written in big black bold letters near the park entrance, a sign read: THE PARK IS CLOSED.

Ron ordered it closed at 10:00am and to remain closed until further notice.

"But sir, this is our busiest time of the year," pleaded Tom Biggs.

"Tom, stay out of my face. We have a bunch of dead people eaten by your inhabitants. This place will be closed until I say it can be open. Got it?"

Grudgingly, Tom agreed, saying, "I got it, Agent Lee."

"I want to see all of your zookeepers up here on this deck within the next ten minutes."

Five minutes later, Tom, followed by 12 others, arrived at the feeding deck.

"Agent Lee, I present to you our entire staff of zookeepers."

"Thank you, Tom. I appreciate all of you for coming in. I'm sure a few of you had the day off, but as you may have heard, we have a situation. It's one that desperately needs your expertise."

The group, as one, acknowledged Ron's words with a collective nod.

"Is there a supervisor or manager amongst you?"

A woman, looking to be in her early thirties, raised her hand, saying, "I'm Sheila McGraw. I'm the manager of the zookeepers."

"Okay, Sheila, here's our situation. Last night someone killed your security guard and fed him to your gators."

"Not Ernie!" someone in the rear shrieked.

"Yes, ma'am, I'm afraid it was."

Wailing began and ran unabated as more than a few of those present expressed their sorrow.

Ron waited patiently… for eight minutes.

"People," he announced with vigor, "if you want to help find who did this to your friend, Ernie, then we have to get going. There will be plenty of time to grieve."

"What do you need done, Agent Lee?" asked a tearful Sheila.

"We need to cull one gator and cut him open."

"To find remnants of Ernie?"

"Possibly. But it is our belief that the man responsible for beheading four women in the past two weeks, used the gators to dispose of the bodies."

"OMIGOD!" screamed a woman in the center of the pack. "No wonder they have appeared less aggressive lately!"

"Ma'am?"

"I am one of the staff that does the feedings, sir. I've noticed, as have a few others, that they, the gators that is, haven't been rushing to the dinner table, if you get my meaning. Many have even remained on the banks sunning themselves. Hell, if fed five human bodies in the past 10 days, I can see why!"

"Meaning?"

"Meaning, that a gator can go two years without eating. But, if they get overfed, especially females, they won't eat. We surely don't overfeed them, Agent Lee. It's bad for business. Feeding time is our biggest attraction."

Ron, while nodding his understanding, stated, "There is one other thing we need you to do. There is a foot stuck in the beams under this deck. We need to get to it. Could you clear the gators, so we can retrieve it?"

"Yes, we can do that, sir," sighed Sheila. "I need you to understand that we, as a group, have become attached to these beasts. Once you get to know them, they ain't all that bad. Killing these creatures for doing what comes naturally, just isn't right."

"Couldn't agree more, Sheila, but if you have another way of retrieving the contents of a gator's stomach without killing it, then be my guest and do it."

Sheila didn't provide an alternative. Nodding her head, she turned to the zookeepers behind her, saying, "It looks like Sid has been feeling more than content over there on that sandbar. He's 32 years old and although that's just the midpoint for these guys, I'm taking it on myself to call it a day for Sid."

No one said a word, but the looks on the faces of these loyal animal-loving people said it all. It would be akin to putting down your beloved dog of 15 years. It would hurt, and painfully so.

"Jack, pick three others and get it done. The rest of you, herd the others toward the south end of the pond. Alex, once they herd the reptiles, get that rowboat, and retrieve the foot from the beam."

Turning back to face Ron, she said, "Anything else we can do, Agent Lee?"

Seeing the depression in her eyes, all Ron could say was, "I'm sorry I had to ask even this of you, ma'am."

****

The fairways of 13 and 14 run parallel to one another at Eagle's Nest. Tom Daniels had been heading down the 14th fairway when he spotted Rick Geslain in the 13th fairway.

"Hey partner, let's run over and talk with Rick and Joe."

"Sounds like a plan."

A moment later, Tom had parked next to Rick's cart.

"You guys playing well?"

"Just okay, nothing special," replied Rick. "How about you?"

"We're minus 14, but I hear Carl Leslie's group was minus 15 at the turn," responded Tom.

"Bad fortunes could befall them," voiced Rick with a tinge of hope. "It's happened on many other occasions."

"Did you see Ron Lee before you teed off?"

"Yeah, he and Tim Pond were just coming out of the pro shop as we were heading to the first tee."

"They have any clues?" asked Tom.

"He didn't say, but he sounded like things weren't going well. Bill Baxter called him before we left."

"Who's Bill Baxter?"

"He's the commander of the State Police here in Horry County. I know him from attending various events held for retired police officers."

"What do you know about the call?" asked Tom.

"I heard Ron mention Alligator Adventure. Apparently, something bad happened over there. He told Baxter that they would get there as fast as they could."

"Hmm. I wonder what happened?" Tom asked. "I'm guessing we'll hear about it on tonight's 6:00 news."

"Maybe even the 4:30 news, or the 5:00 news, or the 5:30 news," added Joe Saffran with a chuckle.

Everyone laughed at Joe's making fun of the redundant newscasts that local stations had resorted to in the past couple of years.

Tom's cart partner, however, only feigned laughter. He realized immediately why the FBI agents had rushed to Alligator Adventure. He had forgotten the garbage bags!

****

Tim had given Alex a pair of tongs to retrieve the foot, and a large waterproof evidence bag to hold it once dislodged. He now held the bag in his hand. Even in the tightly sealed bag, Tim could not deny the odor emanating from Betsy Parker's four-day-old, maggot-infested dead foot.

"I think I'll get a container for this, Ron."

"Good idea. Get it to our lab guys. Tell them to perform a DNA test against the three heads. That foot doesn't belong to our newest gal. It's too decomposed."

They were now in the park's animal hospital where Dr. Paul, the park's resident veterinarian, was about to do a necropsy on the nearly half ton and 13-foot long reptile.

Sid, euthanized by the 4-man zookeeper contingent, now lay on his back on a stainless-steel table. It was painful even for Ron to watch the magnificent animal euthanized, but still a fascinating procedure to observe.

Wondering why it would take a 4-man team to put the animal down, Ron learned that to euthanize a gator, the drug needed to be injected into its tail vein. Since the tail could be a wicked weapon, he now understood why the task required additional help.

With the giant gator lying on his back, Dr. Paul stepped up to the table and sliced open the underbelly. His assistant then took the hide and pulled it wide so that the doctor could make the final incision into the stomach itself.

What came out made everyone, except Dr. Paul, look away, at least momentarily.

First to fall out was Ernie's head, intact except for a missing left ear, and left eye.

"He ate this last night," reported the doctor.

Next came a partially digested upper arm.

"I'll make a good guess and say he ate this about four days ago."

"That would be Betsy Parker," mumbled Ron.

Next came a few rocks.

"What's the story with those rocks?" asked Ron.

"Gators swallow rocks to help them sink to the bottom more easily," answered Sheila.

Last, but not least, came a foot bone.

"My best guess on this would be eight, possibly nine days ago," stated Dr. Paul.

"That would be Laurie Cantor," mumbled Ron.

"How should we proceed, Agent Lee?"

"What do you mean, Doc?"

"Should we recover these people for their loved ones to put to rest, or leave them in the bellies of the beasts?"

Ron gave deep thought to the doctor's question.

When spoken, Ron's words were firm.

"You'll say nothing about this to anyone, Doctor. We'll leave everything as it is. No more euthanizing these animals. No more necropsies. Understood?"

"Yes, sir. Thank you, Agent Lee."

Turning to Sheila and Tom Biggs he spoke decisively, "I can't see how this getting out will help your business. I'm sure the public would view it as disgusting. I know I do, but I'm in the position to understand, while the public will not, and will express their revulsion by staying away in droves."

"What are you implying, Agent Lee?" asked an incredulous Tom Biggs.

"I'm saying that your entire staff must not say a word about us finding the bodies of the slain women. It's too late for Ernie. Besides, we need to have something to explain to the media circus outside the gates. We'll put the story out saying he had an accident… slipped and fell into a pit of gators. An accident the public will understand. Mass murder, they won't. As for the rest of Ernie's body, it's my understanding he has no living relatives."

"And the park, Agent Lee?"

"You can reopen in the morning."

****

It was 12:45 when Ichabod turned onto Barefoot Resort Bridge Road and drove past the park. Cops, like a disrupted ant hill, were scurrying about everywhere. Not seeing Ron or Tim, he dared to stop to ask a gawker standing alongside the road; "What's going on, friend?"

"I don't have a clue to tell you the truth. The cops have been here since about 7:30 this morning. Haven't seen an ambulance, so I'm guessing there are no injuries or deaths."

I can't even begin to tell you how wrong you are, thought a smiling Ichabod.

"Maybe one of their big gators died?"

"Sure seems like a lot of commotion over a dead gator. Doesn't it?"

Not waiting for a reply, Ichabod drove up the road, turned around and drove a final time past alligator park.

"I will need to add finding a new disposal means to my list of things to do, Mr. Lee. Not to worry though. I know a place. Bon appétit, everyone!"

Driving away, Ichabod was already visualizing his next victim in his massively insane mind.

CHAPTER 33
Two More Kills!

July 12, 2018

"**What are your thoughts, Ron?**"

It was two days removed from the findings at Alligator Adventure and that of the fourth severed head at Eagles Nest. It was only 8:00am, but they were already at work, which for Agent Pond was a miracle unto itself.

They were discussing the case in the conference room while drinking coffee and munching on Dunkin' Donuts that Tim had picked up on his way to work.

"I think his overreaction to being called Ichabod has fried his brain. He didn't just kill and cut up the Parker woman, he went crazy and mutilated her far from his normal kill spot. Then he gets caught by the security guard who he ends up killing. I'll bet that he threw that poor bastard into that pond of cannibals while he was still alive."

"I've been thinking the same thing, partner. There was no time to mutilate him, and besides, there wasn't any blood on the deck."

"He's making mistakes, Tim. Leaving those garbage bags was a huge error. His mistakes will continue."

"Yeah, if he hadn't done that, then we, to this day, would still think he had buried his victims. Ernie would just have been an accident."

"You're right, Tim. Baxter would never have had to call us to…"

A knock on the conference room door interrupted their conversation. A young blond-headed woman, with green eyes, and a body to die for, entered carrying two big orange mailing envelopes.

"These just arrived from Columbia, gentlemen."

"Thank you, Marie," said Ron.

They both watched her leave the room and walk pass the glass windows that encircled half the room.

"Damn! If I were just thirty or forty years younger…" Ron said, not needing to finish the thought.

"If I were you," said Tim, "I'd go with the forty just to be on the safe side, and you may as well include an easy 120 pounds."

Even though he knew Tim's assessment was "spot-on," he, nevertheless, shot him the bird.

"What do we have, Ron?"

"Here. You open this one, I'll get this."

After reading what was in their respective envelopes, each reported what they contained. Ron went first.

"He chopped up our newest victim when she was alive! This bastard gets sicker by the day."

"This one," said Tim, "verifies that the foot stuck in the crossbeams was that of Betsy Parker. How did they determine number four was still alive?"

"According to Charlie, the spinal column showed no break in any of the cervical vertebrae associated with a broken neck."

"You mean she had been alive when that bastard chopped off her head?"

"I told you he was crackers."

"Crackers? How far back in time can you go?"

"Would you rather I use, 'nutso'?"

"Stop! You're killing me with these archaic terms," snickered Tim.

The conference room door swung open again, but this time the intruder came in unannounced. It was Jim Braddock.

"Good news, bad news, guys."

"Give us the good," Ron said.

"Your fourth victim goes by the name of Julia Spencer. She lives in Little River. Here's the address."

"What makes you think this is our Jane Doe, Jim?"

"This."

Handing Ron a photo, Jim explained, "The sister gave us this photo. She sure looks better there than she does in the photos you sent out. Do you see the resemblance?"

"Yeah, it looks to be her."

"Let me take a gander, Ron," said Tim, reaching across the table and taking the offered snapshot.

Tim perused the photo and then from a file he had lying on the table, he removed the photo of the severed head taken at the scene. After comparing the two, he stated with emphasis, "That's definitely her."

"A missing person's report came in today," said Jim. "A woman reported that her sister hadn't come home after seeing a play at The House of Blues on Monday night. We sent a cruiser to the House of Blues and found her car. You guys should go down there and talk to the waiters, manager, whoever, and see what they can recall."

"The evening personnel probably doesn't come in any earlier than 11:00am. We'll go then," replied Ron.

"What's the bad news, Jim?" asked Tim.

"The mayor called saying merchants are inundating the Chamber of Commerce with complaints. Apparently, people have been canceling hotel reservations, dinner reservations, and they're not going to the entertainment parks. Hell! Some have even left town!"

"I understand, Jim, but you know this deranged shithead, until this last kill, wasn't giving us a damn thing. He will make a stupid mistake that will let us put an end to this."

"How soon, Ron?"

Hesitating before answering, Ron prefaced his reply with, "I hate to say it, Jim, but unless we get lucky, it will most likely take two more kills."

"TWO MORE KILLS!" screamed a now apoplectic Braddock. "Are you out of your damn mind, Ron?"

"I know it sounds…"

"At whose expense? My wife? Tim's wife? Your neighbor's college aged daughter? You're telling me that a couple more must die before we can put this bastard down for good! That's unacceptable, Ron!"

"Look, Jim. He has been intentionally leaving us a clue at each murder scene. Somewhere up on that board are those clues. We need time to decipher them. He thinks he's smarter than we are and unfortunately, as of now, he is. This is a game to him. He picks his victims at random. That's why it's a bitch to solve. There's no rhyme or reason for who he kills other than to play this game with us. It has intensified because I labeled him, 'Ichabod.' Now he has a vendetta to settle with me."

"We have a combined sketch from two people who talked with him," added Tim. "Perhaps someone at The House of Blues can confirm the sketch or maybe even add to it. Then we could put it in the paper and have posters put in establishments."

"Yeah, Jim. We'll get this guy, but it will take time. I'm sorry."

"I'm sorry too, fellas. I know you're doing your best. I guess I shouldn't let shit from those assholes up in City Hall get under my skin."

"No apologies, boss. I heard it all the time from guys in the Corp who did nothing, but sit on their dumb asses all day, playing God."

"Yeah, you're right, Ron. Sorry for the interruption. I'll let you two get back to work. Keep me posted."

"Will do."

After Jim had left, Ron suggested that they update the board with what came in on the autopsy reports.

Tim did the updating, and they returned to analyzing what they had.

All was quiet as the two men searched the board for anything that might be a clue.

Five minutes later Ron broke the silence when he offered an opinion, "I think his kill spot is close to Alligator Adventure, Tim."

"What makes you say that?"

"It's the timeline. I wonder when the House of Blues opens."

"It's only 9:10. I'll call them. If I get an answer, what should I ask?"

"Ask them the time of the play and its length."

"According to their internet ad, they have a breakfast buffet starting at 8:30am. I guess they will be open."

Tim dialed and immediately heard, *"Hello, House of Blues. How may I help you?"*

"Good morning. Just have a few quick questions."

"I would be glad to answer them for you, sir."

"What time does the Murder Mystery play begin and how long does it normally last?"

"We only have a play on Mondays. It begins promptly at 7:00pm and runs no longer than 90 minutes."

"Okay, thank you."

After hanging up the phone, Tim reported, "The play begins at 7:00 sharp and ends around 8:30."

HEADS FOUND AT:

Tradition - Sara Carson - Hole #7
Indian Wells - Laura Cantor - Hole #15
River Hills - Betsy Parker - Hole #16
Eagles Nest - Julia - Hole #17

Suspect Vehicle

Dark blue or black sedan
Recent model
Michelin Tires 235/55R19 Primacy MXM4 All Season

Picked up Sara - on boardwalk?
Picked up Laura at The Half Shell
Picked up Betsy at Chris's Pizza and Pub
Picked up Julia at The House of Blues

State of Heads - all chopped off with an axe

Sara - frostbite - found within 9 hours of killing
Laura - cool - found within 6 hours of killing
Betsy - no signs of ice - found within 8 hours of killing
Julia - Beheaded alive - killing time not established

Suspect

6'2" to 6'4"
Weight: 210 - 230
Wears white Aussie Hat
Big Head - Large feet
Psychopath
May have a fixed kill site
Thought to have a single disposal site
Man of disguises - different hair, different eyes

Disposal Site

Alligator Adventure - feeds victims to gators

Suspect is Fallible

Abhors the name Ichabod
Getting unhinged - left bags at scene
Killed a security guard

"That security tape we watched had him there at approximately 11:20. Correct?"

"We picked him up at 11:23. Okay, so he arrives, collects the cooler from his trunk, and then walks into camera range. I don't know, Ron, three minutes might be generous."

"All right, let's call it 11:22 when he arrived. What time was it when he left? 11:40?"

"Yeah, I'd say it was close."

"Okay, then he gets back to Alligator Adventure just after midnight."

"Reason?"

"He knows the security guy's schedule. Ernie always left at midnight. He wouldn't go there until after Ernie has left for the night."

"Reasonable. Unfortunately for Ernie, he comes back."

"Yeah. So he took about 20-25 minutes to drive back from Eagle's Nest. How far is that?"

"Way ahead of you, Ron. I knew you'd be asking. It's nine miles and estimated to be a 19-minute drive."

"May have taken longer because of the heavy summer traffic. Okay, so here's what we have. He leaves the theater with or without her..."

"What do you mean with or without her?" asked Tim.

"She goes to the theater alone. No date. She wasn't meeting anyone. What's the chances of her getting picked up by him during a play? He waited for her outside in the parking lot. Either way, it's around 8:45 or later. He grabs her but doesn't kill her."

"Wait, Ron! That should tell us something. If he grabbed her, it had to be in the parking lot before she made it to her car. He doesn't know her before the play, so he can't possibly park anywhere near her."

"Okay, Tim. What's your point?"

"If he grabbed her in the parking lot, someone would have surely seen it happening, especially if she put up any kind of fight. That means he had to pick her up inside the building."

Ron sat on his partner's statement for a few minutes, stewing it over in his mind, before reluctantly agreeing.

"Okay, that makes sense. Let me see that autopsy report one more time, Tim."

After glancing through the report once again, Ron, in a rage, slammed down the paper, saying, "Son-of-a-bitch! That bastard drugged her. The M.E. found traces of a knockout drug in her brain. It says it takes effect within 10-15 minutes of ingestion."

"That's how he got her to his car. He must have slipped her the knockout drug toward the end of the play, otherwise it would have created a scene."

"Okay, so let's assume it's 8:45. He takes her somewhere to do the mutilation. There must be preparation work that has to occur before the chopping task can get underway, so let's assume he doesn't get started until 9:30. Since he arrived at Eagle's Nest at 11:20, he had to have finished the dismemberment by 10:50 at the latest. If he began at 9:30 and he takes 30 minutes to cut up the body, and another 15-20 minutes to clean up…"

Hearing Ron stop in mid-sentence, Tim asked, "What's the matter?"

"Cleaning up. Wouldn't you agree, that if you were cutting someone up, you wouldn't do it on the ground?"

"Yeah, I agree, Ron. Someone might see all the blood and would most likely report it."

"Yes, I'm guessing that they would, but not if you put down something on which to do your dirty work."

"Like sheets or large pieces of plastic."

"My thoughts, exactly! Okay, Tim, tell me, once finished, what would be your next step?"

"Obviously, I wouldn't want to stuff blood-soaked sheets in the trunk of my car, now, would I?"

"No, you wouldn't."

"I throw them in the garbage."

"Yes, you would, but you wouldn't dispose of them in a regular garbage can, would you?"

"Hell no! Even the guys picking up the trash, seeing bloody sheets or plastic, would call the cops. I'd dispose of them where no one would ever see them. In a shithole dumpster!"

"That's a bingo, Tim!"

"Okay, so he dumps the bags in a dumpster. Then what?"

"We'll get back to that in a minute. Let's get back on the timeline."

"Okay, we have him starting at 9:30 and arriving at Eagle's Nest at 11:20. We need to account for that hour and 50 minutes."

"Okay, Tim, of that 110 minutes, we have him chopping and cleaning for at least 50 minutes. That leaves us an hour."

"It takes twenty-five minutes of that hour to drive to Eagle's Nest."

"What do we do with the other 25 minutes, possibly even 40?"

"Being a cold-hearted prick, we go get something to eat," suggested Tim.

"Now, there's an idea. I'll bet if he got something to eat or drink, he did it at a nearby restaurant."

"Yeah, and all you might want would be something quick, like a burger or a sandwich."

"Check the map around Alligator Adventure and see how many fast-food places are within ten blocks."

A few minutes later Tim had a list.

"Some weren't open past 10:00pm, Ron."

"Let's head over to The House of Blues and talk with the folks that were working the theater on Monday."

"According to their online website, you needed reservations. We could check all the names and interview them to see if they saw anything. Hell, old Ichabod must have had a reservation. Damn, we could send a SWAT Team to the residence of every name on the reservation list."

"I doubt he made a reservation in his own name, partner."

"Yeah, that was a stupid suggestion" admitted Tim.

"No argument from me at that point," Ron snickered before adding, "When we're done with the House of Blues, we'll make stops at those fast-food places on your list."

"And after that?"

"After that, we're going dumpster hunting, my friend."

"Gee, I wonder who'll be climbing into dumpsters looking for bloody plastic sheets?"

"Rank has its privileges, Tim-o-thy."

CHAPTER 34
Dumpster Digging

July 14, 2018

"Are we going to take a drive up to Little River and talk with Julia Spencer's sister?" asked Tim as he drove north on Route 17 Bypass.

"We are not. I sent Agents McCauley and Beckett. She was a random pick up. I doubt they'll find anything. I'm sure it will be a waste of time."

A few minutes later they parked in front of The House of Blues.

"This parking lot has an exit that takes it directly onto the Resort Bridge Road. We are but a few hundred yards, as the crow flies, from Alligator Adventure."

"How about a blue jay?" asked Tim.

"What about a blue jay?"

"Are we any closer, as the blue jay flies, from the gator place?"

"You're a true asshole, Pond."

"Probably true, but tell me why is it always as the crow flies? Why not a blue jay or a cardinal or even a sparrow? Don't you think they can fly as straight as a crow?"

Tim kept naming birds until they reached the entrance. That's when Ron turned and said, "Now I understand why the Bureau thinks you're a dumbass birdbrain."

"Good one, Ron." countered Tim. "How about a stork?"

It was 10:30 when they arrived. The breakfast buffet still had a large contingent of people enjoying, what Ron considered, an early lunch.

A young girl with dark hair, too much makeup, and a ring in her nose greeted them.

"Hi, I'm Tina. Can I get you a table?"

"It's 'may I, not, can I,' sweetie," said Ron, correcting her speech, "and no, you may not. We're from the FBI. We would like to talk to someone in charge."

The girl, taken aback by Ron's rebuke of her greeting, lost her smile and tersely replied, "That would be Mr. Manning."

"Would you mind asking if we could speak with him? Please."

The greeter, letting go an exasperated lungful of air, turned, and marched toward the door at the end of the short corridor. Moments later she marched back. She wasn't smiling.

"Mr. Manning is in the office at the end of the hall."

"Thank you, miss," said Ron, with a shit-eating grin.

As Tim passed the girl, he whispered, "He can't help being a dick."

"I heard you, Pond."

"Boy, you must have umpire ears."

Reaching the end of the hallway, Ron knocked twice on the door and heard, "Come in, gentlemen!"

Entering the good-sized office, they saw a middle-aged man seated behind a desk. Rising as they entered, he greeted them in front of the desk with a warm handshake.

"I'm Harold Manning, the manager of The House of Blues. I'm told you are with the FBI."

"Yes, sir. I'm Special Agent Ron Lee and this is my partner, Agent Tim Pond."

"Glad to meet you both. What brings you to our establishment?"

"A murder, Mr. Manning. A murder we believe had its origin in your theater this past Monday."

"Surely, you don't mean our Mystery Theater Murder."

"No, sir, but we believe both the victim and her murderer were in attendance. We would like to talk with anyone who may have come in contact with either."

"Let me look at my schedule to see who worked on Monday evening."

Manning moved behind his desk and selecting a leather-bound notebook, flipped it open and paged through it.

"Yes, here it is. Sue Radford was our manager that night. She would have surely talked to everyone who entered the theatre. If not her, our hostess, Linda Barnes, would have. She greets everyone and has them seated. Also, we had five waiters serving the tables. I don't know which one, but I'm certain one or more of them would have had contact with the people you're investigating. Sue and Linda won't be in until about 1:00. Either one of them could point out the waiter once it's determined where your victim and the murderer were sitting."

"Okay, Mr. Manning, we'll return at 1:00. Please have those two ladies available for questioning."

"No problem, Agent Lee. I will summon them to my office as soon as they arrive."

"Thank you, sir. We'll see you at 1:00 then."

As they left the building, the greeter gave Ron a look that could kill.

"Smile, darlin,' you'll look much prettier, even with that ridiculous ring in your nose."

"F U," she whispered.

"Thank you for the offer, but no thanks," replied Ron.

Once in the car, Tim asked, "Where next, Mr. Manners?"

"Give me your list of fast-food restaurants around here."

Taking the list from his jacket pocket, he handed it to Ron.

"Hmm, small list."

"Yeah, not too many places open that late."

"Well, it won't take much time, that's for sure."

"You know, Ron, we will run into the same thing at these places as we did in there. The people who were working at 10:30 at night will not be at work at 11:00 in the morning."

"Yeah, you're right. Want to get something to eat?"

"Sure. I had nothing for breakfast except a donut."

"Drive out the rear entrance. There's a place right across from Alligator Adventure. I think it's called..."

"The Kitchen Table," said Tim. "I've eaten there. Their food is damn good."

Two minutes later they were pulling into the parking lot where Ichabod had mutilated three of his victims. As Tim turned right to drive to the front lot, Ron spotted the green dumpster at the rear of the restaurant.

"Hold up a second, Tim."

"What is it?"

"Would you look at that! A dumpster! A dumpster across the street from the place of disposal. How convenient. Pull up next to it."

"Can't we eat first?"

"Absolutely not!"

Reluctantly, Tim backed up and then turned into the narrow drive.

"Let's have a look," said Ron.

"You know, they will not appreciate two smelly guys eating in their restaurant."

"Oh, and who, beside yourself, would be the second dumpster digger?"

"What are you two fellas doin' down there?"

Startled by the gruff voice, they turned to see a large man standing on the deck above them. He wore dirty jeans and a sleeveless T-shirt that at one time was white, but now leaned toward filthy gray.

Ron reached into his pocket and while pulling out his identification, said, "FBI, sir."

"Yeah, sure and I'm Donald Trump."

"Glad to meet you, Mr. Trump."

"You gettin' smart with me, mister! Cause if you are, I'll come down there and stick your ass in that goddamn dumpster!"

"No, sir," Tim said. "We are the FBI. We have a case and it may involve evidence thrown into this dumpster. We were just about to check it out."

"It looks full, sir. When was it last emptied?" asked Ron.

"It gets emptied on Saturday morning," answered the man as he made his way down the steps leading to the parking lot.

"That means it has three days of trash on top of the evidence we're hoping to find."

"That's a lot of trash and I'll bet most of it is primarily food waste," surmised Tim.

"No, it isn't," said the man, now standing beside the two agents. "Let me see your FBI identification."

178

They both flashed their badges.

"Are those real?"

"They are real!" Ron stated. "What's your name, sir?"

"I'm Stanley. People call me Stan. I work here doing cleanup and fixing things."

"You said, 'no it isn't,' Stan. What did you mean?"

"There ain't no food waste in this dumpster. We have a garbage disposal for that. The only thing in this dumpster is boxes, cans, and paper. Clean trash."

"Thank God," whispered Tim.

"Tell me what you think might be in there."

"We're looking for plastic sheeting and garbage bags, Stan," answered Ron. "Probably covered in blood and... remnants of body parts."

"You know, when I came out here on Tuesday afternoon, the damn flies were buzzin' all around this dumpster. Flies ain't never around this one. I thought it strange."

"Yeah, well, what we're looking for was most likely dumped here late Monday night or early Tuesday morning," expressed Ron.

"That means it will be down about two-thirds of the way. It will only have Saturday's and Monday's trash under it."

"Two-thirds, eh," said Tim with a tone of disgust.

"It's only boxes and paper, Tim," reminded Ron.

"I think you're forgetting about the maggot-covered plastic, partner."

Stanley gave the two agents the once-over and said, "You two fellas don't look like you're dressed for thrashin' around in a dumpster. I'll get in there and look around for you."

"We sure appreciate that, Stanley," said a relieved Tim.

"We?" whispered Ron.

It only took Stan a few seconds to hoist himself up and into the dumpster. From their vantage point they couldn't see any of Stan below knee level.

"Looks like it's fairly full, Stan," stated Ron.

"Maybe. Some people who throw the boxes in here, don't break 'em down like they should. Those take up a lot of room. You fellas might wanna step back some. I'm gonna toss some of this stuff out to get down to where what you're lookin' for might be."

Minutes later and with only Stan's head now showing above the top of the dumpster, they heard him say, "Damn, this smell would gag a maggot! There's surely somethin' in here that doesn't belong."

"Ron, I think we should put a call in to our lab boys."

"Let's wait until we're sure, partner."

"Got somethin' here, fellas. It ain't pretty."

"Don't touch it, Stan!" yelled Ron. "Tim, I'm sorry, but I need you to get up there and look. We don't need it contaminated if it's what we think it is."

"It's already in the damn garbage, Ron! What difference does it make?"

"Jesus, Tim, for a moment there, you sounded just like Hillary Clinton."

"Screw Hillary Clinton, Ron!"

"No, thank you. I'll pass."

Tim acknowledged Ron's comeback, saying, "Ain't that the truth."

"I take it you don't think it's necessary for you to climb up in there and retrieve those bloody sheets?"

"Correct! Let Stan toss it out here."

Seeing his partner's point and his understandable reluctance to climb into the dumpster, Ron said, "Stan! If you will, just toss it out here."

"It's messy, fellas. Covered in maggots and it's sticky and smelly. I won't be able to toss it out of the dumpster. I'll climb up to where I can drop it."

A minute later first Stan's head appeared above the top, then his shoulders, and finally his arms. Raising his right arm, they could see he had, just as he had described it, a maggot covered plastic sheet. Dried body pieces and blood clung to it. Raising the sheet high above the dumpster's edge, he dropped it to the ground. Hundreds of flies buzzed around it.

"There's a tied garbage bag down here too. It shouldn't be here. You want me to fetch it?"

"If you would, Stan. Thanks," said Ron as he walked toward the dropped sheet. "Now you can call the lab, Tim."

A moment later Stan climbed from the dumpster holding a large brown 33-gallon garbage bag.

Taking the bag, Ron opened it to see what appeared to be clothing and hospital scrubs.

DNA thought Ron. *There has to be DNA on the hospital stuff.*

Turning to Stan, Ron offered his thanks on behalf of the FBI and especially that of Agent Pond who had escaped climbing into the dumpster.

"Is this from a woman who had her head cut off?"

"Yeah, we think it is, Stan. The killer must have been using this spot to mutilate the women. It's invisible from the road, what with the dumpster and all these thick bushes."

"Well, I hope you kill that sonofabitch."

"Yeah, we hear that a lot."

Stan left to go back inside the restaurant. Ron, left in solitude for a few moments, thought *the key to this whole thing was the courses and the holes.*

Tim's return interrupted Ron's thoughts, when he announced, "I'm having an electronic surveillance team come out too, Ron. The chance he will return to this spot again is slim, I know, but if he does, maybe we can catch him on tape."

"Too late for that, Tim, but I guess it won't hurt until the next time."

"The next time?"

"Yeah. He'll be killing again soon, that's for sure. But I doubt he'll be returning here to carve up his victim or to the gator park to dispose of them. I'm betting he has other places to do his dirty work."

"What now, Ron?"

"Well, once the lab boys get here, we'll have lunch and then go back and talk with the gals at The House of Blues."

"I'll bet that greeter, Tina, will be glad to see you again."

"Somehow, I doubt that, Tim."

CHAPTER 35
Interviews and Fast Food

July 14, 2018

It was 12:12 when they sat down to eat lunch at the Kitchen Table. While they ate, the FBI forensic lab techs were behind the restaurant collecting evidence while a security team installed a hidden camera in a tree across from where Ichabod had been doing his carving.

Tim had ordered the meatloaf with mashed potatoes and peas while Ron had a hot turkey open-faced sandwich with fries covered in gravy.

"How's that diet working out for you?"

"Up yours," was Ron's cryptic reply.

"Just how jaded have we become, Ron?"

"What do you mean?"

"Well, take the past few days, for instance. We've seen the head of a decapitated woman. Then we watched a head, a half-digested arm, and a foot, drop out of a gator's gutted stomach. Minutes ago, we had a slime covered, maggot infested sheet of plastic pulled from a dumpster, yet here we are, merrily eating meatloaf and turkey. Doesn't that strike you as... cold?"

"Yeah. Pass the ketchup."

Hearing Ron's disinterested reply, Tim asked, "I know your mind must twirl about all we've come across in the past few days. What are your thoughts?"

"I'm thinking this turkey gravy is beyond delicious."

"No, seriously, Ron."

"You're right. I have so much running through my head, it's hard to keep it all straight. Let me lay it out for you. Now try to remember it for later when we do real detective-like soul-searching."

"Go ahead, partner. Cut loose. I'm listening."

"My biggest questions surround the golf courses."

"The golf courses?"

"Yeah. Look, take the first girl, Sara. We think he picks her up near her motel down on the boardwalk. Right?"

"Yeah. Most likely he did."

"Okay, he kills her. It doesn't matter where or when, that is relatively unimportant, but he drives her all the way up here to dismember her behind this building, and then feeds her to the gators. But then, he drives over 30 miles south to a golf course at least an hour away to leave her head. Why? Why, when just up the road, maybe a quarter of a mile, there are four golf courses where he could have left the head."

"He has reasons, Ron."

"Yeah, but what are they? Take the second woman, Laura. He picks her up way down at the Half Shell. Drives all the way up here, does his thing, and then drives all the way back to leave the head at Indian Wells. Hell, he passes 40 courses on his way there. Why not drop the head off at one of those courses?"

"What about kills three and four, Ron? Those courses were relatively close by to the disposal spot."

"Rage dictated kill three, but, I'll bet the course was the target the entire time."

"Why do you say that?"

"He kills the Parker woman as she leaves work. Why drive the 10 miles to River Hills, when right across the street is Colonial Charters, and straight down Route 9 is Aberdeen and Long Bay?"

"I see your point, Ron. Kill four?"

"Again, and this is the oddest, why Eagle's Nest? He has the four courses just up the road. Why not them?"

"What about the holes themselves, Ron?"

"Yeah, that's been gnawing at my innards too. There's a connection. We're damn close."

By the time they had finished their lunch, 1:00pm had come and gone. After paying their bill, they stopped to see if the lab team had come up with anything.

"Nothing more than what you found, Ron," reported Gary Jones, the head tech. "Those are definitely a woman's clothes in the bag. We'll have the hospital scrubs checked for possible DNA, but after being in the dumpster for two days, anything we find won't be of any use in a court of law."

"This guy won't be going to trial, Gary," snarled Ron.

"10-4 that, Ron."

Five minutes later they were sitting in Harold Manning's office at The House of Blues. Seated to the right and left of Manning's desk were two women and a young man. The two original chairs where Lee and Pond had sat on their previous visit remained open for their use. Manning, standing behind his desk, made the introductions, explained the circumstances, and then turned the matters over to Ron.

Sue Radford, the older of the two women by at least 25 years, was the first to answer the questions directed at them.

"We take reservations, Agent Lee. I believe the man you're talking about called in his reservation the previous evening, using the name Greg Williams. He specifically asked for a two-person table near the stage. I can't help you with the lady, although Linda recalls the events leading to her being seated with the man in question."

Linda Barnes couldn't have been older than 21. She was an attractive girl with blue eyes, light blond hair, and skin that was both clear and soft.

Later, Tim would also note that "she had a great-looking ass."

She wore dark blue slacks and a white blouse buttoned so as not to show what was surely abundant cleavage.

"I remember when the man came in he said if someone needed a table, especially if it were a lady, he would be glad to share his. He was cordial."

"Could you describe him for us, Linda?"

"Well, he was tall and muscular. His face was more oval-shaped than round, and he had a white mustache that perfectly matched his white hair. As far as his clothing is concerned, he wore a blue blazer, and an open collared white shirt. I don't remember the color of his pants, although I'm thinking they were possibly gray. Oh! And his eyes were green. I remember because he winked coyly at me when he suggested that a woman sit at his table."

"You have an excellent memory, Linda," applauded Ron. "How about you Sal? You served them drinks and dinner. What do you recall?"

"I recall that the man was a generous tipper! He paid the lady's bill too. She drank two Manhattans. He ordered a vodka tonic, but I don't believe he ever drank it."

"What's your recollection of his looks, Sal?"

The young man of Italian descent, answered, "I'd go along with how Linda described him. I did, however, took notice of his watchband. The watch was…

respectable… not expensive, not cheap, but the band was all wrong."

"What makes you a connoisseur of watchbands?" Tim asked.

"My father. He was a watchmaker in Palermo. That's in Sicily. I tried it for a while, but it wasn't for me. Still, I know a good watch from a bad watch, like yours, Agent Pond."

Tim, glancing down at his Timex, responded, "Yeah, well, I got this from my kids for Father's Day a few years back."

"Oh yeah, that's a nice," Sal said sarcastically with the phony Italian dialect.

Ron, although enjoying seeing Tim being made uncomfortable by the kid waiter, interrupted the back and forth between the two by asking, "You stated his watchband didn't go with the watch. Why?"

"They made it from cheap leather and it had images of a golfer swinging a club embedded into it."

"Hmm, interesting. What color was the watch? Gold or silver?"

"Neither. It was one of those sport watches. It had a black case and a white face. Sharp. A watch like that costs around $300 to $400 bucks. The band cost $15."

"Anything else that any of you could add?"

All shook their heads, no.

"Show them the sketch, Tim."

Standing, Tim took a folded paper from his inside jacket pocket and opened it. Presenting the list first to Linda, he said, "Is this the man you seated?"

The young girl took her time studying the sketch, before replying, "It could with some subtle changes, yes."

"How about you, Sal?"

Sal took the sketch from Tim's hand, gazed at it for a few moments before handing it back, saying, "Possibly."

"I need not see it, Agent Pond," said Sue Radford. "I saw neither of them that evening."

"We'd like the two of you to come to the office tomorrow morning and sit with our sketch artist. Could you do that?"

"Sure," replied Sal rather quickly. "I'll pick you up at 8:00. Okay, Linda?"

You didn't need to be a detective to see the fire in the two youngsters' eyes. They knew each other well. They had no secrets.

"Maybe you should come earlier," suggested Linda with a well-known twinkle in her eye. "We may have trouble finding our way."

Doubtful, thought Ron with a grin on his face. *I'd bet you both know your way around… each other that is.*

Ten minutes later they were in the car and driving north on 17. It was 2:15.

Ron had the list of fast-food restaurants that Tim had compiled that would be open after 10:00pm. There were only three listed: Zaxby's, Jersey Mike's, and King's Pizza.

"Which one first?"

"Let's try the first one we come upon, which would be Jersey Mike's on 41st. If I were him, I wouldn't want to drive any further than I needed to, what with a chopped-up woman in my trunk."

"Neither would I," agreed Tim, followed by a quick, "There it be, Ron. Jersey Mike's."

Minutes later they were identifying themselves to the young woman behind the counter.

"What may I do for you, gentlemen?"

"Hmm," said Ron, "you should apply at The House of Blues for a greeter's job."

"I beg your pardon, sir?"

"Don't pay him any mind, miss. He loves to ramble. Tell us, is there anyone here that may have worked late last night, say around 10:30 or 11:00?"

"Let me ask Oscar. He's the manager."

A minute later a tall black man approached and introduced himself.

"Patty said you had a question, officers?"

"Is there anyone here now that worked last night, say around 10:30 or 11:00?"

"Only myself, unfortunately."

"How's that, sir?"

"The second shift manager called in sick last night, so I had to cover his shift. It's a long day from 8:00am, to 11:30pm, fellas."

"It sure is. Tell me, sir, did this man," inquired Tim, while handing the manager the sketch, "come in here last night?"

"You know, he may have. I was in the back, but I heard this commotion out here at the counter. By the time I got out here, the man had left. I saw him turn onto 41st headed toward 17."

"What was the commotion all about, sir?"

"Well, according to the server, he ordered a meatball sub and a ginger ale. When it came out, the server noticed a drop of blood on the man's forehead. She told him about it and suggested he may have a cut and to go into the men's room to clean it."

"Then what happened?"

"The guy just ran out the door. He left his order sitting right there."

"Did you see his car, Oscar?"

"I did. It was a Chrysler 300, I believe. Dark color. Black or dark blue would be my guess. Possibly dark green."

"Anything else you could tell us?" asked Ron.

"Not that I can recollect, sir."

"The server. What's her name?"

"Monica Reeves. She'll be here at 4:00. She works till closing."

Handing Oscar two of his cards, Ron said, "Give Monica my card and ask her if she could come by my office tomorrow morning around 9:00. We need to talk with her and have her sit with our sketch artist. The other card is for you in case you remember any other details."

"Was that guy a bad man, Agent Lee?"

"Have you heard of Ichabod, Oscar?"

"Oh, yes. Who hasn't?"

"Well, that was him."

CHAPTER 36
Skinned

July 17, 2018

Having congregated around the bag drop, the Hagan group greeted Ron's and Tim's arrival at the Heritage Golf Club, with mocking moans and groans.

"Boy," exclaimed Ken Hall, "seeing you two here doesn't warm the cockles of my heart."

"Cockles?" said Ron, "You ain't got no cockles, Ken, because you ain't got no heart. Did you forget that you loaned it out to Charles Manson about 30 years ago?"

"Hey, fellas! We have a pool going on which hole we'll find a head," announced John Coughenour. "Hey, Tim! Which hole do you want?"

A defined finger answered the question.

"I'm playing with Fred, Russ, and Fairweather. The punishment never ends, does it?" said Tim with a chuckle.

"You think you're being punished, try Morris, Saffran, and Holsten," commented Gary Whittaker.

"Those guys are your partners?" asked Ron with a grin from ear to ear.

"No," replied Gary. "They're yours!"

The bag drop erupted in laughter.

Having ten foursomes, they were starting off on both the first and tenth holes. The first tee time was 7:52, and the last at 8:24. Thirty minutes later all foursomes were off with Ron's group going off second on the front, while Tim's was fourth on the back side.

Ichabod's team was the third group on the back side.

Ron's cart partner was Joe Saffran who talked Ron's ears off with guitar chatter. A guitar player, Joe was good, playing at different functions both in Myrtle Beach and in Maryland where he lived before moving south. Occasionally, however, Joe would ask about the case.

"Any substantial leads, Ron?"

"Can't say, Joe."

"Any suspects, Ron?"

"Can't say, Joe."

"Getting close to an arrest, Ron?"

"Can't say, Joe."

"You're refusing to answer my questions, right?"

"I believe you've finally caught on, Joe."

Meanwhile, Tim had been with Fred Beermuender, one of the better golfers in the group. Fred's world was not aware of Tim's involvement in the case, so he asked no questions, except, "What did you make on that last hole?"

This is like a day's vacation, thought Tim, tired of his wife's persistence in asking questions he couldn't answer, resulting in her being upset with him.

The first group completed their round at 12:15 and the remaining groups finished in ten-minute intervals. Soon all were present, and the scores recorded by the group leader, John Hagan.

As the early arrivals awaited the remaining groups, they gathered at tables, drinking beer, and enjoying the free lunch provided by the Heritage.

Ron sat at a table with Rick Geslain, who captained the first group out, Ken Hibbert, a Geslain teammate, and Gary Wendt who captained the first team off on the backside.

"Is there anything you could say about the case, Ron?" asked Hibbert.

"There's plenty I could say, Ken, but I won't."

"Well, perhaps you're getting close to an arrest?"

"Perhaps."

The third group was in and reporting their scores to Hagan, who occupied an adjacent table.

Ichabod stood between the two tables closely listening to the conversation at Lee's table.

"I heard the killing up at River Hills was gruesome, Ron. Is that true?" Gary asked.

"It was. It may have been the most sickening thing I've ever seen in my career. I have trouble imagining even an animal being that vicious."

Ichabod sneered.

"How much longer before you end this thing, Ron?"

"I can't go on record about something like that, Rick, but if I were a betting man, I'd say... two weeks. I'll never admit to saying that in a court of law though!"

Ichabod gave thought to Ron's statement. *I wonder what they have to make them think they can wrap this up in two weeks? I'd better get to work. I have four more selections that will reveal all the clues. Tonight, I'll give them the big fifth clue. Oh, to be a fly on the wall as they try to solve it.*

Hagan interrupted his thoughts when he asked for his team's scores.

"Sorry, John. Just doing some daydreaming."

Twenty minutes later all the scores were in and John announced the winners and handed out the money.

"In third place and getting $60, the team of Lee, Saffran, Morris, and Holsten!"

"How the hell did we do that?" asked Saffran. "I sucked."

In second place and winning a $100, Beermuender, Pond, Fairweather, and McElrath.

"Ha-ha, Ron," Tim said as he passed his partner's table. "How's my ass smell back there?"

"Smells just like your breath, Tim."

Everyone, including Tim and Ichabod, exploded in laughter.

"Hey, Ron, are you guys taking bribes?" cried out Ken Hall, whose team finished tenth.

"Oh, compared to our daily bribes, Ken, this is peanuts."

Again laughter.

Laugh long and loud today, my agent friends, for tomorrow, all will not be so hilarious, thought Ichabod while waiting to collect skin money for his birdie on the 17th hole.

"Here are the skins for today, guys. There are seven skins. Beermuender gets two for holes 3 and 7. Al Lowe gets one for 10. Gary Wendt on 11. Bobby-Joe-Gurley for a birdie on 13! Way to go, Bobby Joe! Action Jackson on 15, and the last one goes to Carl Leslie for 16."

"You mean my birdie didn't hold up on 17, John?" asked Ron Lee.

"Nope, and neither did the one I had on 4."

So, you cut my skin, Ron. Well, tomorrow you'll have more skin to deal with, but it will be dead skin.

Hoping to buy tickets to a ballgame, Ichabod left without saying goodbye.

CHAPTER 37
Pelicans and a Vulture

July 17, 2018

Arriving at the ballpark parking lot somewhat early, he pulled to the side instead of heeding the usher's wave to follow the car in front of his to a parking space.

As he sat there waiting, the usher meandered over and asked. "Hey fella, everything all right?"

"Oh, yeah, I'm just waiting for my girlfriend to show. I want to park next to her so when we leave the game, she won't have to worry."

"Gotcha, fella. No problem."

The attendant went back to his job and Ichabod continued to wait patiently as would a spider waiting motionless for its next unsuspecting victim getting tangled in its web of death.

His disguise tonight was simpler than previous masquerades. He wore a Pelicans' baseball cap and T-shirt, a pair of dark blue shorts, sneakers, and sunglasses. There was no facial hair, nor a wig. This was as close to his real appearance as he had ever attempted.

The Pelicans and the Potomac Nationals had completed their warm-ups and play would begin at 7:00. It was 6:42 when she finally arrived in spectacular style. She drove a new blazing red Buick Cascada convertible and, with flowing blonde hair, she looked spectacular behind the wheel. He pulled in behind her and followed until they were both ushered to a parking spot. Glancing over as they both prepared to leave their car, he guessed that she was in her mid-to-late forties.

Exiting their cars simultaneously, he saw that she had left her top exposed. It was an automatic "hello."

"Leaving your top down, miss?" he asked. "Might rain."

"You think?"

"Anything is possible. Better safe than sorry."

"Yeah, I guess you're right. The game will start in a few minutes and I don't have my seat yet."

"You raise your top. I'll buy your ticket when I buy mine. In what section do you like to sit?"

"I prefer sections 103 or 104. They're close to the beer vendors." Then, with a big smile, she added, "and the ladies restrooms."

"Seems reasonable. They go hand-in-hand. I'll wait for you at the ticket office."

"Gee, thanks, mister."

"Call me Hank."

"Okay, Hank. You can call me Ginger."

"Ginger. Hey, why not! What other name could it possibly be?" he muttered to himself as he headed toward the ticket office.

Moments after the beginning of the National Anthem being played, Ginger arrived at the ticket office.

Ichabod had been waiting patiently with tickets in hand.

"I have third-row seats in section 104. I've never sat in that section. I hope you don't mind my sitting next to you."

"No," she said with a hint of uncertainty. "I guess that will be all right."

"I can see you're not comfortable with that. I'll just exchange my ticket for a seat in a different section. It's no problem."

Feeling flushed with guilt, Ginger capitulated with the stranger named Hank, saying, "No, I wouldn't want you to do that, especially after you bought my ticket. Tell you what, buy the first beer, and we'll be ballpark buddies all game long."

"Done! I'll go get the beers... you want a popcorn or a dog?"

"Sure, popcorn sounds great."

"Okay, I'll meet you at the seats in about five minutes. You go catch the first pitch. I'll be along shortly."

"Thank you, Hank. I think it will be a fabulous night."

"Better for me than most, I'm sure!"

She smiled at his self-serving compliment before rushing off to her seat.

He checked his pocket. The tissue where he had wrapped the knockout pill was safe and intact.

It would make its appearance during the 7th inning stretch.

There were two outs in the top of the first by the time Ichabod reached his seat with a beer, a coke, and a large tub of buttered popcorn.

"I'm sorry you had to miss the start of the game, Hank."

"Not to worry. It's not the beginning, but the end that counts."

"I guess you're right, but I've seen plenty of fireworks early in a game that decided the outcome."

"Can't argue with that, Ginger."

He discovered you should never underestimate a world-class beer drinker, like Ginger. She finished the first 20-ounce beer before the completion of the second inning.

He asked if he could get her another, but she insisted on getting it.

"You can get the next one. Besides, I have to stop in the ladies' room."

"Oh, well, far be it from me to stand in nature's way," said Ichabod with a big grin.

It was the bottom of the sixth when she finished her third beer.

"I normally have four beers, Hank, but I think I'll stop at three tonight."

"The next inning will be the seventh inning stretch. It's un-American to not drink in the seventh."

"Un-American, you say? Well, that's a first-time line," she said laughing. "I hadn't heard that one before."

"Well, I plan on buying peanuts and a coke at the top of the inning. Can I get you a soft drink or a coffee?"

"Okay, if you insist. I'll have a coke, but please let me pay."

"Wouldn't think of it, Ginger."

"You are too kind."

As the Nationals came to the plate in the top of the seventh, Ichabod said, "I'll go get in line. Hopefully, I'll be back before the bottom of the inning starts."

"Okay, Hank."

It took nearly 20 minutes to get the two soft drinks and peanuts. After paying for them, Ichabod carried the drinks to a small counter where people collected straws, stirrers, cream, sugar, and napkins. Sitting the cups down, he removed one top, and surreptitiously dropped the pill into the drink. Putting a straw into his cup to distinguish between the two drinks, he proceeded, with drinks and peanuts in hand, back to his seat. When he arrived, there were two outs in the bottom of the seventh, but Ginger had vanished!

Doing a quick scan and not seeing her, he asked the lady who had been sitting to Ginger's left if she had seen where she could have gone.

"She said to tell you thank you for everything, but she had to leave to attend to her dog." Then, holding out a slip of paper, the woman said, "She handed me this to give to you."

Ichabod, taking the slip of paper, opened it to see an address. He smiled.

"Looks like someone might get lucky tonight," said the woman with a knowing smile.

"Maybe," he replied. "Would you like these peanuts? I no longer have a need for them."

"Sure. How about those drinks?"

Handing the woman the drink with the inserted straw, he answered, "You can have this one."

"Thank you, mister."

"Don't mention it, ma'am."

He rushed hurriedly toward the parking lot, only stopping momentarily to deposit the drink with the knockout pill into a trash bin.

The husband of the lady to whom he had given the peanuts, said to his wife, "Pleasant enough guy. What's he rushing off to?"

"My intuition tells me, he's about to get laid," replied the wife.

"Hmm, if it's that blond that had been sitting next to you, I'd say he was a lucky guy."

"I was thinking, she's a lucky lady."

"Maybe we're both right."

"Maybe we are."

CHAPTER 38
Gingerly

July 17, 2018

The address was 914 Ocean Boulevard North in Surfside Beach. It was a typical beach house; built on stilts, with two floors, each having a balcony facing the ocean, and painted a Charleston pastel pink and white.

She had parked the convertible in the parking spot underneath the building. He didn't pull into the driveway, but instead drove down the street until finding one of the beach access parking spots. From there he walked in the shadows along the beach, to reach her home. He carried with him the tools he would need later that evening.

Climbing the obligatory winding stairs that all beach houses seemed to possess, he made it to her doorway unseen. He placed the axe, the ice-filled cooler, hospital garb, and plastic bags on the floor away from the door so when she greeted him, they would be out of her view.

A doorbell presented itself, but instead he used a gentle knock.

Barking sounds, of what he presumed to be a large dog, replied to his knock. As he waited for her to answer, he gave thought to what to do about such a dog. Those thoughts quickly dispersed with the sudden opening of the door. There, in the silhouetted doorway, stood a beautiful woman still wearing the colorful shorts and the white sleeveless blouse she had worn to the game. As she lingered there, the word "stunning" easily came to mind.

"Hank!" she cried with mild surprise. "Thank you for coming. I thought I had upset you to where you'd never want to see me again."

"Nonsense! Although I must admit, it surprised me when I returned from the food vendor and your seat was vacant. I thought you may have gone to the restroom, but then the woman sitting next to you gave me the note. That was kind of you."

"Oh, thank you. Come in and meet Bruno, my best bud and protector."

Entering the house, a massive animal greeted him with low growls.

"Wow! What do we have here?"

"Bruno's a Rottweiler. He's four-years-old and as lovable as they come."

"I can see why you needed to get home. He's magnificent."

The animal growled softly at first when Ichabod reached out to pet him on the head.

Drawing his hand back, the man who was here to kill the dog's master, said, "You said he was lovable?"

"Bruno," purred Ginger. "It's okay, buddy."

There would, however, be no denying Bruno's canine suspicions.

The growl grew more intense. They could see the hairs rising on the back of Bruno's neck. His entire body went rigid, as if he were ready to spring, which, in fact, he would if the stranger made any aggressive move.

Knowing dogs and seeing Bruno's body language, Hank said, "Maybe I should go, Ginger. It appears as if Bruno isn't all that fond of me."

"I've never seen him like this before. I wonder what's wrong?"

"It's clear there is something about me he doesn't care for. Dogs do, as you probably know, have an inner sense, right or wrong, about people."

"I don't want you to leave. I had hoped we could spend time together."

"As was I," he answered with a deep hunger in his tone.

"I'll put him in one of the other bedrooms. He'll be okay in there."

"You sure?"

"Oh, yes. He may whimper for a while, but he'll be fine for a time."

It was now 10:30.

Does she have a busy evening planned for us? thought Ichabod. *Maybe I'll take advantage of her offerings before...*

Bruno resisted Ginger's initial attempts to take him to a back bedroom, but eventually she had him secured.

Returning to the living room, she said, "There! I'm sorry about that. He's never been that way before with anyone."

"No apologies needed, Ginger."

"Can I get you something to drink? A glass of wine, perhaps?"

"I'll just have a soda if you have one. I'm not a big drinker as you may have noticed at the game."

"Yeah, well, okay. I have some soft drinks in the fridge. Wait, here. I'll get you a glass. Ice?"

"No ice, thank you."

She disappeared into the kitchen, giving him an opportunity to check out the view from the back patio.

I'll close these curtains. No sense in taking any chances.

When Ginger returned with the drink, she had abandoned her shorts and blouse. All that covered her now was a loosely worn white bath robe. As she handed him his drink, the upper portion of the robe parted, and two magnificent breasts made a not-so-subtle appearance.

"I must say," said Hank, "dreams do come true."

Setting his glass aside, he took her in his arms and as he did; the robe slipped to the floor exposing Ginger as a true blond.

Picking her up as if she were a feather, he whispered, "Point me to the bedroom."

They spent the next hour making love, not once, but twice, with "Hank" bringing out the woman in Ginger each time. Her moans of ecstasy, however, brought ferocious barking and growling from Bruno, locked in the adjacent bedroom.

"He's having difficulty with your enjoyment."

"Um-hmm," she purred as she kissed his body from top to bottom, stopping for a long stretch somewhere south of his navel.

She had an insatiable appetite for sex, which normally isn't a bad thing. But this wasn't normal.

Their third encounter turned out to be murderous.

She had climbed on top of him, but as she bent down to kiss him, he took her face in his hands and snapped her neck. He was still inside her as he rolled her over onto the bed.

"Wait here, Ginger. I'll be back in a moment."

Bruno, sensing something was wrong, bellowed.

"Can't have that, Bruno," whispered Ichabod. Putting on his pants, he ran to the front door, and opening it, reached around the corner to grab the axe he had propped against the wall.

Reentering the house, he first turned out the living room lights and closed the drapes leading to the patio. Next, he made his way to the room where Ginger had put Bruno. Slowly he opened the door just enough so that Bruno could get his head through the opening. Using the back side of the axe, Ichabod brought it down on the top of the dog's head, knocking the animal out cold.

"Good boy, Bruno."

Returning to the front door, Ichabod collected the rest of his materials.

After dressing in the hospital garb, he spread sheets of thick plastic onto the bedroom floor. Dragging Ginger down on the floor and taking the axe in hand, he quickly removed her head with three powerful chops.

"Such a shame," he whispered. "What a beautiful creature, in so many ways."

An hour later, Ginger was in pieces and bagged. He cleaned the room up, but blood spatter from a swinging axe covered the ceiling. The ceiling fan, which had been running at full speed during the entire ordeal, spread the blood around the room's walls in a repeating pattern.

He had filled three garbage bags. Two contained Ginger's hacked body parts. The other carried his bloodied hospital scrubs. After placing the bags outside the front doorway, Ichabod returned inside to gather the axe and the cooler.

A check on Bruno revealed the dog's labored breathing while blood trickled from the animal's left ear.

"Sorry, boy."

Leaving the front door open a crack, he gathered the three bags, the cooler, and the axe and in the darkness made his way down the winding stairs. Upon reaching the driveway, he found himself somewhat winded.

It had been a busy day. He had played 18 holes of golf in the July heat, attended a ball game, made love to a beautiful woman, not once, but twice, then killed her, and mutilated her body. The long day was far from being over, however. There was still much to do.

Walking under the raised beach house, he made his way out onto the sand and began the quarter-mile hike to his car.

Quickly the weight of his load, combined with the uneven sand, took its toll. After having traveled only a hundred yards, he became winded and his legs felt heavy, necessitating a few moments of rest. Another time, the cooler slipped from his hand and Ginger's head rolled out onto the sand. Dropping all that he carried, he quickly gathered the head and returned it to the cooler which was now void of its bloodied ice as it too had spilled onto the sand.

Gathering the bags, the axe, and the cooler, he continued his trudging through the sand. It took another three excruciating minutes to get to the car. Upon reaching the car, he put all he had carried into its trunk, slammed it closed, and fell against the vehicle in total exhaustion. Slowly he slid down the vehicle's trunk until his ass hit the ground. The back of his head rested against the rear bumper. He stayed in that position for a dangerous ten minutes before pulling himself up. Getting behind the wheel, he drove to Route 544 just a mile away.

Midnight had passed well over an hour earlier, and he still had so much work to do.

CHAPTER 39
The Witch

July 18, 2018

The quickest way to the Witch's 17th green was to park right next to the clubhouse and walk down the cart path leading to the par four 18th hole's tee box. The 17th green was to the left of the 18th tee box, down an embankment of some 20 feet.

As he made his way down Route 544 he met only sporadic light traffic. As he approached the Myrtle Ridge intersection, he spotted an Horry County Sheriff's cruiser parked in the Sonic Restaurant located across from the Witch entrance.

The restaurant had been closed since 10:00, so the officer was obviously not there to eat. It was, however, an excellent location to spot a speeder or anyone who looked suspicious. Feeling as suspicious as he had ever felt, Ichabod found that his palms were sweating. *But then, why wouldn't they be?* he thought. *Heck, all I have in my trunk are two garbage bags filled with body parts, along with a cooler containing a decapitated head.*

The presence of the police car temporarily voided his plan. He needed to come up with an alternative to gain access to the Witch. A glance to his right and seeing the convenience store gave him an idea. Turning onto Myrtle Ridge Drive, he pulled right in front of the store's front door. Leaving his vehicle, he proceeded to the store's doorway, stuck his head inside, and with an urgency in his voice, exclaimed, "Call 9-1-1. There's a robbery in progress down the road at McDonald's!"

Seeing the clerk make the call, he returned to his car and eyed the police cruiser. As expected, within moments, the cruiser's blue lights were flashing as the vehicle ran off.

As soon as the cruiser disappeared, Ichabod left the convenience store's lot, made a right turn onto 544, and drove the hundred yards to the Witch's entrance. Turning left into the driveway, he drove down the dark road with headlights darkened.

Traversing the dark road with caution, he eventually found himself next to the bag drop. Parking, he exited the car, popped open the trunk, and removed the cooler. Taking a final look around, he began his trek to the 17th hole.

The 600-yard journey from his car to the 17th green, being made in complete darkness, took 12 harrowing minutes. The cart path he traveled had more than its share of issues. Most of these resulted from tree roots, growing under the cart path, pushing the asphalt upward. This inconvenience had him tripping multiple times, although none resulted in his falling.

Having reached the area of the 18th tee box, he had two options. The first would be to cut across the tee box and then make his way down a weeded slope to the 17th green. The second required that he continue to follow the cart path as it weaved its way behind the 18th tee box and down a steep grade to his destination. Not wanting to chance falling, he opted to follow the cart path as it snaked its way to the 17th green.

Reaching the green, he found the flagstick planted in the green's upper right corner. Extracting it from the hole, he removed its flag and tossed it aside into an adjacent sand trap.

Opening the cooler, he removed Ginger's head. Taking the flagstick in his right hand and holding Ginger's head in his left, he jammed the stick up through the torn neck and continued pushing until he felt it butt up against the inner top of her skull.

Placing the stick back into the hole, he turned it so that Ginger's head faced westward.

"I truly enjoyed sticking it to you tonight, Ginger."

He giggled at his double entendre while taking a moment to admire his work. Satisfied, he gathered the cooler and took but two steps before stopping in his tracks.

He had heard something.

Plunk. Plunk. Plunk.

Turning back toward the flagstick, Ichabod smiled when he saw the source of the sound.

Ginger's brain matter had seeped from the skull and dripped into the flagstick's hole.

Grinning, Ichabod headed to his car.

It was already 2:15am, but despite his near total exhaustion, there remained much work to do.

****

As he made his way off the Witch property, it occurred to him that the police cruiser may have returned to the Sonic's parking lot. Exiting a driveway that shouldn't have traffic at this time of night would, with little doubt, raise the officer's suspicions.

He stopped well short of the exit.

Leaving his vehicle, he walked the remaining 200 yards toward the exit, and using vegetation for cover, surveyed the Sonic lot and those of other nearby establishments. Seeing nothing, he sprinted, as best he could, back to his car. Driving to the exit, he made a right onto 544 but, as luck would have it, caught the light at the intersection with Myrtle Ridge Drive.

As he sat waiting for the light to change, he glanced over at the convenience store where he previously had the clerk make the bogus 9-1-1 phone call. There, near the rear of the building, sat a large green dumpster.

The sprint to his car had taken all his remaining energy, and his exhaustion was now complete. Knowing he could not complete the remaining tasks; he took the easy way out. Turning left onto Myrtle Ridge, he made the turn into the store's lot and parked near the dumpster.

Still being cautious, he scanned the immediate area and saw nothing of consequence. Exiting the car, he walked to the trunk and opened it. Grabbing one bag, he carried it to the dumpster and with a noticeable grunt tossed it over the container's lip.

Returning to his trunk, he selected a second bag, this one much lighter. *This one must be the hospital scrubs,* he thought as he carried it to the dumpster and easily flipped it over the top.

A final return to the trunk had him about to grab the third bag when from behind, he heard, "Hey fella, what the hell do you think you're doing there?"

Turning to face the voice, he saw that it was the store clerk.

"Hey! You're the guy that had me make that 9-1-1 call! What's in those bags you're throwin' in our dumpster?"

"Come see for yourself," replied Ichabod.

"No, thanks, but I am gonna call the cops!"

The clerk had done nothing more than turn around and taken a step, possibly two, before Ichabod shot him in the back of the head.

He had hidden the now smoking gun beneath some rags in the trunk. Ichabod removed the third bag and tossed it into the dumpster. Wiping the gun clean, it also found its way into the big green container. Having pilfered it, along with a few others, from a pawnshop in California many years earlier, authorities would find it to be untraceable.

Closing the trunk, he took a brief look at the dead clerk, got in his car, and was about to drive off when he froze, while whispering, "Cameras!"

Leaving the car idling, he rushed into the store. Seeing a door behind the cashier's counter, he made his way to it. Opening it, he saw only a messy desk and file cabinets. However, another door presented itself beside the desk. Turning its doorknob, he found it locked. Searching the desk drawers, he found a set of at least ten keys. Frantically he tried each one until, finally, the seventh key unlocked the door. He cried with giddiness upon seeing the video equipment. After removing the CD from each of the four recorders, he bent each of them until they snapped in half.

Exiting the store, he saw a car pull in next to one of the gas pumps. Holding his head down, he ducked around the corner of the building. Taking time for a quick glimpse, he watched the driver exit the car. Convinced no one saw him, he headed to his vehicle, stepping over the body of the clerk as he made his way.

Having left the car running, he quickly pulled out of the lot and drove east on Myrtle Ridge Road. As he drove, he randomly tossed pieces of the CDs out the window.

Twenty minutes later he was safely home. He went straight to bed where he had a well-deserved good night's sleep.

CHAPTER 40
Clue #5

July 18, 2018

It was 7:15am when Ron's phone rang.

"Ron, this is Captain Baxter. Sorry to call you so early."

"That's okay. I'm preparing to leave for the office. What's up, Bill?"

"It's the Witch, this time. Hole 17. You gotta see this."

"I'll be there in twenty minutes."

He dialed a number. Hearing his partner's voice, Ron said three words, "Tim. The Witch," and then hung up.

It was ten minutes to eight when they, along with about a dozen others, stood staring at the blond-haired head jammed atop the flagstick.

"He stuck her head on top of the damn flagstick," said an unusually solemn Ron.

"What's the message this time?" asked Bill Baxter.

"I don't know, but, I think she'd make a hell of a pole dancer."

"Not funny, Tim. Not funny," said Lee with a grin.

"Did you notice the sand stuck to the base of her neck, Ron?" asked Baxter. "It's as if he planted her in sand before sticking her on the pole."

"That's an explanation. We'll get the sand analyzed. Maybe we can determine its origin."

"I'm wondering why he stuck her head on the flagstick and not at its base like all the previous times," said Captain Baxter.

Moving closer to the stick, Lee bent down and peered upward.

"What are you doing?" asked Tim.

"Where's the damn flag?"

"Oh, that. They found it lying in the sand trap over there on the right side."

"I've been in that trap a few times in my illustrious golfing career."

"Don't you mean non-illustrious?"

"Oh, you mean like your FBI career?"

Tim gave him the mental middle finger before saying, "Obviously he had to remove it, so it's being dusted for prints."

"I wish you good luck on that."

"Why do you say that?"

"He didn't care if we found it. He likely just tossed it on the ground and the wind blew it into the trap. He wouldn't have bothered to walk over there."

"Maybe he forgot about it."

"This guy will not leave any obvious clues, Tim. You can bet he's leaving messages though. We still aren't smart enough to figure them out... yet!"

"Well, this is, with little doubt, a different message than those that came before," surmised Tim.

"Yeah, and I think it may be the key to cracking the code that this guy uses to talk to us."

"Code?" inquired Bill.

"Yes, code. He's telling us something, but we're too blind to see it. This, however, may be the key. I'll bet money on it."

No one spoke for a while before Tim voiced three words, "Top and bottom."

"High and low," mumbled Ron.

"What's that?" asked Captain Baxter.

"High and low. What's high and low?" asked Ron.

"The tides," answered Tim.

"Temperatures," added Bill.

"Emotions," contributed a passing technician.

"What other description could you attach to this?" Ron asked.

"What do you mean?"

"Well, instead of 'high and low' maybe he's saying something like, 'up and down'."

"Oh, I see," said Tim. "How about 'tall and short'?"

"Yeah, things like that."

"How about 'raised and lowered'?" suggested one of Bill's officers.

"Lift and drop?"

"How about, 'elevated and grounded'?" asked another.

"Those are all good, fellas. I'll keep them all in mind, " said an appreciative Agent Lee.

"Hey, Bill."

"Yeah, Ron."

"I saw a lot of your guys across the street at that convenience store. What's going on over there?"

"Oh, the convenience store night clerk got himself killed. Took a bullet to the back of the head."

"Was it a robbery gone bad?"

"I doubt it. They found him lying in the parking lot."

"Parking lot? What's he doing there?"

"We're trying to figure that out. Earlier, around 1:30am, he had called 9-1-1 to report a robbery at the McDonald's about a half-mile down the road."

"How would he know about that?"

"A citizen stopped by and asked him to make the call."

"A citizen?"

"Yeah. Don't hear about that too much lately."

"No, you don't. I'd like to have a look at the scene if you don't mind."

"Knock yourself out, Ron. Be glad to have your two cents."

"Tim! Let's go across the street. A convenience store clerk got himself killed. We have a decapitated head over here and a dead clerk across the street. That's too coincidental for my taste. I'll bet a dollar to a donut, there is something connects them."

"Ron."

"Yeah, Tim."

"That would be a fair bet as a donut runs about a buck. You'd know if you bought occasionally."

CHAPTER 41
Another Dumpster

July 18, 2018

Upon their arrival, they found Trooper Michaels, whom they had first met at the alligator park a week earlier, investigating the crime scene. Ron noticed that the trooper now had Sergeant designations on his sleeve.

"Congratulations on your promotion, Michaels."

"Thank you, Special Agent Lee."

"Who found the body and when?"

"A guy working a construction job in Florence stops to get gas and coffee around 3:00. He calls for the clerk, whose name is Bobby Harrell, but gets no response. He goes looking for him outside and finds the body lying on the ground around that corner," reported Michaels, tipping his head to the left.

"Show me."

As they turned the corner, they saw a white sheet covering a body. Blood sopped the sheet where the victim's head lay.

Bending down, Tim pulled the sheet back. Seeing the wound, he said, "This isn't an execution style killing, Ron. Someone shot him from ten or more feet."

"That's the way you found him, Sergeant?"

"Yes, Colonel."

"It appears as if he's walking back toward the store and someone shoots him in the back of the head."

Ron hadn't noticed the big green dumpster up to that point but, when he did, he froze in his tracks.

"Has anyone checked out that dumpster, Michaels?"

"Not to my knowledge, Colonel."

"Get someone up there and tell me if there are brown plastic bags lying near the top."

"Yes, sir. Trooper Adams!"

"Yes, Sergeant?"

"Get up in that dumpster and tell me if there are any brown plastic bags lying on top."

It took less than two minutes to get a report from the trooper.

"I see three bags, sir."

"Pick them up and carefully hand them to someone on the ground, trooper," ordered Lee.

Minutes later, the three bags were all lying on the pavement.

"Let's open them up, gentlemen," commanded Ron.

"Damn!" cried the first trooper after opening a bag. "There are body parts in here!"

"All right! Stop! Don't open the other bags! Secure the one you opened, trooper. Captain Baxter!"

"Yeah."

"Have this dumpster taken to the police lab. Go through it with a fine-tooth comb. No one is to go near it other than your lab people. Understood?"

"Yeah, Ron. I'll get on it immediately."

"Good. Has anyone looked at the security footage?"

"Sorry to say, sir, but the room was unlocked when we arrived. Someone had taken all the security computer discs."

"He's a smart son-of-a-bitch," pronounced Lee, with clenched teeth.

"Do you think he had the clerk make the 9-1-1 call?" Tim asked.

"Yeah, I do. Why though, I haven't pieced together."

"I think I might help you out with that one, Ron," said Captain Baxter.

"How so?"

"The first person to respond to the supposed break-in at McDonald's was an Horry County Sheriff. He received the call while parked at the Sonic across the street."

"But of course," Ron said. "He saw the cop car sitting there and knowing he couldn't enter the Witch without drawing attention, he had it called away by reporting a robbery. Brilliant!"

"Then what, Ron?"

"Then what? It appears he waited for the sheriff to take off before he drove over to the Witch. I'm guessing he parked right near the clubhouse, then walked down the cart path to the 17th hole where he stuck the woman's head on the flagstick."

"Why would he come back to the store?" Tim asked. "It's chancy, don't you think?"

"Yeah, it was. But I'm guessing our boy had himself a busy night. We don't know where he made his kill, but we know he was here at 1:30, because that's when they received the 9-1-1 call."

"So, he drives back over here to dump the bags in this dumpster because what... he's tired?" queried Baxter.

"I don't know, but it had to be near 2:30 or later. I'm guessing he parked right near the dumpster and unloaded the bags. The clerk, seeing what's happening on the store's monitor... I'm assuming there is a monitor near the cashier's counter, Sergeant Michaels."

"You would be correct in that assumption, sir."

"Okay, so the clerk sees the guy unloading bags into the dumpster and comes out here to confront him. I'm guessing he recognized him from the earlier encounter with the 9-1-1 call. He decides he'll call the cops, but... bang, he's dead."

"Then the guy, realizing there are security cameras, enters the store, finds the security equipment and removes all the discs," said Tim, finishing Ron's theory.

"That's about it, gentlemen."

"It's the same story all over again, Ron."

"Not quite, Bill. We have the victim's body that matches the head."

"We hope," added Tim.

"True, partner, true."

They were about to wrap up the convenience store crime scene when Captain Baxter's cell phone rang.

"No doubt it's my wife calling to remind me about my kid's swim meet this afternoon."

Ron and Tim were on their way to the car when they heard Baxter call out, "Follow me, Ron."

"Where?"

"Surfside."

"Why? What's happening there?"

"A wounded dog."

CHAPTER 42
Bruno

July 18, 2018

A grandfather clock in Ginger's living room signaled the time Bruno regained consciousness, as 8:00am.

As the Rottweiler lifted himself, facial skin and hair pinned in dried blood for most of the night, tore away resulting in excruciating pain. Ignoring the pain, Bruno struggled to his feet and immediately sought his master.

Pushing the door fully open, he staggered into the living room. Sensing that something bad had happened to his master, he emitted a mournful howl. Making his way to his master's bedroom, he picked up the smell of death. Immediately, he became frightened. First the ears involuntarily laid down, followed by a low growl, and then the hair on his back stood up. Lowering himself into a semi-crouch stance, he backed out of the room, clumsily at first, then regaining his balance, much more steadily.

Feeling a draft at his back, he turned and sprinted to the front door. It was open a crack. Nudging his nose into the small gap, he opened it enough to escape and stumble his way down the stairs, falling the final three steps. Confused and scared and with labored breathing, he laid on the concrete at the base of the steps. Shaking badly, he needed a hug, but he needed a vet even more.

He appeared horrendous. Dried blood caked the entire left side of his head. Fresh blood, a result of torn facial skin, drizzled down his face. Being way past thirsty, his long tongue hung out the side of his mouth. Glazed eyes made him appear mad.

Thankfully, he had been lying in that position for only a few minutes when a neighbor, Barbara Smith, a good friend of Ginger, walked by with her miniature poodle Brenda.

"Bruno!" she called out to the big Rottweiler. "You shouldn't be out here by yourself."

Bruno could barely wag his tail. He knew the voice. It was the hug he needed. The vet would soon follow.

"What's the matter, Bruno?" said the soothing voice of Barbara as she and Brenda made their way toward the injured animal.

"Oh, my God!" Barbara screamed. "Bruno, what in God's name has happened to you?"

Rushing back home, she yelled for Bob, her husband, to come quickly.

"What is it?"

"It's Bruno, Bob. He's covered in blood. He needs a doctor!"

"Where's Ginger?"

"Oh my. Where's Ginger?" said Barbara. "Go see if Ginger's hurt. Hurry. I'll call the police."

"The police! Why do that?" asked Bob, taken aback by his wife's hysteria.

"Just do as I ask, Bob! Go!"

Still in his pajamas, he had been enjoying a cup of coffee while reading the paper, when his hysterical wife came barging into the house and ordered him to check on their neighbor, Ginger Evans.

Stepping into his slippers, Bob made his way to the neighbor's house. As he approached the stairs, his breath left him when he saw the injured Bruno.

Looking up the stairs toward the open door, Bob felt fear. Afraid of what he would find, he approached the partially open doorway with a great deal of caution and trepidation. As his shaking hand reached for the door handle, a Surfside Police squad car pulled into the drive, and its young driver exited the car yelling, "Don't touch the door, sir!"

"Sir! Do not go in there," barked a second officer. "We'll take care of this."

Nodding, Bob quickly descended the stairs and watched as two officers bounded up the steps and fearlessly entered the house.

Moments later a rescue squad vehicle appeared. A man, obviously a trained volunteer, asked, "Is there someone hurt, sir?"

"I don't know. The police are up there where the owner of this injured animal lives."

Seeing the injured Bruno, the man yelled to another man in the ambulance, "Bring some medical supplies to treat a bloody wound, Joe. We have a dog here who appears to be in bad shape."

Turning back to Bob, the man asked, "You know this animal, sir? Is he dangerous in any way?"

"He's as gentle as they come, sir. You needn't worry about Bruno."

Ten minutes later, informed by the police officers that there was no one in the house, the rescue team left, taking Bruno to the Ark Animal Hospital a few blocks away.

Ten minutes after that, the FBI arrived.

CHAPTER 43
Spatter

July 18, 2018

"**Let's hear it, officer,**" said Ron, standing in the driveway of Ginger Evans.

"Well, sir. We received a call from a Barbara Smith... that would be her standing over there with her husband Bob. She reported that she had found her neighbor's dog lying in the driveway with severe wounds and that the neighbor's door," he said while pointing to the door at the top of the stairway, "was open."

"And?"

"We arrived at 8:32 and entered the house, sir."

"We searched it thoroughly."

"And?"

"You'd better come in, sir, and see for yourself."

Making their way up the stairs, Ron saw the convertible and called out to Bill Baxter, "Captain, have someone go over that car."

"We're on it!"

Entering the living room, they saw that everything was neatly in place. No furniture eschewed, no damage to walls. There were, however, multiple pictures of a woman whose head they had found impaled on a flagstick earlier that morning.

Following the police officer, he first showed them the massive blood stain on the floor leading into a bedroom.

"We believe the dog had been lying here, sir. He had a serious wound on his head. You can see dog hair in the dried blood. We think he was unconscious for most of the night."

"Okay, what else?"

"In here, sir."

Stepping into Ginger's bedroom they found someone had left blankets piled in the middle of the bed, but the rest of the room was neat, but for one unsettling exception. Blood spatter covered all the walls and most of the ceiling.

Upon seeing the revolving ceiling fan, it took Ron only a moment to ascertain what had happened.

"He killed her and chopped her up right here on the floor. Every time he raised the axe, blood would fly off the blade and get caught in the wind stream created by the fan, spreading splatter on all the walls."

"There are women's clothes lying on this bedroom bench, Ron. There's a pair of shorts, a blouse, bra, and panties. There's also a white robe."

"She had sex with him. Be sure to have the forensic team check the bedding for DNA."

Seeing photographs on a dresser, Tim said, "I don't blame him. She's a knockout."

"Was a knockout," corrected Ron.

A thought exploded in Ron's head as he looked out the bedroom's window at the beach.

"Damn! Baxter! Get people down on the beach and look for footprints."

"Footprints in the sand?" Tim asked. "You know it's a useless venture. Sand crumbles, gets walked on, and then gets washed away."

"True, Tim, but I'll bet he didn't park his car in this driveway. He wouldn't want anyone to take notice of his vehicle. That's for sure."

"True."

"A head covered in sand indicates he used the beach to come and go."

"Tough to argue that point," quipped Tim.

"There's not much doubt he puts the heads in a cooler. Agreed?"

"Agreed," nodded Tim. "And do you know why, Ron?"

"No. Why?"

"Because of that old saying."

"What old saying?"

"Cooler heads will prevail?"

Everyone in the room laughed except Ron, who just shot Pond a grin before he continued with his theory.

"I'm just guessing now, but I think there's a strong chance he dropped the cooler somewhere down on that beach and out rolled the damn head. Would anyone want to make a wager on that being a fact?"

"Nope," Tim answered, forever admiring his partner's cognitive skills.

"Surfside has beach access parking every three blocks, Agent Lee," said one of the Surfside officers who had led them into the house.

"I'm sure he parked in the closest one, Officer. Could you determine where that would be? Maybe someone on patrol last night noted it."

"I'll check into it, sir."

"Thank you."

A moment later, Sergeant Michaels entered the room and hailed Ron, "Agent Lee."

"Yes, Sergeant?"

"We checked out the car and found this, sir."

Taking what appeared to be a colorful piece of paper, Ron saw it was a Pelicans' baseball ticket stub, dated July 17, 2018.

"Holy crap! She met him at the Pelicans' game last night! He must have followed her… no wait… she invited him here! Tim, call the Pelicans' ticket office. Maybe they could tell you who paid for this ticket, and who sat next to this woman or even near her. As stunning as she was, she wouldn't go unnoticed. I bet he sat within a few seats if not right next to her. If we could find someone else who sat near them, maybe we could get a good I.D. Let's get on it! This could be the big break!"

CHAPTER 44
Wheat from the Chaff

July 19, 2018

It was only 7:00am but Ron was already at the office anxiously awaiting the day to begin. He expected to uncover many pieces of the puzzle from the previous day's events.

These pieces included the autopsies on both the decapitated head and the body parts found in two of the bags. Also expected were the DNA reports on the bedding and any found on the hospital scrubs found in bag three. Bag three also contained the bloodied plastic sheets where the decapitation and mutilation of the body had occurred.

He was most eager to see if the Pelicans ticket personnel could come up with the names of those who may have sat near Ginger Evans. Ron surmised they could track anyone who paid for their ticket with a credit card. He also hoped that possibly the area may have had season ticket holders.

Having stayed late last night, he had already received news that the police lab had discovered a 38-caliber revolver in the dumpster. They had identified it as the weapon used in the murder of the clerk. Stolen from a California pawn shop some 17 years earlier, it was no surprise to anyone it was untraceable.

He had been enjoying the early morning solitude while drinking coffee and reading all the relevant news in the local paper. The office phone rang just as he had turned his attention to the Jumble and the Sudoku puzzles.

His enjoyment was about to end.

"Hello. FBI. Special Agent Lee speaking."

"Agent Lee?"

"Yes, this is he."

"I'm guessing that you have wanted to speak with me for some time."

A shiver ran down Ron's back as he knew immediately it was the man he had labeled, Ichabod. He disguised his voice, perhaps with a cloth of some type being held over the phone's mouthpiece, an old but still an effective ploy.

"You only have four more clues coming, Agent Lee. If you can't solve the clues, I've generously left for you, well... you too will be a failure just like all those before you. I'll be blowing in the wind and you'll be the town clown."

"Listen, you piece of shit. When I catch you, and I will catch you, the only thing that will be blowing in the wind will be your fucking ashes!"

"My, my. The language. So infantile. Stay calm, Agent Lee. Maybe you'll be able to piece it all together before the deadline."

"Deadline? You had better pay attention to the first syllable of that word, because that's what you will be, real soon, you bastard!"

"I thought, being a big thinker, you would have been a better adversary, Agent Lee. Your small-minded partner, Mr. Pond, doesn't bring much to the table now, does he? Shoring up your manpower should be a priority. In a word, you have been a great disappointment, Ron. I grade you with the local police at my previous locations."

"Your clues suck. Admit it."

Then, hoping to insult and enrage him to the point he might make a fatal mistake, Ron said, "You're afraid to give a meaningful clue because you know I'd have you by the balls, that is, if you even have any balls!"

"The clues are there for the solving, Agent Lee. Maybe, due to your ineptness, you'll need someone else to spell it out for you, since you're incapable of adding it up by yourself."

"You won't think I'm inept when I have my gun halfway up your ass! I'm coming for you, ICH-A-BOD!"

"Make sure you write this down, Agent Lee. Just four more clues. Goodbye."

Hearing the click, Ron knew it would be useless to trace the call. Over the next 15 minutes he replayed as much of the conversation as he could recall.

"... four more clues... stay calm... piece it all together... big thinker... small-minded... write this down... just four more clues... spell it out... add it up..."

"Damn! That bastard is planning to kill four more women."

"Oh, and how do you know he will kill four more?"

Ron almost jumped out of his skin. Being in deep thought, he never heard his partner enter the room.

"He called to tell me."

"Ichabod called you!"

"Yeah. He said I disappointed him. Thought we'd have given him a better challenge."

"What else did he say?"

"Well, he said, and I quote, that 'I was a big thinker and that you were small-minded'."

A big grin crossed Ron's face when he saw and heard Tim's reaction to his last statement.

"That sonofabitch had better hope I don't catch him, because 'old-small-minded Timothy' ain't bringing that useless prick in alive. I guaran-fucking-tee you that, partner."

"Is that a fact, Tim-o-thy?"

"Yeah, that's a hard-ass fact, Special Agent Lee."

"Okay, Tim, let's get to work. He didn't just call to say hello. He said something in that conversation that was a clue."

"Tell me everything he said."

Ron watched Tim jotting down on a notepad all that Ron could recall from the conversation.

"See anything that stands out, Tim?"

"Well, the obvious thing is, like you said, he's going after four more women."

"Yeah, that's disconcerting enough on its own. What else jumps out at you?"

"You stated he covered up his voice."

"Yeah, he did. That's for sure."

"Don't you think it strange? Give me your best reason for him doing that."

Realizing something so apparent had escaped him, Ron sat staring at Tim, processing his partner's most obvious revelation.

"Because I know him."

"Yeah, you know him."

"What do you think he meant when he said, 'piece it all together'?"

"Yeah, I've been giving that some thought. The other thing that puzzles me, Tim, is why he repeated 'four more clues'."

"Why did he tell you to 'write it down, Agent Lee'? Why emphasize that with your name?"

"I know the 'small-minded' thing upset you, but that set me to thinking about that discussion we had on the green the other night."

"What discussion?"

"I asked for examples of how else you could say 'high-low.' Remember?"

"Yeah, I do. We came up with 'up-bottom,' 'tall-short,' and some others."

"Yeah, but no one said, 'big and small,' did they?"

"Not that I recall. You think he gave us a clue regarding high and low?"

"Maybe he did, Tim, but I guarantee you everything he said had one of two purposes."

"What might those be?"

"He's either trying to throw us off track, or, he's teasing us with a clue to show how smart he is and how stupid we are."

"I'm small-minded, Ron. But if you're right, then most things he said were to throw us off the trail."

"I agree."

"With which part? That I'm small-minded or…"

"Shut up, asshole," scolded Ron while laughing at Tim's self-depreciating sense of humor. "No, he gave us one clue in that conversation. The rest was dog shit. All we need to do, in a manner of speaking, is separate the wheat from the chaff."

CHAPTER 45
Puzzle Pieces

July 19, 2018

Ever since 8:30am the office had been humming with activity.

Footprints found on the beach all but assured that the killer had traveled along the beach to a parking spot a quarter-mile from the Evans home.

The autopsy of the body parts had been even more surprising.

"She definitely had sex with someone that night, Ron. I'd say multiple times based on the amount of semen found in her vagina. It matched that found on the sheets."

"Did you run a DNA test to see if it matches with any known felons, Charlie?"

"Hey, this ain't my first rodeo, you know."

"Okay, cowboy. So tell me, did you?"

"Yeah, I did, and we found a match with a guy picked up on suspicion of assault back in 2001 in California. When arrested, his name was Gerald Williams."

"What do you mean, when arrested?"

"It wasn't his real name, but an alias."

"So what you're telling me is we have squat from the DNA."

"I guess that's what I'm telling you."

"Is there any other useless information you need to tell me, Charlie?"

"That's about it, Ron. The hospital scrubs came up negative, but they were so contaminated by the bloody plastic sheets, anything I would have found would have been useless in a court of law."

"Okay, Charlie. Thanks."

"Well, what did Charlie have to tell us?" Tim asked.

"Nothing we didn't already know. What's the word on the baseball ticket?"

"The ticket office opens at 9:00. Want to take a ride over there? It's just a few blocks from here."

"Yeah, let's go."

It was 9:10 when they reached the Pelicans ballpark. There was a single car parked near the ticket window. They pulled in beside it.

Occupying the ticket window was a man who had inquired about seating and pricing. The options were being explained to him by a female employee.

Ron and Tim stood by patiently until the man had completed his business. Stepping up to the window, they identified themselves as FBI agents and asked to speak with the manager.

"That would be me," voiced the spirited middle-aged woman. "Go around the corner. There's a door. I'll let you in down there."

"Can I get you guys a coffee? I made it about 20 minutes ago."

"No thanks, ma'am. We're just here to pick up reports that a... Mr. Lepine... implied would be ready this morning."

"Call me Jenny. As for some reports, let me see if Ray left anything on his desk that might be for you fellas. What's it supposed to be, anyway?"

"It should be a list of names or credit card numbers of people who purchased tickets last night in section 104," answered Tim.

"You don't say! That's an unusual request. Can I ask why?"

"It has something to do with a woman killed last night after leaving the game. We believe she sat with the suspect. We were hoping to get information from the spectators who sat next to, or around her."

"Did you say in section 104?"

"Yes. Why?"

"Well, I work the ticket office out by the entrance and I recall a guy buying two tickets in that section. It was late. I remember him saying that his girlfriend needed that section or section 103 because they were close to the beer vendors and the bathrooms."

"How did he pay for the tickets?"

"Cash."

"Do you recall what he looks like, Jenny?" Ron asked.

"Was the woman a blond?"

"Yes."

"Okay, then I remember. After buying the tickets, he stood just a few feet from the ticket window, waiting for her. Being it was just a few minutes before game time, there wasn't much ticket selling. I can remember her arriving and him saying he bought seats in section 104 for two. I also heard him say, which at the time I thought was strange, that he'd exchange his ticket for another in a different section, but he didn't."

"What did he look like, Jenny?" asked Ron with a hint of impatience.

"Oh, I'd say he was at least 6'2" and weighed about 220. Strong-looking guy. He wore a pair of dark-colored shorts and a Pelican T-shirt. He had on a pair of white low-cut sneakers—maybe they were deck shoes—I'm not sure. He wore dark wraparound sunglasses, and a Pelican ball cap."

"What about facial hair?"

"No, there wasn't any facial hair."

"What about his head?"

"What about it?"

"Did he have hair?"

"You know, I think he was bald."

"What else?"

"Well, his head was more egg-shaped than most heads. He had a very pronounced chin and a high forehead."

"Ears?"

"Hey, what do you want, a photograph? That's all I have."

"That was exceptional, Jenny. Now, can you find anything that Mr. Lepine may have left for us?"

Searching Lepine's desk brought no results, but a look atop an adjacent filing cabinet, did.

"Here's an envelope with the name 'POND' written on it. Ain't one of you guys named Pond?"

"That would be me, ma'am."

"Well, here you go then."

Opening the envelope, Tim found two sheets of paper. One sheet listed three credit card numbers, and the seats purchased using those cards. The second sheet listed names, addresses, phone numbers and seat numbers of section 104 season ticket holders. There were seven names on this list.

"What seat did Ginger occupy, Ron?"

"Row C, seat 11."

"Well, we have Mr. and Mrs. Granger sitting in seats 9 and 10 of that row. We also have Bruce Miller sitting in row D, seat 11. He had to sit right behind her."

"Boy, I can see why you guys are in the FBI. Such deductive powers, Wow!" Jenny said, with a big grin.

"Since I'm a gentleman, I won't respond to you in a manner that is not polite," said Tim with a returning smile.

"Gotcha, honey. Just having fun with you, is all."

"We appreciate your time, Jenny," said Ron. "We might need to call on you again. May we have your address and a phone number?"

"But of course, you can. I love giving my phone number to a good-looking guy, especially one who carries a gun," Jenny said with a wide grin.

Ron gave her a returning grin and a nod.

Ten minutes later they were on their way to 101 Prescott Drive, the home of Mr. and Mrs. Granger, in Socastee. It had just turned 10:30 when Ron said, "Those little phrases that Ichabod used in our conversation."

"Yeah, what about 'em?"

"The one where he stated in so many words that 'I can't add it up by myself' sticks in my craw."

"How so?"

"What do the holes, where he left the heads, add up to, Tim?"

"Let's see: Tradition was 7, then Indian Wells was 15, that's 22, then River Hills was 16 for 38. Eagles Nest was 17 for 55, and finally the Witch was 17, that's 72, which, coincidentally, is par on most courses."

"Maybe it's not coincidental. What is par on those holes?"

"In order of appearance: a 4, 5, 5, 4, and 3. That adds up to... 21... blackjack!"

"I can't make any sense out of those numbers, Tim, can you?"

"No, not while I'm driving. Look, there's Prescott Drive."

Two minutes later they were ringing the doorbell of a modest ranch with a brick façade. A single-car garage sat at the end of the driveway. The yard was small but well-kept. Parked in the driveway was an older model Chevy.

The door opened and a man that Ron estimated to be in his mid-sixties greeted them with, "Yes, how may I help you fellas?"

"Are you Mr. Bob Granger, sir?"

"I am, and who might you be?"

"FBI, sir. I'm Special Agent Lee and this is Agent Pond."

"FBI! My, my, what could I have done to deserve a visit from the FBI?"

"To be truthful, sir, you attended a baseball game last night. Is that correct?"

"You mean going to a ballgame is now a federal crime!"

"No, sir, it is not. May we come in, sir, and we'll explain ourselves?"

Ushering them in, Bob called to his wife, "Helen, put on some coffee, we have guests."

"That won't be necessary, sir."

"I beg to differ, Agent. I'd like a cup, but she won't make it just for me."

"Oh, well then, I'll join you in a cup," said Ron grinning.

Moments later, Bob's wife Helen joined them and as Bob and Ron drank coffee, Tim asked questions.

"Last night you were at the Pelican's ballgame."

"Yes, we were," answered Helen.

"Did a blond-headed woman sit next to you?"

"Why, yes, she did."

"Was there a man with her, Mrs. Granger?"

"Yes. I believe they had just met too."

"Why do you say that, ma'am?"

"There are many reasons, but the most telling is that she gave him her address."

"Now how would you know that, ma'am?"

"Well, he went to go get drinks and peanuts to have something for the 7th inning stretch. Shortly after he left, she received a phone call from a neighbor saying that her dog had been making a helluva fuss. Since the fella hadn't returned, she wrote her address and asked if I would give it to him when he returned."

"Did she say anything else, ma'am?" asked Tim.

"Her final words as she rushed off were, 'Tell him I'm sorry to have to duck out like this,' and then she left."

"When he returned, you gave him the address."

"Yes, I did. You could see the surprise in his eyes. In fact, he gave me one drink and the bag of peanuts he had bought. We both thought it was mighty kind."

"Then what, ma'am?"

"Nothing. He left immediately." Then, with a twinkle in her eyes, she added, "I told Bob that someone may get lucky tonight."

"For a second, I thought she was talkin' about me," said Bob. "I occasionally get delusional."

Laughing nervously at her husband's comment, Helen asked, "What's this all about, officers?"

Ignoring her misstep of their titles, Ron answered, "Someone killed the woman who sat beside you, ma'am. Most likely, by the man who gave you those peanuts."

They watched as Helen, her eyes immediately filling with tears, placed her right hand over her mouth as she mumbled, "Oh, my. How horribly dreadful."

"We hate to ask, folks," said Tim, "but could you give us a description of the man?"

For the next ten minutes the couple described the man virtually to a "T" as had Jenny, the Pelicans ticket clerk.

As they thanked the couple and said goodbye, they heard Bob say to Helen, "I guess someone wasn't so lucky."

CHAPTER 46
Gardening

July 19, 2018

 While the FBI and the other police forces were trying to piece together clues left at what was now eight crimes scenes, Ichabod spent a Friday afternoon at one of Horry County's finest attractions, the beautiful Brookgreen Gardens.

 Since its founding in 1931, by Archer and Anna Hyatt Huntington, Brookgreen, with its unique melding of art, nature, and history has been a cultural center for the community.

 Today it would also be a hunting ground for a madman.

 Arriving at 11:00 he walked the gardens, barely noticing the sculptures or the flowering plants. Instead, he searched for victim number six. Having learned his lesson with the insatiable Ginger, he now sought an elderly woman, perhaps in her 60s, but whose appetite for sex was tepid or better yet, nonexistent.

 Today he dressed in neatly pressed khaki pants, a buttoned collared shirt, and a comfortable pair of walking shoes. He wore wire-rimmed spectacles with rounded lenses, and a sky-blue roll up bucket hat. A well- trimmed white beard completed his facial features.

 Using a four-foot wooden walking stick, he moved along briskly even though he feigned a slight slouch.

 It was 1:30 when he spotted her. She had been admiring the magnificent sculpture of Pegasus. Watching her make her way around the carving counterclockwise, he moved to encircle the statue in a clockwise motion. He met her at the 11:00 position.

"Breathtaking, wouldn't you say?"

"Oh, my, yes I would," she responded with a voice that spoke of awe.

She stood not much over five-foot and weighed only 120 pounds. Her physical features still held up to the test of time. Her face had lines where a face pushing 65 should have wrinkles. She wore no makeup, except for a light covering of eyeshadow around a pair of soft brown eyes. Her hair, thick and dark brown at one time, was now thinning, but ever so slowly as it succumbed to being taken over by strands of gray. Her body was firm and showed no signs of infirmities.

"Look! Can you see the four-piece construction? Can you imagine the patience and the skill to create such a masterpiece?"

"I see only three pieces," she answered as she peered ever more intently at the sculpture. "Where do you see a fourth?"

"There, at the rear, near the back of the legs."

"Oh, yes, now I see. You must have good eyes to have seen that."

"Oh, if only that were true. I must wear these spectacles nowadays, but there was a time when my eyes were sharp and clear. Besides, I've been here so often, I know these sculptures inside and out, just as if I were their creator."

"Well, wouldn't you make a great tour guide!"

"I never thought of it that way before, ma'am."

"Oh, please call me Sophie. I'm from Cleveland. I'm down here visiting my niece for a few days."

"Well, hello Sophie. My name is Barney. Barney Barnes. And yes, that's my real name. My folks had a wicked sense of humor."

"That is funny, but I like it, Barney."

Knowing fair well that she was alone, he still asked, "Is your niece here with you?"

"Oh, no. She's teaching summer school in Pawleys Island. Being a Brookgreen member, she had a free pass, so I came over to see what it offered. I've heard so many wonderful things about this place."

"Oh, it's a great place, to be sure. Have you seen the Botanical Garden or the Butterfly House?"

"Why no, I haven't!"

"How about the zoo?"

"Haven't been there either."

"Would you like me to escort you around for a part of the day? I'd be happy to do so."

Feeling not in the least intimidated by this older gentleman who walked with a cane, Sophie instantly replied with a slight giggle, "I had been hoping you would ask... Barney Barnes."

"I'm honored that you would say yes... Sophie."

"It's Sophia McDougall. But I prefer Sophie."

"Okay, Miss Sophie McDougall, right this way."

Two hours later it was apparent that Sophie had enough sightseeing for one day.

"Barney, I appreciate you escorting me around this beautiful park, but I must admit, I'm bushed."

"I'm quite winded myself. I'm glad you're raising the white flag," he added with a chuckle. "It has been a pleasure sharing my knowledge of the gardens with you. I hope you enjoyed the day."

"Oh, I most certainly did! I'm thinking we might get a bite to eat and possibly have a drink. Do you know of an appealing place nearby?"

"Matter of fact, there's a place called the Salt Creek Café. It's about two or three miles north on Route 17."

"Oh, I know exactly where that is. I've passed it a few times this week. My niece lives within hailing distance of the place."

"It would be my honor to have you join me. If you like, you could follow me."

"I'd like to freshen up first, Barney. You go ahead, and I'll meet you there."

"Okay, I can do that. Is there a drink I could have ready for you when you arrive?"

"Yes, that would be considerate of you. I'd love to have a cold vodka and tonic... with a lime."

"Fear not! Both I and your vodka tonic will await your arrival, Miss Sophie."

****

She arrived just ten minutes after his being seated. As promised, her requested drink, cold and sparkling, waited for her arrival. As usual, he drank a ginger ale.

It had been 4:45 when she arrived. According to Ichabod's digital it was 7:00 when they completed the main courses of their dinners. Sophie, at Barney's insistence, had the lump crab cakes.

"They are to die for, Sophie."

He had the seafood platter of shrimp and oysters, which he shared with her.

They had finished the meal with coffee while sharing a slice of Peanut Butter Pie topped with chocolate ganache.

Barney's coffee was regular with cream. Sophie had decaf with cream, sugar, and a knockout pill.

They were on their second cup of coffee when Sophie disclosed she would like to leave. She felt exhausted.

"All that walking apparently took a lot more out of me than I had thought."

"Gosh, Sophie. I'm so sorry."

"Oh, don't be sorry, Barney. I loved spending this time with you."

"I have a feeling we'll be spending more time together in the immediate future."

"That would be enjoyable, I'm sure," she replied, not realizing the morbid significance of his statement.

"I'm sure it will."

Barney knew he had about ten minutes to pay for the meal before Sophie would fall unconscious.

"Well, let me get the check, and we'll get out of here. Miss! Check please."

Quickly paying the check in cash and offering a generous tip, "Barney" took Sophie's hand and helped the quickly fading woman from the restaurant.

Making their way to the parking lot at the rear of the restaurant, it was soon evident that Sophie could not stay on her feet. The parking lot, having no real organization, was dirt covered, interspersed with large live oak trees. Cars parked at obtuse angles played directly into Ichabod's hand. It made it easier to put her into his car without being seen. At that moment, there were no other cars arriving or departing. It couldn't have gone better... for Ichabod.

One could not say the same for Sophie McDougall.

****

Leaving the Salt Creek Café, Ichabod, along with his unconscious passenger, headed south on 17 for six miles. Reaching the Litchfield area, he turned onto Willbrook Boulevard. Traveling down Willbrook, he passed the 7th green where he had left the head of the girl named Sara. A mile further, he turned onto Old River Road and drove to the entrance of the Litchfield Plantation.

The guard at the gate, recognizing who it was from his position in the guard hut some 30 feet away, just waved as Ichabod knew he would. Driving up the Avenue of the Live Oakes, Ichabod turned left onto All Saints Loop, then made a quick right onto Landings Road. This road would take him back to the marina where only a few boats docked, including his own. Parking at the furthest end of the gravel lot, Ichabod hurriedly removed Sophie from the car, but as he did so, he snapped her neck. He hadn't enjoyed decapitating Julia while she was alive.

After all, I'm not a monster, he told himself.

He didn't bother laying out the covering of plastic here. The ground was a mixture of dirt and ground oyster shells. The blood would seep into the ground in just a matter of days and animals would eat any remaining "Sophie morsels" resulting from the mutilation.

Removing Sophie's clothes, he put them in a bag and threw the bag in the back seat of his car.

"I'll drop those off at Goodwill," he whispered.

Donning his hospital scrubs, he took to the task at hand.

He had Sophie's head in the cooler within five minutes.

I'm getting good at this.

Forty minutes later, Ichabod had Sophie's body, now in pieces, in a 33-gallon garbage bag. Instead of putting the bag in his car he carried it down a path that led into the marsh where alligators lived and even better, crabs.

Reaching the bank of the creek, he scattered her body parts and organs along a 50-foot stretch of mud.

Counting the number of crabs that came out of the mud would have been superfluous, as the count would have easily reached into the hundreds of thousands.

Bon Appetit, my little friends.

Returning to his car, he removed the bloodied hospital scrubs and put them into the bag, that just minutes ago, had housed Sophie's mutilated body. He then stuffed the bag into a garbage can next to the dock.

Taking the cooler, he set it behind the driver's seat and headed to The Heritage, just a few miles up the road.

Upon reaching Heritage's security gate, a guard approached his vehicle.

"Yes, sir."

"I feel stupid, but I left my golf clubs at the bag drop earlier today. I called, and the guys in the pro shop said my clubs would be at the drop. I just need to pick them up. I'll be right back within five minutes."

"Been there, done that," the grinning guard replied as he raised the gate.

Speeding, Ichabod drove the half mile to the bag drop, and leaving the car's engine running, grabbed the cooler and ran down the cart path toward the 18th hole located a scant 100 yards away.

As his eyes adjusted to the darkness, he could see the flagstick in the upper left corner of the green.

"Perfect!"

Reaching the flagstick, he opened the cooler, grabbed Sophie's head, and placed it against the base of the pole. Then bending down, he opened her mouth and slipped something into it.

"Goodbye, Sophie, my little messenger. It has been my pleasure showing you around the Gardens."

Running back to the car, he circled the driveway and sped back toward the gate, waving at the guard as he drove past.

I'll be home before 10:00 tonight. That should make Deni happy for a change, he told himself as he sped down Old River Road.

It would indeed make her happy, but it would be a short-lived happiness.

CHAPTER 47
The Heritage

July 20, 2018

"He's killing at a faster rate, Ron."

"Yeah, that he is for sure."

The call came in at 7:30. It was from Captain Baxter who said they received a call from the Heritage Golf Club in Pawleys Island.

"One of their greenskeepers found a head on the 18th hole, Ron."

"I love that course," said Tim. "We played there on Tuesday."

"I wonder if I'll ever feel the same about these courses once this is all said and done."

"I don't think I will," Tim said, shaking his head.

"Nor will I," confessed Ron with a heavy exhale.

Flashing their badges as they passed through the gate, they made their way to the clubhouse. Upon reaching the circular drive they saw a dozen or more police vehicles parked, with blue lights flashing. Captain Baxter greeted them as they exited their vehicle.

"Morning, Bill."

"Good morning, fellas. Tough way to start a day, isn't it?"

"It's getting old," said Tim. "This makes six mornings in the past three weeks."

"This one has another surprise for you."

"Oh? What did he do this time?" Ron asked. "Put the flagstick through the victim's ears?"

"No, nothing that gross. C'mon, let's head over to the green."

It took only a minute to get there and with the pin location in the upper left side, they could see the head propped against the flagstick from fifty yards away.

"Well, he's back on the ground, I see," said Ron, "but that's what I fully expected."

"Why is that?" asked Baxter.

"The head on top of the flag was significant. Its meaning isn't clear yet, but he didn't do it for show."

Baxter nodded his head in obvious agreement.

"Okay, so what's the surprise?"

"Look in her mouth."

Peering downward, Ron saw someone had inserted something in the open mouth.

"It looks like a piece of paper," said Tim, who had squatted to get a better look.

"Remove it," ordered Ron.

"Do I have to?"

"I let you out of crawling into that dumpster. You owe me one."

Tim reached into the mouth with his index and middle finger and slowly extracted a folded slip of paper.

"I have a feeling it's for you," he said as he handed it to Ron.

Opening the folds, he saw that Tim was right. He read it silently:

Agent Lee,

This will be number six and counting. It's a pity you cannot decipher my clues. Your archaic methods have left you up the creek without a paddle. If you had just a gram of common sense, you might be worth your salt. Once I complete my work, I'll be leaving as the true king of murder. There will be three more. I have my sights on Ana.

So, should you. I've told you all you need to know. Better luck in your next career, Ron.

"How did you know this was in her mouth, Captain?"

"Sergeant Michaels discovered it. He said with her mouth wide open, he could easily see the folded paper. He didn't touch it though."

"There wouldn't be any prints anyway, but we can analyze the handwriting. There's nothing more to do here. Send the head to the lab."

"She appears to be much older than any of the previous women he has taken," surmised Tim. "We're thinking he's in his early to mid-forties. I wonder how he seduced an older woman like this."

"He's a master of disguises, Tim. Who knows?"

"Agent Lee!"

It was Sergeant Michaels.

"What's up, Sergeant?"

"Just received a call from the Sheriff's Department. A woman, Elisa Gardner, just reported that her aunt, a Sophia McDougall, never came home from visiting Brookgreen Gardens yesterday."

"Did you get a description?"

"Yeah, and I'd say, this head fits the description."

"Let's head over to Brookgreen, Tim. Maybe someone saw something."

"Did this Elisa say what time her aunt visited the Gardens, Sergeant?"

"Being a teacher, she wasn't home when her aunt left."

"Do we even know if she ever made it there?" Tim asked.

"The Gardner woman told us she gave her aunt a pass," explained Michaels. "If the gate has the pass, then we'll know she was there."

"Yeah, and if her car is still there, we'll know she didn't leave."

"I can't imagine where in Brookgreen he would dare kill her, and do all he does without being seen," said Tim.

"Ron, sorry to interrupt," said Captain Baxter.

"That's okay. What is it?"

"Got a call from the Horry County Sheriff's Department. They received a complaint from the Salt Creek Café. Someone left a white Buick Regal with Ohio plates in their parking lot last night. It's registered to a Sophia Angela McDougall, who lives in Cleveland."

"Lived in Cleveland," mumbled Tim.

Hearing Bill's report, Ron abruptly ripped out the note he had put into his jacket pocket and reread it.

"Son-of-a-bitch!"

CHAPTER 48
Pegasus

July 20, 2018

"I'm sorry, Agent Lee, but it's impossible to remember any one person when so many people are roaming the gardens. Do you realize that there are 9,000 acres here, and we have thousands of visitors each day?"

"Yes, ma'am, I do. Let me ask; are there security cameras on the premises?"

"Yes, there are. We wouldn't dare take our eyes off the invaluable sculptures."

"We would like to see yesterday's recordings."

"That would be Mr. Sullivan's territory. He's across the way," she said, pointing toward the gift shop building.

They walked over and asked to see Mr. Sullivan.

A clerk behind the gift shop counter informed them, "Mr. Sullivan is up those stairs there to your right. Just knock on the door at the top of the stairs."

Following the clerk's directions, they knocked on the door, and heard a boisterous, "Come in!"

"Mr. Sullivan?"

"Yes. And to whom do I have the pleasure?"

"I'm Special Agent Ron Lee and this is Agent Tim Pond. We're with the FBI."

Sullivan, an older man, well into his 70s, stood only 5'5" but he was well-fed. His complexion was smooth for a man of his age, and his hair, what there was of it, was white.

"What brings the FBI to Brookgreen Gardens?"

"Unfortunately, sir, it's a matter of murder."

"Murder! You don't say! What can we do to help?"

"We wanted to look at your security tapes of the property from yesterday, sir."

"Hmm, now that may be a problem, fellas."

"How's that, Mr. Sullivan?"

"We have limited recording capacity, so if nothing occurred on the previous day that would require us keeping the recording, then we erase the data."

"Have you erased yesterday?"

"All but two areas, I'm afraid."

"May we see those, please?"

"Yes, you may. I have one of the parking lot. It starts at 9:00am and ends at 8:00pm."

They sat and watched it for a few minutes before Tim asked, "Could you speed it up, please?"

"Can do!" replied Sullivan.

Watching the cars whizzing in and out of parking spots for a few minutes, Ron, having spotted something, yelled, "Stop!"

Sullivan stopped the recording. A timestamp reading 11:17 appeared in the screen's lower-left corner.

"Go back slowly, for about two minutes."

Sullivan backed up the recording and once again Ron yelled, "Stop!" although not as boisterous.

"There! Exiting that white Buick. That's her, Tim."

They watched her walk through the parking lot until she left the screen.

"No one was with her."

"No, you're right, Tim, there wasn't. What other recordings do you have, Mr. Sullivan?"

"The camera that covers the Pegasus sculpture is all I have, Agents."

"Okay. Let's have a gander."

The recording of Pegasus began at 9:00am.

"Speed it up to at least 11:30, Mr. Sullivan."

"That's logical," Sullivan replied. "She didn't get here until much before then, did she?"

It was a question that didn't need answering.

"Since we know how she dressed," said Ron, "we should be able to spot her fairly easily."

They watched the camera roll past noon, then 1:00 and then, there she was, at 1:25.

"Slow it down, sir," ordered Tim.

Both men moved closer to the screen as they watched the woman strolling around the magnificent sculpture. A few moments passed before they spotted an old man, slightly stooped over and using a walking stick, moving clockwise around the sculpture. It was obvious his focus wasn't on Pegasus, but was instead, on the woman.

"That's him! I'd bet my life on it!" exclaimed Tim.

"I think I agree with you there, partner."

The camera shot was too far away to secure legitimate facial recognition. They could, however, determine he had a white beard and wore glasses. The camera, however, only recorded in black and white, making it difficult to determine clothing colors.

They watched intently as the two met and carried on a conversation for an extended period. Then, some 15 minutes later, they saw the couple walk off together and out of the camera's range.

"What do you think, Ron?"

"Let's see the parking lot tape again, Mr. Sullivan."

With the camera going at five times regular speed, they watched, concentrating on her vehicle. It was 4:05 when she arrived at her car.

"Slow it down to regular speed, Mr. Sullivan and back it up a minute or two," ordered Ron.

Watching the tape at regular speed, showed no signs of the man with the walking stick. They continued watching long after Sophia McDougall had left the lot. No sign of the old man came into their view.

"Maybe he didn't pick her up here in the Gardens, Ron. Maybe he picked her up at Salt Creek."

"That's probably the scenario, partner."

They were about to leave when Ron stopped and asked, "Mr. Sullivan, would you mind going back to about the 3:40 mark?"

"Not at all, sir."

A moment later they were watching the screen starting at 3:38.

At the 3:47 mark, Tim cried out, "There he is!"

He had the same clothes. He wasn't, however, walking stooped, nor did he use the walking stick.

Ron described his gait as hurried.

"I'd say even quicker than that," suggested Tim.

"Let's see what kind of car he's driving," Ron said with great anticipation. "Maybe we can get a plate number."

It was, however, not to be. Either by luck or by guile, with the latter being the more plausible, he had parked far from the eye of the camera and under a tree, where his car would be nothing but a blur.

"We need to get to Salt Creek and verify they met there," declared Tim.

"Agreed," said Ron. "Thank you, Mr. Sullivan. We would ask that you not destroy those tapes, sir."

"Not to worry, gentlemen. Good hunting."

As the two FBI agents were leaving Brookgreen Gardens and heading to Salt Creek, an unplanned bloodletting was underway.

CHAPTER 49
Two Boards

July 20, 2018

    Arriving at the Salt Water Café, Ron and Tim spoke with the manager who vividly recalled the couple.

"He came in first, right around 4:00. He ordered two drinks: a ginger ale and a vodka tonic. Robert, their waiter, didn't realize the vodka was for someone else. The vodka drinker, a respectable looking older lady, arrived about fifteen minutes later. They had a long dinner. Didn't finish eating their meal until after 7:00. Then they had coffee and split a dessert. It would have been close to 8:00 when they left. Oh, look, here comes Robert. He might tell you more."

After introductions, which made Robert visibly nervous, Tim asked, "Did they leave together, Robert?"

"Yes, sir, they did. I thought it strange how the old man became overly eager to get the check, but then I heard the woman say she wasn't feeling well. He paid in cash and they left. She appeared somewhat unstable as he walked her to the door."

"Oh? How many drinks had she had?"

"Just two. Both vodka and tonic."

"Did he drink?"

"Just ginger ale."

"Anything else you can recall that seemed strange or out of the ordinary?"

"Just one thing, but it might have been just my imagination."

"And what was that?" Ron asked.

"He arrived stooped over and using a cane or walking stick. When leaving and while helping the woman, he stood tall and did not use the cane."

Ron glanced at Tim and both gave knowing nods.

"Okay, Robert. We'll get back to you if needed."

"Yes, sir."

"Oh, and Robert."

"Yes, sir?"

"Stay away from reefers before you come to work. It's probably not something the customers need to smell."

Taken aback by Ron's assertion, Robert's mouth fell open and he nearly messed himself.

As they rode to their office, Ron blurted, "He's getting way too cocky, Tim."

"What do you mean?"

"In that note he left in Sophie's mouth, he told me about Salt Creek, not directly, mind you, but it was right there in black and white. I'm sure there is much more to uncover in that note. He's begging us to catch him."

"Well, I wish he'd beg a lot harder."

"When we get back, we will put everything we know on the whiteboards, especially the words he said on the phone and the things he wrote in that note. I hate to admit it, but like he wrote in the note, 'he told us all we need to know'."

Then, holding up his hand with his thumb and index finger an inch apart, he added, "This close, Tim! This damn close to catching that son-of-a-bitch."

"I hope so, Ron. I'm tired of lying to my wife."

Upon returning, Ron went into Jim Braddock's office to brief him on all that had happened since finding Sophia McDougall's head earlier that morning.

"He wants to get caught," said Braddock.

"That's exactly what I told Pond."

"Go wrap this up, Ron."

"We're getting close, Jim. We need to see just a sliver of daylight," remarked Ron as he left and headed toward the conference room.

Two hours later they had filled two whiteboards with all the useful data they had accumulated.

Tim erased the previous boards as they no longer served a purpose. The new boards had all the clues. All they had to do was to decipher them.

"You see those comments 'creek without a paddle' and 'worth your salt,' Tim? That was his way of telling us Salt Creek Café."

"It's certainly obscure if you're not looking for it."

"True, but now we know to look for the obscure."

"You know the one that bothers me the most, Ron?"

"Which one?"

"The fifth one under 'Note'."

"How's that?"

"Most people would say 'an ounce of common sense' yet he says 'gram.' Why?"

"I've heard many people say 'a bit of' or 'a drop of' too. How many grams in an ounce?"

"Glad you asked because I looked it up while you were talking with Braddock. There's slightly more the 28 grams in an ounce."

"Twenty-eight, eh? How does that relate to anything?"

"I don't know, but that statement is so far off the wall, he had to be telling us something."

"What else up there makes little sense?"

"How about 10?" said Tim.

Victim	Course	Hole #	Date Killed	Picked Up at
Sara Carson	Tradition	7	6/28	Boardwalk?
Laura Cantor	Indian Wells	15	7/2	Half Shell
Betsy Parker	River Hills	16	7/5	Chris's Pizza
Julia Spencer	Eagle's Nest	17	7/9	House of Blues
Ginger Evans	Witch	17	7/17	Pelican's Game
Sophia McDougall	Heritage	18	7/19	Brookgreen Gardens
Ana?				

PHONE	#	NOTE
four more clues	1	number six and counting
stay calm	2	cannot decipher my clues
piece it all together	3	archaic methods
big thinker	4	creek without a paddle
small-minded	5	a gram of common sense
write this down	6	Need to shore up your manpower
just four more clues	7	worth your salt
spell it out	8	the true king of murder
add it up	9	There will be three more.
	10	I've set my sights on Ana and so should you
	11	all you need to know

"Could he be telling us he will kill a woman named Ana, and we should try to find her before he does?"

"I doubt that's the case, Ron. He may know Ana, the woman he's targeting, but we have no clue where to look for her. He couldn't possibly expect us to find the woman before he kills her. No, that can't be it."

"I have to agree with that deduction, Tim. But I think you're right about ten. Something there just doesn't add up."

They sat quietly for five minutes before Tim spoke up, saying, "You know, Ron. I've known a few girls in my time by that name, but that's not the way they spell it. It's A-n-n-a."

"Hot damn, Tim. You're right! He's not telling us a woman's name! We've been looking at this all wrong!"

Another ten minutes went by as they gnawed on the "Ana" clue, but between them, nothing popped.

Tim asked about the eighth entry on the list.

"Why would he brag about being such a great criminal?"

"Where are you going with this thought?"

"The phrase 'the true king of murder.' What's that all about, Ron?"

"Good question. Maybe it's a red herring."

"It appears to be too obvious to be that. He said it for a reason. I believe he's telling us something."

"Who's the all-time serial killer, Tim?"

"That's easy. It's Gary Ridgeway, better known as 'The Green River Killer'."

"Right!" agreed Ron. "If I recall, they had him for something like 50 victims, even though he confessed to another couple dozen. Maybe this guy wants to beat Ridgeway's numbers, at our expense."

"He's saying that he'll exceed Ridgeway's numbers if he kills three more women here in Myrtle Beach. Does that mean he has at least 40 previous kills?"

"It's either that or he stinks in math."

"That may be true," said Tim with a big grin, "but I believe he's telling us something when he says, 'the true king of murder'."

Before Ron could respond, Keith White, another Special Agent who worked in narcotics, entered the conference room. Seeing the whiteboards, he asked, "What are you guys up to, Tim?"

"Trying to figure out what this demented killer wants us to know by feeding us these cryptic phrases."

"I see he impaled the Evans' woman's head on the 17th flagstick at The Witch."

"Yeah, that was gruesome," replied Tim.

"I play there at least twice a month. That's their signature hole."

Ron, having not paid much attention to the conversation, practically snapped his neck when he heard White's remark.

"What the hell did you say, Keith?"

"I don't know. What the hell did I say?"

"Something about the 17th hole at the Witch?"

"I noticed he impaled her head on its flagstick."

"Yeah, but then you said..."

"That's their signature hole."

"JOE SAFFRAN!" Ron roared.

CHAPTER 50
Shopping and Chopping

July 20, 2018

Ichabod decided he would sleep in this morning even though he had made it home much earlier than usual from his killing sprees.

It would be a tragic mistake!

The 50-year-old grandfather clock had been chiming 9:00am when Ichabod's wife, Deni, left the house to do some needed food shopping at the local grocer.

Entering the garage, Deni seated herself in her Toyota and pressed the remote button on the visor to open the garage door. She was about to pull forward but looked up to see that her husband's car blocked her exit.

Having keys to her husband's Chrysler, she left the Toyota and drove his car to the supermarket.

Buying far more than she had planned, she wheeled the fully loaded grocery cart out to the car's driver's side rear door. Opening the door, she saw a large brown trash bag lying on the back seat. Curious why her husband would have this bag in the back seat, she lifted it out and peered inside to see the contents.

She dropped the bag like it was on fire.

She stood there, at first seething, but then after giving it more thought, her mood changed to fear. It couldn't be she told herself. Her need to know had her bending down and lifting the bag a second time. Opening it wide, she deliberately removed its contents one item at a time.

First, there was a blouse, then a bra, followed by a pair of panties, next came a pair of slacks, and finally two women's loafers.

Shaking, she stuffed the clothing back into the bag, set the bag on the ground, and began putting the groceries in the car. That's when she noticed the cooler sitting on the floor behind the driver's seat. Lifting it up onto the rear seat, she opened it and immediately muffled a scream. Floating in the cooler must have been at least an inch of watery blood. *It must be blood,* she thought, *what else could it be?* Closing the cooler, she replaced it where she had found it.

She emptied the bags of groceries from the shopping cart onto the back seat. Finished, she lifted the bag of clothing off the ground and tossed it onto the floor behind the passenger front seat. Then, as if it were the entrance to hell itself, she slammed the door shut.

Eyeing the trunk, she told herself not to, but, just as she needed to open the bag a second time, she also needed to open the trunk.

Taking the trunk key in her quivering hand, she stepped to the rear of the car, inserted the key, and turned it until the lid popped open. It took all that she had to raise the trunk to where she could fully see its contents.

There amongst a slew of plastic liners, garbage bags, and a box of hospital scrubs, lay the item that clinched her suspicions... the bloody axe.

She now knew. Her husband was the monster they were calling "Ichabod."

Slamming the trunk closed, she jumped into the car and started the engine. Putting it in reverse, she backed out of the parking spot, but slammed on the brakes when she heard, "Hey bitch! Watch where the hell you're going!"

A young teenager had been doing the screaming. She never saw him walking behind her vehicle. Putting the gear shift into the park position, she sat shaking and crying. What was she to do?

Then doubt crept into her thoughts.

Maybe there's an explanation for this, she told herself. *Someone was framing him.*

She knew she was lying to herself.

As she drove home, she put together a plan. She would wait until her son came home from summer camp, and then they would run safely away from the monster they had been living with for all these years.

She thought back to when she first met him in Vancouver. He was charming, good-looking, well-spoken, intelligent, and had a good sense of humor. Told that his previous marriage ended strangely, she now suspected the truth. His wife, an avid hiker, went into the mountains one day and never returned. Weeks of searching turned up no signs. Given up for lost, the search ended. Some speculated that she had run away from married life to start anew elsewhere.

Now she knew better. He had, without a doubt, killed her. But for what reason? Had she discovered his secret? Has he been a murderer all these years, well before she met him, possibly even before his first marriage?

All these questions were running through her mind when she inexplicably found herself at home.

There, standing in the middle of the driveway, waiting, his arms folded against his chest, and a smirk on his face, was the devil himself.

She trembled with fear as she sat there pondering what to do.

Start the car and drive away! An inner voice screamed.

But my son! Another voice answered.

Without warning, the car door swung open, and he asked, "Need help with the groceries, hon?"

She tried to disguise her fear as she replied with a false smile, "Thank you, that would be nice."

"No problem. " he said, opening the rear door and grabbing bag after bag.

There were but two bags remaining when he went stock-stone rigid.

The bag! Screamed the small voice in his mind. *You fool! You left the brown garbage bag in your car!*

Stunned that he had forgotten to drop it off at Goodwill on his way home, he momentarily stopped breathing.

Did she look in the bag? He wondered.

She had seen his shock. He saw that she saw, and he knew immediately that she had seen the contents.

Displaying a far better facade than she had attempted, he announced, "I have all but two bags, Deni. You sure bought a lot."

Carrying the bags of groceries, he walked through the garage and into the house like nothing was wrong.

Hesitating, she knew the best thing to do was to get into the car and drive off, but she feared he would go to the camp and get her son. She was right, for that's exactly what he had planned to do if she failed to come into the house.

Grabbing the two remaining bags of food, she took a last glance at the brown trash bag, then walked into the house where death awaited her.

The grandfather clock was reporting ten bells as she stepped inside. Deni would only hear two of its chimes.

She had only just closed the door when he stepped from behind, grabbed her head and snapped her neck before she could fetch a scream.

Carrying her into their bedroom, he quickly undressed her before tossing her limp body into the large walk-in shower. He went to the kitchen and mustered a series of knives that occupied a drawer, including a meat cleaver.

Returning to the bedroom, he undressed and entered the shower, knives in hand. Turning on the shower head to where the raining water was warm, but not hot, he went to work.

It took 75 minutes to dissect Deni's body in the tight confines of the shower. It took another 20 minutes to flush all the blood from her body and to wash it down the drain.

Stepping from the shower, he shivered, not from what he had done, but due to the water getting cold after having been running for more than an hour and a half.

He scolded himself when he realized that he had forgotten to retrieve the garbage bags and the cooler from his car.

Donning a pair of shorts normally only worn when doing yard work, he went to the car and gathered three bags and the cooler. As he returned to the house he heard a voice say, "Hey, neighbor, you plan on cutting your grass?"

It was Bruce Langley, his next-door neighbor, a widower, and at this moment, a real pain in the ass.

"Possibly," replied Ichabod, "but I have other things that need my immediate attention."

"Well, can I borrow your mower for about an hour? Mine's in the shop getting the blade sharpened."

Knowing he had little choice, he answered, "Sure, Bruce. I'll bring it over in just a minute. Let me make sure I have gas in it."

"Oh, don't bother. I've plenty of gas."

"Okay then. Just give me a minute."

Rushing the bags and cooler inside, Ichabod returned to the garage and opening the second door, pushed his lawn mower over to Bruce's yard.

"There you go, buddy. If I'm not home when you're done, just leave it by the garage door."

"Much obliged, neighbor."

"Don't mention it, Bruce."

Returning to the house he grabbed the cooler and rinsed it out in the kitchen sink. He then took it into the bathroom and deposited Deni's head in it.

He undressed again to place her body parts in the three bags. The shower, still showing remnants of blood, took over an hour to scrub thoroughly with bleach. When done, there were no signs of the carnage that had taken place just a few hours earlier.

It was now 1:00 and his son would be home at 4:00. He needed to dispose of the bags and to hide the head until he could drop it off at the golf course he had selected to be the next clue.

He needed a foolproof plan and believed he had one.

After placing the bags and the cooler in the trunk of Deni's Toyota, he transferred his killing axe and a pistol from his trunk into the Toyota's. He also took Sophie's bag of clothes and put them behind the passenger seat of the Toyota. Taking a box of insecticide from a shelf in the garage, he placed it on the car's passenger seat. He then moved his car to the opposite side of the driveway.

It was at that moment that Bruce returned the lawn mower.

"Thanks, Gary, for the use of your mower."

"Anytime, Bruce. Say, listen. I'm thinking of taking the boat out on the river. Would you like to join me?"

"Boy, I surely would, but I'm waiting for an important phone call. If you could wait about a half-hour, I'd be more than happy to accompany you."

"I have a few errands to run. I'll meet you at the marina, in say, an hour?"

"That sounds perfect. I should be there in plenty of time," Bruce replied with a big smile.

"Great. And hey, say nothing to the neighbors. They might get upset I didn't invite them."

"My lips are sealed."

Ahh, if only you realized that you know of what you speak, Bruce, for soon they will be sealed... forever, my friend.

Driving Deni's car out of the garage, Ichabod headed to the marina with a stop at McDonald's where, going through the drive-thru, he bought a cheeseburger, a large fry, and a large drink. He pulled over for a minute to lace the drink with enough insecticide to kill a small horse.

It took fifteen minutes to drive to the marina. Upon his arrival at the gate the attendant he knew as Dennis greeted him.

"Mr. Whittaker, how are you doing, sir?"

"Doing fine, Dennis. How about yourself?"

"Fine, sir. I take it the boat needs some exercising?" he asked.

"Yes, it does, Dennis," smiling at the attendant's metaphor. "A friend, Mr. Langley, will join me. He should arrive in about a half-hour driving a white Chevy truck."

"I'll send him on his way, sir."

"I take it you're working solo the entire day, Dennis?"

"Yes, I am. I'll be here until 6:00."

"Listen, I bought this food just a few minutes ago, but I won't be able to eat it. If you're hungry, it's yours."

Weighing 265, Dennis was always hungry.

"Thank you, sir. I'll be more than happy to take it off your hands. Are you sure I can't pay you for it?"

"No, no, definitely not! It's yours to enjoy. I hope you like cheeseburgers."

It was a rhetorical statement. Dennis never met a food item, especially cheeseburgers, that he didn't love.

"Oh, yes, sir. One of my favorites!"

"Okay, Dennis. See ya later."

"Okay, Mr. Whittaker. Thank you!"

Reaching the marina parking lot, he placed the bags containing Deni's body parts, along with the axe, in his boat.

While he awaited Bruce's arrival, he sauntered down the path that led to the area where he had dumped Sophie just a day earlier. Although the crabs had done a decent job, to his surprise, Sophie was still hanging in there.

He had hoped a gator or two would chip in with the disposal as gators are notorious for eating rotting meat. Sophie's remains, however, were still a day away to qualify as rotting.

It was 2:05 when Bruce arrived. Ichabod was glad to see that he had worn his signature beige Panama hat. The neighborhood knew he would never leave home without it.

"I'm sorry that I took so long, Gary, but I received an important phone call from my insurance agent just minutes before leaving. He would have talked my ear off if I had let him."

"Is your life insurance paid up, Bruce?"

"What in the hell is that supposed to mean and what the hell is that gun doing in your…"

The bullet went straight through Bruce's left eye and exited out the back of his head.

Wrapping Bruce's head in a plastic bag so it wouldn't leak blood, he carried the body to his boat. There he laid him on the floor and covered him with a blanket.

Leaving the slip, he steered down Waverly Creek until it met the Waccamaw River. Heading south at full speed on the Waccamaw, he made a turn at the first tributary on the right and traveled up it for the better part of a mile until finding another tributary. After traveling a short distance up the second tributary, he found what he had been searching for, a large gator. The reptile, upon seeing the approaching craft, hustled itself, without hesitation, into the safety of the water.

Using caution, he steered the boat through the marsh grasses until it gently bumped the bank of the tributary. Tossing his anchor into the grasses to ensure the boat wouldn't drift off, he then emptied Bruce's pockets of any identification. Hoisting the dead neighbor's body over his right shoulder, he stepped from the boat and carried it for approximately thirty yards through the tall grasses, before unceremoniously dumping it onto the ground.

After removing the bag from Bruce's head, he pulled the gun from his belt, and tossed it, along with the hand axe, alongside his neighbor's body. "You may need these, Bruce, to keep the gator away."

Chuckling at his little joke, he returned to the boat to collect Deni's remains.

Returning to where he had dropped Bruce's body, he sprinkled Deni's body parts all around that of his neighbor, while saying, "Deni wants to keep you company,

Bruce. She's all yours... well, except for her head. That's needed elsewhere."

Having supreme confidence that finding Bruce and Deni would require a miracle, especially if the gator had anything to do with it, Ichabod retraced his steps to the marina. As he made his way back, he tossed the torn-up contents of Bruce's pockets into the waters of the tributary.

After arriving back at the marina, he stuffed the plastic bags that had held Deni's remains, and the bag that had covered Bruce's head into a garbage can. He then moved the cooler containing his wife's head from Deni's Toyota to Bruce's truck.

After wiping down the interior of Deni's car and satisfied that all went well, he headed home in Bruce's new truck, but not before taking time for a quick stop to clean up one more significant item.

Exiting Litchfield Plantation required passing through an unmanned automatic gate. After exiting the gate, Gary headed north on River Road but only for a quarter mile, for that is where the entrance gate was.

Arriving at the gate entrance, he was not, as he expected, greeted by Dennis, although he could see the attendant's feet through the hut's open door. Leaving the truck, he rushed to the hut to find the gate attendant sprawled on the floor, with a half-eaten cheeseburger lying just a few feet away. A plastic 20-ounce cup lay nearby, with its former contents flowing like a slow-moving stream across the uneven floor.

A white foam gurgled from Dennis's mouth and nose. It was streaming down his cheeks and puddling on either side of his head. His eyes, having a look of shock, literally bulged from their sockets, as they stared, unseeing, upward toward the ceiling.

"I've seen you when you looked better, Dennis," quipped a grinning Ichabod.

After dragging Dennis further into the hut so that his feet weren't visible in the open doorway, Gary located the daily logbook of entrants to the property. Tearing out the page where the last two names entered were his and Bruce's, he ripped it into as many pieces as was possible.

Stepping to the doorway he took one last look around, saying to himself, *Job well done, Gary.*

Returning to the truck, he circled around the property and exited once more through the unmanned gate and headed home. As he headed north on Old River Road, he held his hand out the window and released a shower of confetti.

Wearing the Panama hat and a pair of sunglasses, he pulled into his now deceased neighbor's driveway, opened the garage, pulled in, and lowered the door behind him.

Leaving the hat on the car seat, he let himself into Bruce's house, and touching nothing inside, exited the back door.

Walking across the adjacent backyards, he entered his house and made his way to the living room. There he found Doug playing a computer game.

It was 4:10.

"Hey, champ, how was camp?"

"Dad! Where have you been?"

"Next door. I was talking with Mr. Bruce."

"Where's mom?"

"She told me she might be late, and that I should fix dinner tonight. I was thinking of making mac and cheese. How does that sound to you?"

"Sounds great, Dad! You know it's my favorite!"

CHAPTER 51
Signatures

July 20, 2018

"What about Joe Saffran?" asked Tim, somewhat startled at Ron's sudden outburst.

"Tim, do you remember when we came out of the pro shop at Eagle's Nest, and we ran into Geslain and Saffran who were on their way to the first tee?"

"Yeah, we had just finished watching that security tape."

"That's right. I can't recall exactly how the conversation started, but someone mentioned the 17th hole. That's when Joe mentioned 17 being the signature hole."

It took Tim only a second to follow Ron's thinking.

"Are they all signature holes?"

"Let's find out."

Tim went to a computer and typed in "Tradition signature hole." A moment later, up popped a box describing the 7th hole as the course's signature hole.

He next typed "Indian Wells signature hole." The 14th popped up.

"We have found the mother lode, Ron."

Tim continued the search for the signature holes of River Hills and the Heritage and found them to be the 16th and the 18^{th,} respectively.

"Okay, it's a given he's leaving the heads on the signature hole of each course," stated Ron, "and will continue to do so until we catch the bastard."

"The question is, what does it all mean? He's telling us something, but what is it?"

"Obviously, Tim, it has to mean something else. Let's have a look. What's the sum of the holes?"

Tim calculated the sum of the holes to be 90.

"I'm thinking red herring, Tim."

"I'll go along with that."

"He claims he has three more kills. If the sum of the holes means anything, we would have to wait until he's finished. We can't wait for that to happen."

"Let's take what we know, Ron, and put it up against the whiteboard. Maybe now, we can make heads or tails out of some of this stuff."

They first perused the left side of the board where they had listed the victims. They perused the kill sites. Nothing rang the bell for either of them.

"That name 'Ana' still bugs me, Ron."

"Are you talking about the spelling?"

"Yeah. Something is wrong there."

They moved their attention to the second board and Tim took notice of two blurbs under the "phone" category.

"Look at the 'write this down' and 'spell it out' quotes he gave you. What do you think he wants us to 'spell out'?"

"I'm not sure. I can't see anything in either the names of the victims or the courses."

"I still think the thing with 'gram' is a key, Ron."

"Yeah, that and the 'set my sights on Ana' and 'so should you'."

"Gram and... Holy crap, Ron!"

"What? What do you have?"

"Gram and Ana!"

"What about... them..."

Realizing what Tim had hit upon, Ron stopped his question in mid-sentence before bellowing, "Anagram!"

"He's telling us something in an anagram, Ron."

"Yes, but what?"

"Let's look at the other blurbs. Something has to be there that tells us what it is," suggested Tim.

They spent the rest of the day and much of the evening going over every blurb; dissecting them, examining them, looking for a hidden meaning, but nothing jumped out at them.

It stymied them, but even more so, it frustrated them.

The call came into the office at 10:00.

It was Captain Baxter.

"What is it, Bill?"

"I received a report of a missing woman, Ron."

"Who?"

"I think you both know her husband."

CHAPTER 52
Missing

July 20, 2018

    "Doug, I need to run to the store. I'll be back in a few minutes. I want you to stay in the house."

    "Okay, Dad."

    It was 8:30 and total darkness was just minutes away. He made his way to Bruce's back door, walked through the house, and entered the garage.

    Putting on the hat and glasses, he opened the garage, backed out, and drove off to his destination. He noticed no one out and about in the neighborhood.

    He reached the Myrtle Beach National parking lot in fifteen minutes. There were three courses here, but he was only interested in the premier course: King's North.

    Hurriedly exiting the vehicle, he grabbed the cooler and headed toward the course's tenth tee. Reaching the tee area, he jogged down the fairway of the long par five. It took three minutes before he passed the 10th green. Following the cart path, he continued jogging past the 11th tee box and up its long fairway. Ten minutes after leaving his car, he had made his way to the twelfth hole tee box. As he stood on the tee box, sucking wind, he fell to his knees. This was the signature hole of King's North. Time had become a factor. Although the green was only 130 yards away, he calculated it would take him another five minutes to take the head to the flagstick and return to where he now stood. Convincing himself it was the right thing to do, he instead extracted Deni's head from the cooler and plucked it down on one of the white tee markers.

    "I had hoped this would never have been necessary, Deni, but you left me no choice. But, on the bright side, you saved me the inconvenience of going out and finding my next gal."

Giving Deni a slight wave goodbye, he rushed back to Bruce's truck and, sweating profusely, drove home.

Upon arriving in Bruce's driveway, he repeated the scenario from earlier in the day when he walked out the back of Bruce's house and walked into his, via the rear door. It was 9:20.

"How's it going, Doug?"

"Going good, Dad. What about mom? Why isn't she home?"

"Yeah, I'm getting worried. I'll call Margie and see if she knows anything."

Doing as he said, he called Deni's best friend. Margie told him she hadn't seen Deni since early this morning. She conveyed to him that Deni planned on doing grocery shopping and then that the two of them might go to the mall, but Deni never called.

"Maybe she got caught up with something else," said Margie. "I've seen your car in the driveway all day, but not Deni's. I figured she must have gone off somewhere."

"Yeah, well, we're worried. Hearing you haven't seen or heard from her, makes me even more worried. I'll call the police. Thanks, Marge."

****

A police unit arrived at 9:30.

"When's the last time you saw your wife, sir?"

"It was shortly after noon. She went grocery shopping, came home to drop them off, did housework, cleaned up, and then off she went. She mentioned something about meeting friends at Coastal Grand Mall. I'm thinking they would shop, have lunch, and see a movie.

She said she wouldn't be home for dinner and suggested that I should make something for Doug and myself. Doug is our son."

"Do you know who she was meeting, sir?"

"I don't think she mentioned names. I assumed it was Margie Layton or Carol Conner. Those are the two with whom she normally does things of that ilk."

"When did your son last see his mother?"

"Well, the bus for summer camp picks him up at 7:30. Deni makes him breakfast and packs his lunch so that's when he last saw her. I was here when he came home from camp."

"What time was that?"

"It was 4:00."

"Were you home all day, sir?"

"I was. I normally do my class planning on Friday. I'm a professor at Coastal Carolina."

"Do you have a recent photo of your wife, sir?"

"Ahh, sure. Do you think it's necessary?"

"Well, it might, sir. We'll be checking the area hospitals…"

Faking concern, he asked, "You don't think she's been in an accident, do you?"

"It's possible, sir. We don't know, but in a missing person situation that's one place we check first."

"I see. So if she had no identification with her, the picture would help."

"Yes, sir."

It was 10:05 when the phone rang.

"Excuse me, officer. Maybe it's my wife!"

Playing the role of a distraught husband to perfection, he answered excitedly, "Hello! Deni!"

"Sorry, Gary, it's not Deni. It's Ron Lee. I heard about Deni. Obviously, she's still missing. Any details you could give me to help find her?"

Gary Whitaker, aka Ichabod, with an irrepressible grin on his face, replied, "Yeah, Ron, thanks for calling. She went out today to be with some friends, but it's 10:00, and she hasn't come home. I expected her home by 7:00 or 7:30 at the latest."

"I'm sure she's fine, Gary. Maybe she had car trouble, or even more probable, she and her friends are having such a good time they haven't noticed the hour."

"Maybe, Ron, but I called her friends. They haven't seen her all day."

Hearing Gary's response gave Ron pause.

"I'm sure she'll be home shortly, Gary. Call me if you need anything."

"Did you call me because you think she's a victim of…"

"No! No! Not at all," Ron lied. "Due to the current situation, it's mandatory that any reports of missing women come into my office. When I saw it was Deni, well, I thought I'd call to see how things were going."

"I appreciate that. I'll let you know as soon as she gets home."

"Okay, Gary. Don't worry. Deni wouldn't do anything crazy."

He couldn't help himself. He had to say it, "Yeah, I have to admit, she's pretty level-headed, that's for sure."

CHAPTER 53
King's North

July 21, 2018

It was 8:15am when Ron rolled over in bed and answered his cell phone.

"Yeah, what is it, Tim?"

"Not good, Ron."

"Meaning?"

"King's North."

"Let me guess. Number twelve?"

"Yeah, but somewhat different, Ron."

"How's that?"

"He didn't leave it on the green. He left it on the tee box."

"Tee box? I wonder why?"

"I'll give you my take when you get here."

"Anything else?"

"Yeah, but it's the bad part."

"Don't tell me… it's Deni."

"Afraid so, Ron."

"Damn! Is Gary there?"

"Not yet. We sent someone to get him."

"Okay. I'll be there in about 20 minutes."

Ron pulled into the course parking lot 30 minutes later, where Tim, sitting in a golf cart, had been waiting.

"How come she was found so late, Tim?"

"Well, from what I gathered from the maintenance guys, they cut the greens and the fairways first, and the tee boxes last. A group of guys visiting from Syracuse, who had teed off on the backside, found it. It so happened they reached twelve before the mowers did."

"Must have been a shock, hey?"

"It may sound funny, but one golfer thought someone had left their 'head' cover."

"Not funny, Tim," Ron said with a huge smirk.

"Well, if that's so, wipe that grin off your face."

"When did Gary get here?"

"He arrived 15 minutes ago. He's taking it hard."

"Wouldn't you if it were your wife's head?"

"Sure, I would."

"You told me on the phone you'd give me your take on why he left it on the tee box instead of the green. So let's hear it."

"Well, since he had to walk it out here…"

"Maybe he didn't. Perhaps he lives around here and has a golf cart."

"You asked me for my take. Can I expect continuous interruptions or was that it?"

"Keep talking."

"Okay, so he has to walk out here. The distance from the parking lot to the 10th tee is easily 200 yards. The 10th is over 500 yards. The 11th is over 400 yards. So, at a minimum he had to travel 1100 yards, and that's as the 'sparrow' flies, partner. It's also the better part of two-thirds of a mile."

"Crows are smarter than sparrows."

"So?"

"They fly straighter."

"Bullshit!"

"Okay, so what's your point?"

"Time and distance, Ron. How long would you want your car parked in the parking lot if you were running around with a severed head?"

"Not long, that's for sure."

"Yeah, well this guy, going both ways, had to cover approximately a mile and a half. I'm thinking he's flat out wasted upon arrival. Being winded, he decides not to walk down to the green, which would have added another 170 yards, even though the length of the hole itself is only about 125."

"That's because you must go down the little hill and walk around to the back to gain access to the green."

"Right. So round trip that's 340 yards… with a good 50 of it uphill. Add that to what he already traveled, and you have used up a great deal of time."

"How much, do you estimate?"

"Walking and jogging, I'd say 20 minutes if you're in excellent shape, which, according to the descriptions we have, he is. Don't forget, he's doing this in the dark too."

"I like your estimate and I also like your theory, partner. It makes sense. Hell, I'm winded just thinking about it."

"Hell, you get winded taking a dump."

"Screw you."

"Is that a statement or a question?"

★★★★★★★★★★★★

"No notes or anything like that, Bill?"

"Nothing. He just stuck the head on a tee marker."

"Where's Gary?"

"He's over there by the restrooms."

"How's he doing?"

"If you ask me…"

"I'm asking, Bill!"

"Well, I'd say he's doing damn good! Took it hard when he first arrived. But within 10 minutes he was well under control, but… that's just my observation."

"Did he cry? Get choked up? Eyes get teary?"

"No, yes, and yes."

"Tim."

"Yeah, Ron."

"See anything different about the decapitation?"

"Yeah, I noticed that right off. He didn't use an axe that's for damn sure."

"Maybe we have us a copycat?" suggested Ron.

"Possible. He left her on a tee box instead of a green. The cut is different. Much neater, that's for sure."

"No note, either. I would have thought he would continue to berate us with something. I had been expecting another message."

"Maybe he didn't have time to write one."

"Perhaps. Get the head to the lab. Maybe they can determine how it was severed. I'll go talk to the grieving widower."

****

"Gary, we're sorry for your loss. Deni was a great gal."

"Thanks, Ron."

His eyes were red. He had been grieving.

"Do you think it was this 'Ichabod' guy?"

"Possibly. There are differences, though."

"Oh?"

Ron, hearing how Gary had emphasized "Ichabod" like he had a mouth full of shit, gave him pause. *I guess,* he thought, *if it had been my wife killed like that, I would have most likely spoken the name in the same manner.*

"I can't say what the differences are, but as soon as it is practical, I'll let you know."

"Thanks, Ron, I'd appreciate that."

"I know others have asked these questions but humor me for just a moment."

"Sure. Anything to help catch her killer."

"When did you last see her?"

"I'm guessing it was around 12:30. She had gone food shopping. I met her outside when she returned and helped her carry the groceries into the house. She did a little housework, and then shortly after noon she left to meet some of her friends at Coastal Mall. That's the last I saw of her."

"You didn't work yesterday?"

"No. I usually take Fridays off. That's my class planning day."

"Your son?"

"He's at summer camp. Leaves at 7:30, comes home at 4:00."

"I'm told you called the police around 9:20 last night. Is that right?"

"Yeah, I guess that's correct."

"Why so late?"

"What do you mean? She was only about two hours late."

"Doesn't she usually have your dinner ready around 5:00 or 5:30?"

"Usually, yes."

"Weren't you concerned when she hadn't come home by dinnertime?"

"As I explained to the officers earlier, she had told me she'd be late and that I should cook dinner for Doug and myself. I made mac and cheese. That's Doug's favorite. We ate about 5:30."

"When did you become concerned about her not being home?"

"It was around 7:30, Ron."

"Did you call any of her friends at that hour?"

"No, because I thought she was with them. Why call them? They wouldn't be home."

"Did you call her cell phone?"

"She doesn't have one. There's a landline at home."

"If you expected her home around 7:00, why did you wait two hours before calling the police?"

"I don't know, Ron! I gave her some rope, you might say. What? I'm not a suspect, am I?"

"You damn well know you're a suspect, Gary! You're the husband! The spouse, especially husbands, is always a suspect in a wife's death. You're not stupid. You should know that."

"Yeah, I do. Sorry for getting testy."

"No problem. You go home. We'll be talking to you later. Get some rest. Where's Doug?"

"He's at camp. You're not questioning him, are you?"

"I doubt that will be necessary."

"Okay, thanks, Ron."

"Okay, Gary."

Ron watched Gary walking toward the golf cart that would take him to the parking lot. It was only then he came to realize Gary's overall physique. *He's well over six-foot,* thought Ron. *He's well built, bald, smart, and then there's the clincher.*

Taking a long glance back at the crime scene, triggered a thought.

"Tim!" he yelled.

"Yo!"

"Let's get back to the office. There's something on that board I need to see."

CHAPTER 54
Anagram

July 21, 2018

"Shouldn't we be out there trying to track down Deni's abductor, Ron?"

"Someone abducted her?"

"You know it's the way the guy works! He abducts, in a manner of speaking, the women he winds up killing."

"Let's wait until we have something to chase, Tim. As of now, we have nothing but a head."

"Yeah, I guess you're right."

"Update the left side of the board with Deni, Tim."

Grabbing an eraser, Tim removed the reference to Ana, and then filled in the remaining four columns.

"Now, look at the right side of the board, Tim. Can you pick out something relevant to Deni?"

Tim spent five minutes reviewing the phrases before saying, "Have you spotted something?"

"Yeah."

"Give me a hint. Is it under 'phone' or 'note'?"

"Note."

Tim spent another couple of minutes before saying, "Well, the word 'king' is up there and they found Deni at King's North."

"Good job. That's it."

"That's somewhat vague, Ron."

"Maybe, but I'll bet you that one of the two remaining courses is True Blue."

Tim looked back at the board and viewed the phrase "the true king of murder."

Victim	Course	Hole #	Date Killed	Picked Up at
Sara Carson	Tradition	7	6/28	Boardwalk?
Laura Cantor	Indian Wells	15	7/2	Half Shell
Betsy Parker	River Hills	16	7/5	Chris's Pizza
Julia Spencer	Eagle's Nest	17	7/9	House of Blues
Ginger Evans	Witch	17	7/17	Pelican's Game
Sophia McDougall	Heritage	18	7/19	Brookgreen Gardens
Deni Whittaker	King's North	12	7/20	????

PHONE	NOTE
four more clues	number six and counting
stay calm	cannot decipher my clues
piece it all together	archaic methods
big thinker	creek without a paddle
small-minded	a gram of common sense
write this down	Need to shore up your manpower
just four more clues	worth your salt
spell it out	the true king of murder
add it up	There will be three more.
	I've set my sights on Ana and so should you
	all you need to know

"You may have something, partner. That would account for eight of the nine courses. Do you think the 9th is up there, somewhere?"

"I do. But to be honest, I can't, for the life of me, see it."

"I'm getting coffee. You want a cup?"

"Yeah, thanks," said Ron. "Just cream."

Giving the board one long look, Ron shook his head and turned away, saying aloud, "I need to get away from this for a few minutes."

"Here's your coffee."

"Thanks."

While drinking his coffee, Ron spotted the morning paper lying on the table. Picking it up, he turned to the comic page and worked on the two puzzles he did religiously each day.

Finishing the Sudoku puzzle in no time, he began the Jumbo but stopped before even solving the first word.

Turning to Tim, he said, "Grab something and jot down the first letter of each golf course."

"What?"

"The first letter in the name of each golf course. Write them down!"

Grabbing a sheet of paper, Tim jotted down the first letter in the name of each golf course, stopping to ask, "Should I include the first letter of the second name?"

Ron, at first not recognizing Tim's meaning, glanced at the names to see that Indian Wells, River Hills, Eagle's Nest, and King's North had two-part names.

"Make two lists. Include the letters of the two-part name in the second list. Don't put it on paper. Write it on the board."

"Good idea," acknowledged Tim.

FIRST ONLY	FIRST & SECOND
Tradition	Tradition
Indian	Indian Wells
River	River Hills
Eagle's	Eagle's Nest
Witch	Witch
Heritage	Heritage
King's	King's North
True	

Two minutes later a third list was on the board.

"Is there software that can scramble letters, Tim, and determine all the words that could come from those letters?"

"I've never needed to use anything like that, but, I'm betting there is. Let me check."

Keying into Google the search phrase, "Scramble Letters into Words" resulted in finding dozens of sites that would satisfy their need.

Selecting one site, Tim entered the letters from the "first only" column. Revealed were the words: *whiter, writhe,* and *wither.*

"It only used six of the seven letters, Ron."

"Okay, do the other side."

Keying the 11 letters generated the words: *whither, rethink, thinner, thinker, writhen.*

"It didn't use all 11 letters, did it?" Ron asked.

"No. Not even close. Seven was the most."

"Then we don't need the second part of the course's name."

"Are you sure, Ron? It could be multiple words he's giving us."

"Yeah, you're right, but let's hold that thought. I'm thinking of one word. Go back to the single list and add another 'T'."

"For True Blue, I take it."

"Exactly."

The search returned only a single word: *whitter*.

"It didn't use all the letters, Ron. It omitted 'K'."

"The ninth course starts with the letter 'A,' Tim."

"How did you come up with that?"

"He's giving us his name. It's his signature. Clever, he was. Each 'head hole,' if you will, was the course's signature hole. He impaled Ginger Evans' head on top of the flagstick at the Witch for a very precise reason which I now understand."

"You do?"

"Upper and lower, Tim."

"Upper and lower?"

"Upper and lower case."

"The Witch... a capital 'W'?"

"Yep. Take that word you have there and put the missing 'k' in front of the 'e'."

"Whittker. Whitt... ker. Whitt... a... ker. Holy crap, Ron! Gary Whittaker is Ichabod!"

"If he's not, then I'm Santa Claus."

"All you need is the white beard and a red suit, that's for damn sure."

"I wish your detective skills were within hailing distance of your sarcasm skills. If they were, you might be of some use."

Shaking off Ron's attempt at being funny, Tim asked, "Do we have enough proof? I mean this... anagram. Hell, a shitty attorney could twist it into something else. Would this hold up in court?"

"No, it likely wouldn't."

"He has a late model dark colored car. His build matches the various descriptions we got from witnesses."

"You know, Tim, I was with him once, and he expressed something about how gruesome Sara Carson's head was. It occurred to me his team was way back on the 7th tee. He couldn't have seen her head."

"Again, circumstantial. Someone could have described it to him."

"Yeah, you're right. Everything we have is circumstantial, Tim. We need solid proof."

"Proof? This guy hasn't made a mistake yet."

Oh, but Ichabod had made a huge mistake. The problem is, he wouldn't realize it until he prematurely gloated.

CHAPTER 55
Dennis

July 22, 2018 – Dennis

The call woke Ron at 6:45.

Seeing the caller ID, he answered, "What the hell do you want, Bill Baxter, at 6:45 in the damn morning? A Sunday morning at that!"

"Geez! Has anyone ever mentioned that you're overly obnoxious when called early in the morning?"

"Yeah, but who gives a rat's ass?"

"Listen, Ron. Earlier this morning, around 5:30, we received a call about the gate attendant at Litchfield Plantation being found dead."

"Okay, so what the hell does that have to do with waking me on a Sunday morning at 6:45?"

"Poison killed him. We think it was insecticide."

"I'm still waiting for the punchline, Bill."

"I had my guys do a scan of the property. Guess what they found?"

"I'm peeing the bed in suspense, Bill."

"Deni Whittaker's car."

Ron sprang up in the bed and put his feet on the floor.

"What's her car doing at Litchfield Plantation?"

"Someone parked it at the marina."

"I didn't know Litchfield had a marina."

"It's secluded back along the Waccamaw River. Whittaker has a boat there."

"You're shitting me, Bill!"

"No, I am not."

"Let no one near that boat or car. I'll be there in less than an hour."

"An hour? What are you gonna do? Braid your hair?"

"Lots of funny people in this world," Ron said as he hung up the phone. "Speaking of which."

Dialing, he waited while the phone rang five times before he heard, "Yeah."

"Were you getting laid, partner? It sure took you a long time to answer."

"I'm not good at multi-tasking, Ron. Having an orgasm and answering the phone falls under that category. What the hell do you want?"

"Get dressed and come pick me up."

"Why? What's happened?"

"They found Deni's car at the Litchfield Marina."

"Where the hell is that?"

"In Litchfield, dumbass."

"Damn, that makes sense. Do you have a map?"

"Just get dressed and get over here."

Thirty minutes later, Tim was driving south on Route 17.

"When you get to Willbrook, turn right."

"Hey, we go right past Applewood's. Would you like to get...?"

"No!"

"There's where it all started," said Tim, as they drove past Tradition's 7th hole.

"You'll turn left about a mile from here onto Old River Road."

A minute later Tim made the turn, and they were traveling south.

"That's my favorite Willbrook hole," Tim declared, as they passed the course's third fairway.

"There's Tradition's 15th green and the 16th fairway," said Ron, pointing to his left.

"That 16th hole is a bear."

"Yeah, it is," agreed Ron. "Look! The entrance to Litchfield Plantation is up here on the right, just past River Club's third tee box there on the left."

"Now I remember this place," said Tim as he turned into the gated property and stopped by a uniformed State Trooper.

Tim rolled down his window and Ron leaned over saying, "We're FBI. Where's Captain Baxter?"

"Take this road to the end, make a left, go about a hundred yards, and turn right. Follow the road to the marina, sir."

"Thank you, officer."

Minutes later, they were standing beside Deni's Toyota.

"Has anyone touched the car, Bill?"

"You said for no one to get near it or the boat. No one has."

Sensing Bill's irritation at him for implying his people couldn't follow orders, Ron replied, "Sorry, Bill. Nothing meant by it. I wasn't thinking."

Bill, seeing Ron had been sincere in his apology, nodded.

"Have you found anything else?"

"One guy found what he believes to be blood spattered on the ground over there to our right. It will take a lab tech to verify that."

Ron walked to the area where Bill had been pointing and seeing what appeared as dried blood, nodded his agreement.

"It appears to be blood, no doubt."

Returning to the car, he opened the driver's door and without getting in, gave it a thorough examination.

"It looks clean."

"What does that tell you, Ron?"

"It tells me that someone other than Deni drove the car in here. Does the attendant keep a record of who comes onto the property?"

"Yeah, there is a logbook, but yesterday's page has gone missing."

"I'm just theorizing here, but I'm thinking whoever drove this car in here was someone the guard knew."

"He would know Deni Whittaker, wouldn't he?" asked Bill.

"Yes, he would," admitted Ron, "but she would have no reason to remove the page. Besides, she was most likely already dead. She either died here or brought here for disposal. Have your men scour the area, Bill. See if they can find any signs of foul play."

"Sure thing."

"If someone brought her here in her own car, then where did the killer go?" asked Tim.

"I'm guessing there are two options. Either he already had a car here, which is unlikely, or someone picked him up."

"How about if he took off in a boat?" asked Tim as he circled Deni's car looking for something, anything, that might be of some help.

"That's a viable alternative, that's for sure. Let's get a list of the folks who keep their boat here and determine if any may be missing."

"Hey, Ron," said Tim, after opening the rear door on the passenger side. "There's a 33-gallon garbage bag on the floor behind the passenger seat."

"Take it out and set it on the hood. Be careful."

Tim, taking a pen from his jacket's front pocket, slipped it through the bag's red-colored tie strings and, lifting it out of the car, placed it on the hood.

"I'll open it," announced Ron.

"Why not? Be my guest," replied Tim, offended that Ron didn't trust him to open the bag.

Realizing that he had slighted his partner, Ron quickly pivoted, saying, "On second thought, you found it, you open it."

Glad to know his partner trusted him, Tim carefully opened the bag and peered inside to check the contents.

"It appears to be women's clothes. I see a bra."

"Take them out, Tim. You don't have to be too careful. We can't get prints off clothing."

One by one Tim laid the articles of clothing onto the hood of the car.

"Recognize anything?"

Taking a second to give the clothes a closer look, Tim smiled, saying, "Yeah, I do. It looks like the clothing the woman at Brookgreen had been wearing."

"Yep, it appears we have found Sophia McDougall's clothes. I'll bet she isn't too far away."

"Ron! Tim!" yelled Captain Baxter. "Come look!"

"No doubt they have found Sophie."

"It could be Deni," Tim offered.

"It could well be both!"

Rushing across the lot, they followed Baxter down a pathway leading into the marsh. A few moments later, they stood aghast at what they saw.

"Damn! What the hell is that!" exclaimed Tim, covering his mouth and nose to prevent breathing in the ghastly smell.

"Rotting flesh," answered Ron, who had also covered his mouth and nose. "My guess is that's Sophia McDougall. Deni wouldn't decompose that much in a day's time."

"Ron, come over here for a minute," Tim said, motioning his partner as far away as possible from the rotting body parts, now covered with hungry crabs.

"What is it?"

"The clothes."

"What about them?"

"The killer knew someone would find the car. Correct?"

"Definitely."

"So why leave the clothes?"

"Tell me."

"It wasn't intentional. He forgot they were there."

"You're thinking he's made a mistake?"

"That's what I'm thinking. I'm guessing he's thinking he has pulled off the perfect crime. Missing wife, no cadaver in sight, no signs of a struggle, and witnesses who confirm his car was in the driveway all day. Everything is perfect. But... in time he will realize, if he hasn't already, that he left the bag."

"It's the only thing that could trip him up."

"Those could be his thoughts, Ron."

"So, you're assuming he'll come to get it?"

"Maybe he will."

"If he does, that's an admission of knowing the car was here," stated Ron.

"Correct, and only the killer would know that."

"CAPTAIN BAXTER!"

"What the hell are you yelling about, Ron?"

"Bill, get all your people out of here. Leave someone to attend to the front gate."

"Why?"

"We believe our killer will soon realize that he left something behind that could incriminate him. He could be on his way here, right now! Get all your people out, Bill! Pronto!"

"What about the body over there in the marsh?"

"I doubt she'll mind spending a few more hours in the mud, Bill."

"That's cold, Ron."

"That it was, but if we don't catch this guy, two more women will be real cold, real soon. Like dead cold."

"What are you two going to do?"

"Plant a few seeds."

****

The knock at the door came at 3:15.

Gary, grinning all day about what he had pulled off, had been watching a movie when he heard the knock.

He had shipped Doug off to his maternal grandmother's home. Gary decided his son would remain with his grandmother until matters concerning Deni were concluded.

Rising from his recliner, Gary hastened to the door and opened it to find Ron Lee and Tim Pond.

"Ron! Tim! Come in. Have you found Deni's body?"

"No, I'm sorry, we haven't," replied Ron.

"Have you come up with anything?"

"Again, we haven't."

"We're searching for her car, Gary," said Tim.

"We're hoping that it might tell us something, either by its location, its condition, or anything we may find inside the car or its trunk."

"You found no witnesses at Myrtle Beach National? I mean, there is only one way into their parking lot. Surely someone saw something."

"We questioned every resident on that street," stated Tim. "They saw nothing."

"What about security cameras?" asked Gary. "That outfit must have security cameras around the clubhouse."

"They do, but…" muttered Tim.

"But what?"

"They're just for show."

"You're kidding me!"

"Sorry, but we're not."

"Look," said Ron, "we've been talking to your neighbors. They have confirmed your story about being home all day. Some remember seeing you and Deni carrying groceries into the house too."

"One neighbor said he saw you giving your lawn mower to the next-door neighbor… Mr. Bruce Langley," added Tim.

"Yeah, apparently his mower is in for repairs. He asked if he could borrow mine."

"We're having trouble locating Mr. Langley. You wouldn't know where he might be, would you?"

"Gosh, no. I haven't seen Bruce since he brought my mower back later that day."

"Someone reported that they saw Deni talking with Mr. Langley the other day as she pulled out of the driveway. Any idea what that discussion could have been?"

"No idea, Ron."

"His truck is in the garage. He said nothing about going off somewhere, did he?"

"Not that I recall," answered Ichabod. "Might he be a suspect, Ron?"

"He may have been the last person to see her alive. As you know, she never met her friends, nor did she intend to meet them, at the mall that day. None of them knew anything about getting together."

"You're not implying that Deni had been having an affair, are you?"

"We can't find anything that points to that, Gary," answered Tim.

"As you know, the husband is always the key suspect in the murder of his wife. Even though you have a tight alibi, we still need to check out a few things. We'd like to look around the house. Do you mind?"

"Not at all, Ron. Take all the time you need."

"Thanks, we shouldn't be but a few minutes."

As he watched, Tim took the steps to the upstairs bedrooms while Ron headed toward the kitchen. *Damn!* he thought, *I forgot about the thing that started all this, Sophie's damn clothes! They're still behind the passenger seat! My prints are all over that bag.*

Ron interrupted his thoughts when from the kitchen, he heard, "Gary, would you come to the kitchen for a moment?"

Entering the kitchen, Gary replied, "What is it, Ron?"

"Would you mind if we took some of your cutlery? We need to have it tested."

"Tested? For what?"

"I hoped you wouldn't ask, but it would be for Deni's blood."

"So, since I'm the main suspect, you're implying that I used those knives to cut off her head. Is that right?"

"I'm just doing my job, Gary."

Having run the knives through the dishwasher at least a half-dozen times, not to mention having soaked them in bleach for two hours, he had no qualms in letting Ron test the knives.

"Yeah, I'm sorry. Go ahead, take them. Take them all. There's some in that other drawer too."

"The bathrooms will need a thorough scrutinizing."

"Check the entire house, Ron. I'll wait in the living room."

Twenty minutes had passed when Tim and Ron reconvened in the Whittaker living room. Gary sat staring at the television screen, watching, but not seeing, the movie he had been viewing before they had arrived.

"Okay," said Ron. "We're done here, buddy." Then watching for a suspicious reaction, Ron continued, "Sorry we won't be seeing you at golf on Tuesday. I don't know if you heard, but we're playing True Blue for $50."

If Lee could have heard Gary's heart, he would have heard it pounding by an extra 20 beats a minute. Outwardly though, the only physical reaction Ron could decipher was a slight, barely noticeable, clenching of Gary's left hand.

"Golf may be the furthest thing from my mind, fellas."

Ironically, he wasn't lying. Foremost in his mind at that moment was a brown garbage bag containing the clothes of a woman he had killed just three days earlier.

"I'm sorry, Gary. That was insensitive. We'll do everything we can to get this Ichabod monster. You have my word."

Ron had been pushing buttons, but Gary wasn't biting, at least not outwardly. The term "Ichabod" had rankled him, but he didn't let it show.

"I'm hoping that you catch him soon before he does this to some other woman."

"We'll be going now, Gary. Talk to you soon."

"Okay, guys. See you later."

He watched them leave and head toward Bruce's house. He also saw Mrs. Laverty, Bruce's other neighbor, standing in the driveway. Apparently, she had been expecting them.

Why is the old lady Laverty standing in Bruce's driveway?

Then he saw it. She handed Ron something small and silver. It was a key to Bruce's front door.

"What do you expect to find, Ron?" whispered Whittaker.

He watched as they entered the house.

"You won't find Bruce, I can assure you of that," he articulated slightly louder and with a wicked grin. "Bruce sleeps with the fishes," he announced, paraphrasing a famous quote from *The Godfather*, one of Gary's favorite movies.

****

"You saw Mr. Langley pull into his garage around 9:15 last night, Mrs. Laverty. Is that correct?"

"Yes, Agent Pond. I had been sitting on the front porch in my rocker. Bruce drove past the house and pulled into his driveway. He sat there for a few seconds as the garage door opened. A few moments later, he pulled in and closed the door behind him."

Noticing that all the downstairs lights were in the off position, Tim asked, "Did you notice any lights being turned on in his house, ma'am?"

"Can't say I did, but I can't say I didn't either. I'm sorry, but I wasn't paying attention."

"That's okay, ma'am."

"Tim, look at this."

Ron had been standing at the rear door.

"What is it?"

"It's unlocked. I wouldn't think someone would leave his door unlocked."

"Mrs. Laverty," called Tim, "is Bruce a person who would leave his doors unlocked if he weren't home?"

"Never!" she replied. "Bruce didn't trust too many people. He liked the Whittaker's, especially Gary, who would often take him out on his boat."

"Is that a fact?"

"Let's have a look at his truck," suggested Ron.

Tim flicked on the garage lights as he led Mrs. Laverty down the three steps to the garage floor.

A Chevy 4-door truck took up most of the garage.

"Ron, check out the tires."

Bending down to look at the rear left tire, he immediately picked up on Tim's observation.

"Oyster shells."

"Lots of crushed oyster shells at the marina parking lot."

"Do you know how often Bruce drove to the Whittaker's marina, ma'am?"

"I wouldn't have a clue, Agent Pond."

Ron opened the driver side rear door, looked inside, and seeing nothing, closed it and opened the driver's door. There, lying on the driver's seat, was Bruce's hat.

"Nothing here except a hat," reported Ron.

"I'm sorry, but what did you say, Agent Lee?"

"I was just saying, ma'am, that the only thing inside the truck was a man's hat."

"Is it a beige Panama hat?"

"Yes, ma'am. Does that mean anything?"

"Yes, I'd say so."

"Tell us what it means, Mrs. Laverty."

"Mind you, I'm no detective, Agent Lee, but if Bruce's hat is in that truck, and he's not in this house, then I fear that Bruce is dead."

"Ma'am?" asked Tim, seeking an explanation.

"Bruce never leaves the house unless he's wearing that hat. I mean, never!" she repeated emphatically. "His wife Ginny, may her soul rest in peace, gave him that hat a week before she died. It is Bruce's connection to the woman he adored. He goes nowhere, and I mean absolutely nowhere, without that hat on his head."

Ron and Tim gave each other a nod, then Ron said, "Ma'am, you have been a great help. Thank you."

"You're welcome. I hope you fellas catch the son-of-a-bitch who killed Deni."

"We may be close to catching him, ma'am."

Opening the garage door, they watched her walk down the driveway and turn right toward her home.

"What are you thinking, Ron?"

"I'm thinking he drove the Toyota to the marina with Deni's body in the trunk. How he made his way out of the neighborhood without being spotted is a question for another day. Somehow, he had Bruce follow him in this truck to the marina. Once there, he killed Bruce and took him and Deni out on the river to dispose of their bodies."

Interrupting, Tim added, "Don't forget the gate attendant could have identified him as the person driving Deni's Toyota into the marina. He took care of that problem by slipping the guy a Socrates' special."

"Not much doubt about that, Tim. Now, knowing Bruce always wore this hat, he puts it on and drives right into the garage. Anyone who sees him, just as that lady did, sees the hat and automatically assumes that it's Bruce. He walks through Langley's house, leaves through the back door, and enters his house, all while his car sits in the driveway, giving the impression he's been home all day. Solid alibi!"

"He had to drop Deni's head off at King's North last night."

"I totally agree, Tim. When Mrs. Laverty saw 'Bruce' pulling into his garage, she was actually seeing Gary returning from King's North. When he returns, he calls the cops and reports Deni missing. All that's left is the window dressing."

"That's a solid scenario, Ron. When do you think he'll make a run to the marina and claim the bag?"

"If it were me, I'd try to get there as fast as possible. The discovery of the car increases the longer it sits there, although, that's what he wanted to happen."

"If he swallowed the bait, he's most likely just waiting for us to leave."

"Then, let's oblige Mr. Ichabod, Tim-o-thy."

CHAPTER 56
Springing the Trap

July 22, 2018

Watching their movements from behind a closed sheer curtain, he saw the two agents leave the house, get into their car, and drive off.

Retrieving another gun from his dwindling collection, he rushed to his car. An elderly neighbor, Giles Porter, who lived three doors down had been passing by as Gary was about to enter his car. He called out, "Gary!"

Stopping in his tracks, Whittaker whirled around to see the neighbor.

"Yes, Mr. Porter?"

"Brenda and I want to say how sorry we are for your terrible loss."

"Thank you, Mr. Porter, I appreciate your sympathy."

"If we can do anything to help you get through this, please let us know."

Gary's immediate thought was, *you can get the hell out of my way,* but instead he answered, "I appreciate that, Mr. Porter. You must excuse me; I'm needed at the funeral parlor."

Knowing they had recovered only the wife's head, Whittaker's proclamation confused Porter, but he let it slide.

"I apologize. We'll talk later."

"Yes, sir."

A minute later he was out of the neighborhood and heading toward Litchfield Plantation. As he drove, he gave little thought to Lee's visit to his house or the search, but Lee's comment about True Blue had sounded an alarm.

Did he know? Has he figured out the clues? Why would he mention playing golf to a man who had suffered such a horrific loss? Was Lee that insensitive?

Paranoia overtook Gary's thoughts. Then unaware, his thoughts became vocal, and he began a two-way conversation with himself.

"They haven't found the car yet, Gary."

"Surely, they found Dennis. I would think a poisoned man would cause an investigation of the entire plantation."

"Did they call the local cops to the scene, Gary? They wouldn't know enough to do an exhaustive search."

"Yeah, maybe that's it. They're a bunch of buffoons. They wouldn't be smart enough to search the whole area."

"Besides, that marina is so isolated few people ever go back there."

"Maybe, after I get the bag, I should make an anonymous call and tell them a car has been back there for quite a while."

"I don't think it would be wise, Gary."

"Why not?"

"It might draw suspicion on us."

"Yeah, maybe you're right. Let them find it on their own."

"This couldn't be a trap, could it?"

"A trap? Lee is too dumb to set a trap."

"If you think he's dumb, look at that partner of his."

"Pond? How in the hell did he get into the F-B-I?"

"Maybe he knew somebody."

"Don't you mean, maybe he 'blew' somebody?"

Laughing as he pulled up to the familiar Litchfield entrance and, seeing an unfamiliar face, he turned serious.

"Where's Dennis?"

"There's been a problem, sir. Dennis is no longer with us."

"Oh? He always seemed to be a capable guy."

"Yes, sir. I'm sorry, but I don't know you, sir. State your name and your business."

Gary's thoughts once again began their own dual conversation.

"How could you be so stupid, Gary? If you give your name, once they find the car, this guy will remember you being here."

"Yeah, you're right. I guess there's only one solution."

"I beg your pardon, sir?" asked the attendant. "Were you addressing…"

Before Gary's inner voice could react, Ichabod shot the undercover state trooper right between the eyes.

Flooring the Chrysler, he shot down the Avenue of the Live Oaks.

"What about the body, Gary? Are you going to leave it there?"

"It will only take a few minutes to get the bag and get out of here."

****

"Your man at the gate knows the vehicle, right Bill?"

There were only five men located around the marina. Ron, Tim, and Bill were standing near the Toyota. They placed a marksman, covered by a tarp, on the transom of a large boat docked in the last slip, less than 40 yards away. They had a fifth man, Sergeant Michaels, stationed

306

under the walkway leading from the parking lot down to the docking pier.

"Yeah. I told him it was a dark blue Chrysler 300. He'll radio us as soon as he lets it pass."

"What do you mean, 'when he lets it pass,' Bill? He can't greet this guy! He won't leave anyone alive that could identify…"

They all heard the gunshot some 400 yards from their position.

Baxter immediately lifted his radio and called to the man at the gate.

"Corporal Winston. What was that shot?"

Dead silence was the reply.

"Corporal Winston! Come in."

Nothing.

"Forget it, Bill. He's dead! Find cover! He's on his way here!" screamed Lee.

Together the three men scrambled down the pathway where earlier in the day they had found Sophie's half-eaten body. There they waited.

Their wait was short-lived. They could hear a vehicle coming down the winding, pothole filled dirt road that ended in the marina's parking lot.

"We don't take him until after he takes the bag out of the vehicle," reminded Ron through his radio.

"Roger, that," came two replies.

They heard the car stop, but the engine remained idling. A minute passed at glacier speed. They heard a door open and there was quiet except for the humming of the car's engine.

It stayed quiet for the better part of five minutes. Then they heard a door shut, followed immediately by cautious footsteps.

Ron counted the footsteps, stopping at twelve when he heard a car door open and then shut, followed by running footsteps.

Ron was about to give the order to arrest the suspect when he heard another door open.

Damn, thought Ron. *He opened the driver's side back door, saw the bag on the opposite side, and ran around the car to get it.*

Moments later the door slammed shut and they could hear footfalls treading across the oyster-based gravel.

"Now!" yelled Ron into his radio.

The marksman fired a shot that hit three feet in front of the suspect and sprayed gravel onto his pant legs.

"Don't move, Gary! We would relish the opportunity to shoot you dead, right where you stand. Drop the bag and get your hands up! High!"

Whittaker, immediately recognizing the voice of Ron Lee, called out, "Well played, Ron. My congratulations. I didn't think you were that smart."

"Couldn't have done it without your stupidity, Ich-a-bod," replied Ron knowingly and purposely rubbing the grain the wrong way, hoping that Whittaker would give him cause to blow him away.

Lee's words gnawed at the rage filling Whittaker's head. He was a volcano about to blow. His first instinct had been to go for the gun tucked in his belt, but he resisted, knowing the marksman would shoot him dead before his hand ever neared the grip.

No, he told himself, *there would be a much better opportunity.*

He would be right.

CHAPTER 57
Hook, Line and ...

Safely handcuffed, they put Whittaker in the back seat of a State Police cruiser.

Ron and Tim, along with Bill Baxter, were standing alongside the open rear door.

"Took you long enough to figure it out, Ron. If you had been just a wee bit smarter, you may have saved a few of those women."

"If you hadn't been so stupid, maybe you'd still be out there chasing Gary Ridgeway's number. You will fall short of your goal. So sad. You're just another 'also-ran'."

"I have a question you may choose not to answer, Gary."

"What's that, Agent Pond?"

"Why your wife? You had to know killing Deni would be the end."

"Why would that be the end? I killed a previous wife, she was number 17, and things continued merrily along for another 10 years."

"Why Deni?"

"Same reason I killed my first wife. She found out who I was and what I did. In Deni's case, she found the bag in the back of my car."

"Jesus! You really are a piece of shit!" yelped Ron. "You forgot about the same bag twice? What a complete asshole!"

Whittaker took those words hard. If looks could kill, Ron Lee would be stone-cold dead.

A moment later Pond asked, "What did you do with your neighbor, Mr. Langley?"

"Bruce?"

"Yeah, Bruce."

"I did to him what I did to that gate attendant just a few minutes ago. I put a bullet in his head."

"You're a no-good son-of-a-bitch!" screamed Bill Baxter. "That was just a young kid and a good cop you killed in cold blood, you motherless prick!"

"That's a nasty vocabulary you have there, Captain."

Baxter, out-of-his-mind enraged and completely out-of-control, reached inside the car, grabbed Whittaker by the neck, and choked him while screaming, "You motherless bastard... I'm gonna kill you..."

"Bill! Bill! Stop!" yelled Ron, pulling him off the monster, but wishing he hadn't.

"Officer Michaels," called Tim. "Take your captain someplace where he can cool down."

They watched as Michaels escorted Baxter to another cruiser.

Turning to Whittaker, Ron asked, "Where are Deni and Langley's bodies, Gary?"

"Why should I tell you that? You can't prove I killed them. Everything you have is circumstantial."

"Does that include you coming down here and removing that bag from your wife's car? Only the killer would have known it was here."

"I may have been coming down to go out on my boat. I saw her car and naturally looked inside. I found the bag which, being the victim's husband, I was bringing to you. Can you prove otherwise? See, like I said, all you have is circumstantial."

"You may be right, Gary, but it doesn't matter. You're gonna fry for killing that young cop to which you admitted to in front of three witnesses, not to mention we've recorded everything said."

Smiling, Gary nodded his head, saying, "Okay, you have me there, Ron. I also admitted to killing my first wife, but you'll never find her body."

"Why not?"

"Well, that's when I lived in Vancouver. I killed about a dozen people during those years. I used fire back then. Cremated my victims using the services of a crematorium. They never had an inkling that someone had been using their equipment all those years. Amazing! Don't you think?"

"Yeah, amazing, Gary," Tim said with no intention of hiding his sarcasm.

"Where's your wife, Gary?" Ron asked.

Ahh, thought Gary, *finally, the hook.*

Nodding his head westward, he said, "Out there."

"In the river?"

"Come on now, Tim," blurted Gary, acting offended. "Do you really think of me as an amateur? Bodies in water normally find their way to the surface and eventually float right past someone. Neither Deni nor Bruce are in the river."

"Where are they?" asked Ron.

Repressing a smile, Gary thought, *Now the line.*

"I took them out to some grassy field alongside a tributary. You'll never find them."

"When did you do this?"

"Friday."

"Do you remember how to get there?"

"I do, but I won't show you the way."

"Think of your son, Gary. A few years down the road, he'll want to know if you had enough decency to give his mother a proper burial. Deni deserves that."

Hoping they would eventually get around to being sentimental, he replied, "That's playing dirty, Ron. Bringing my son into this."

"Your son was in this the minute you killed his mother, asshole!" shouted Tim.

Gary sat there staring at them for a minute before surrendering to their wants.

"Okay. I'll take you. We can go out there in my boat."

"How far away is it?" asked Tim.

"Less than an hour."

"Tim, inform Baxter what we plan on doing. Ask if we can have Trooper Michaels join us. Tell him to have the Coast Guard on standby. Oh, and Tim, don't forget to grab a flare gun. We'll signal them once we find the bodies. While you're doing that, I'll put this useless dick in the boat."

CHAPTER 58
...Stinker

July 22, 2018

"If you like, I'll drive," remarked Gary with a smile that belied a smugness.

"You are nothing but a piece of shit, Gary, so just sit and point the way!" Tim shouted in anger as he steered the craft down Waverly Creek.

"Aye, aye, Captain Pond," responded Gary. "Upon reaching the river, turn to the port side."

The turn took them south on the Waccamaw.

Gary's boat, white with blue trim, was a 20-foot Yamaha with a 120 horse-power inboard engine. It had a center console with a fishing deck off the back and a four-person sitting area in the front.

With his hands handcuffed behind his back, they seated Whittaker in a forward-facing seat. Sergeant Michaels sat beside him holding a baton he hoped he could use to smash Gary's face if he dared to make a single wrong move. Ron Lee, in a rear-facing seat, sat directly across from Whittaker.

Looking down at the floor, Ron asked, "Is this where you put them when you brought them out, Gary?"

"Yeah, right where your feet are. Bruce was all in one piece except for a large hole in his head, but I had Deni in three bags. I sure miss feeding those gators at that alligator place."

"You fed Ernie to the gators too, didn't you?"

"Yep, I sure did. He was a friendly guy too. It's unfortunate he came back. He forgot to turn on the alarm system. You should have seen it, Ron."

"Seen what?"

"I had him by the neck, holding him over the railing and wham! Damn, if a monster gator didn't rise out of that water and snatch him from me. Incredible!"

"Sorry that I missed it, Gary."

"Hey, Captain Pond, you'll be heading up that tributary on the starboard side."

"How far up the tributary?"

"Oh, I'm guessing a mile. I'll let you know."

"Tell me about Ginger Evans."

"What do you want to know, Ron? About the sex? Yeah, it was great. That woman had a helluva appetite for sex. She was more woman than I could handle. She had that dog too. What was its name… Bruno? Yeah, that was it. Bruno. I had to knock him out just to get her out of the house. Did he come out of it, okay?"

"Yeah, he'll be fine."

"Big son-of-a-bitch! Fun girl though. Good looking, loved baseball… oh, and did I tell you, she could put away some beer. What a woman!"

"What about Betsy Parker?"

"Now that one's on you, Ron!"

"Me? How's that?"

"You pissed me off by calling me that infernal name on television. I was so pissed… well, I just lost it, is all."

"Oh, you mean Ichabod!"

"You'll pay for that, Ron. I promise."

"If you say so, Ichabod."

Gary, seeing the smaller tributary he had taken the previous day, shouted, "Next starboard turn, Captain."

"We'll be there shortly. Do you have the stomach for what you're about to see?"

"Hell, I've had the stomach to sit here with you. Anything else should be a walk in the park."

"Bear to the port side, Captain Pond, and lower your speed to a crawl."

"Where are we going?" Tim asked.

"Steer the boat into these reeds. Just creep along until you bump into the bank."

A moment later they felt the expected jolt.

"It's best you toss the anchor into the grasses so that the boat doesn't drift off."

"Where are they, Gary?"

"I'll take you, Ron, but I can't get out of this boat or walk in the grasses with my hands tied behind my back. There's three of you, all armed, and me… unarmed. I think you'll have the advantage."

Ron assessed the situation, then said, "You might still run off, and I will admit, it might be tough finding you in this grass."

"Good point," nodded Gary in agreement.

"Sergeant Michaels, undo his right-hand cuff and put it on your left. That way, if he runs, he won't get far dragging you along."

Michaels, laughing, answered, "I'm a lot to drag, Colonel. I don't think Ichabod will go far."

You'll be the first one I kill, thought Whittaker.

Seeing the killer securely cuffed to Sergeant Michaels, Ron said, "Lead the way, Gary."

"Right this way, gentlemen."

Walking side-by-side, Gary and Trooper Michaels led the way through the six-foot tall grasses. Ron stayed a few feet back, with Tim bringing up the rear another half-dozen steps behind.

Gary smelled it first, but the others were quick to pick up the wretched scent.

"Rotting flesh," remarked Tim in a mumble.

Sensing the bodies were just a few steps ahead, Whittaker took a lead on Michaels. After almost stepping onto the decomposing and partially eaten body of his neighbor, the killer jerked Michaels off balance just enough to allow him to pick up the maggot covered axe and bury it into the trooper's head, killing him instantly.

Ron, screened by the tall grasses from the horrors happening just a few feet away, knew immediately that something had gone wrong.

"Michaels!" screamed Ron. "What happened?"

"Michaels is dead, and now it's your turn, Lee!"

A hail of bullets came whistling through the reeds flying over and around the diving FBI agents.

Blinded by the height and abundance of the grasses surrounding him, Gary, having found the pistol he had left behind, fired reckless shots into the reeds where he felt the FBI agents would be standing.

Having escaped being hit, the two agents returned fire. However, the abundance and height of the reeds also hindered the accuracy of their shots.

Suddenly, the shooting gave way to silence.

There were no sounds, other than the rustling grasses being caressed by an always present wind.

Moments later, there was a thud. Followed by another.

"What was that?" whispered Tim.

They heard a third thud, followed by the sound of thrashing grasses.

Ron and Tim, guns drawn, cautiously moved forward. As they separated the grasses, they saw the remains of Gary's neighbor. It appeared as if a bomb had blown open his chest cavity, but when later autopsied, it would prove to have been the work of a bear.

Then, covered in maggots and crabs, was a scattering of arms, legs, and a torso of what they presumed were Deni's remains.

Finally, there was the body of Trooper Michaels, his head split open right between the eyes. Lying next to the trooper was his amputated left hand.

"Now we know what the thud sounds were all about, Ron."

"Yep. It was that bastard chopping off Michaels' hand with that damn axe."

"He went off that way. You can see the disturbed grass."

"He could be anywhere in these grasses, Tim."

"Yes, and the lousy bastard has Michaels' revolver."

Ron turned to Tim saying in a semi-whisper, "Tell me you have the key to the boat!"

Tim's eyes answered the question long before Tim said, "They're still in the ignition."

"Let's get back to the boat before he does!"

Following the trampled grass of their inward journey, they found themselves within 20 feet of the boat when they heard an ungodly scream to their right.

Gunfire followed and again they hit the ground, but no bullets came their way.

Ichabod's horrifying screams continued as the two FBI agents regained their feet.

Gary had every intention of making his way back to the boat. His plan was to locate the edge of the tributary and follow it to the boat's location. What he found instead was a nest.

Alligators lay their eggs in late June and early July. The female stays on or near the nest until the eggs hatch, normally in 65 days. Now when the eggs hatch, the baby gators are on their own and they often become a meal by the male gator who fathered them. During incubation, however, the mother will guard the nest with her life from all intruders, including a decapitating serial killer.

She had been lying perfectly camouflaged alongside her mud, stick, and grass nest, when the intruder appeared.

Seeing the edge of the tributary bank, Gary, sweating profusely and breathing heavily, paid no attention to where he was walking. He was just a few feet from the bank when his left foot came within inches of stepping on the nest. The step would be his last.

Before Ichabod could advance another inch, she sprang from the mud and applied a 2500 pound per square inch bite on his left calf. Being 12 feet and weighing 600 pounds, he was no match for her. He fired three shots into her hide. It may as well have been a mosquito trying to draw blood from a corpse.

Being a California boy, he didn't know the only place to shoot an alligator was between the eyes.

He screamed as she dragged him into the water.

Ron and Tim, following the cries, made it to the bank just in time to see the gator pull Gary into the water and begin a death roll. Each time he surfaced, he reached out to them screaming, "HELP!"

Reaching out his hand as if to help, Ron, reminiscent of a Roman emperor who would display his verdict on whether a conquered gladiator should live or die, made a fist, and flipped his thumb downward.

Tim, meanwhile, raised his right hand to shoulder height and just wiggled his fingers in a "goodbye" gesture.

Smiles creased their faces as they watched a monster doing monstrous things to a monster.

They watched the brownish tannic acid waters of the river infused with red blood as she perforated the femoral artery.

Then, unexpectedly, Gary was free! Swimming as best he could with a mortally wounded leg, he headed toward the bank while screaming at the two agents, "Help me!"

They made no move to do so. He was within an arm's reach of the shoreline when she rose from the water to clamp her jaws on his neck. They both blanched as the gator, with Gary's neck firmly locked in her jaws, violently rolled her head first one way and then the other. Abruptly Gary's head was severed.

As his head momentarily bobbed in the water, their attention turned toward the gator as she took Gary's body under, leaving a massive red stain on the water's surface.

Standing and watching for the body or the gator to reappear, they instead saw neither. They redirected their attention toward the bobbing head. It had flipped over on its side. Gary's horrified eyes were looking directly at them as the head slowly rolled until it was face down. Then it popped upward for a brief second before sinking like a rock into the depths of the murky waters.

"That was interesting," Ron said, displaying about as much emotion as he may have while watching a National Geographic report about mushrooms.

Nodding his agreement, Tim asked, "Just how long do you think he can hold his breath?"

"I believe he may have a few things going against him, Tim. The first being he's lacking lungs."

"That could be an obstacle, partner. Anything else?"

"The other being, he's dead. Listen, that gator's nest is right over there. She can do to us what she did to him. Let's get the hell out of here."

After returning to the boat, Ron called Bill Baxter and gave him the bad news.

"Sorry, Bill. We didn't see it coming. He led us into his own little trap."

There was a moment of silence, then Tim heard Ron say, "We're sending up a flare as we speak."

Twenty minutes passed before a Coast Guard boat, carrying the forensic team, came up the tributary.

Ron escorted the coast guard to where they had last seen Whittaker's body being taken under by the gator.

"I'd be careful, guys. Her nest is right there. If I were you, I'd go back to your boat. What's down there, ain't worth bringing to the surface."

Tim watched the baskets containing the body of Sergeant Michaels, then that of Bruce Langley, and finally the remains of Deni Whittaker, taken to the Coast Guard boat. After their removal, he made his way back to Gary's boat where Ron was waiting.

"Let's get the hell out of here," said Ron.

Tim slowly backed the boat out of the reeds and into the waters of the tributary.

"When you get to the river's entrance, Tim, make a left. There's a restaurant about eight miles upriver. Let's go get drunk."

"Who's buying?"

"The good-looking guy."

"Damn, I'm always buying. When will the fat-looking guy be buying?"

Ron laughed as he replied, "Rank has its privileges, Tim-o-thy."

EPILOG

Myrtle Beach Sun News – July 23, 2018

The murdering crime spree of the man known as "Ichabod" has ended. South Carolina State Troopers, led by Captain Bill Baxter, report the suspect, Gary Whittaker, suffered a mortal wound during a shootout with FBI Agents late yesterday afternoon in the rice fields of the Waccamaw River near Litchfield Plantation.

Lost in the line of duty, were South Carolina State Troopers, Sergeant Randy Michaels, and Officer Anthony Sanders, both victims of Whittaker.

Responsible for the murders of seven women, including that of his wife, over a four-week period, Whittaker decapitated his victims and left their heads on various Grand Strand golf courses.

He also murdered Ernie Cavanaugh, a security guard, Robert Harrell, a convenience store clerk, Dennis Pritchard, an employee of Litchfield Plantation, and Bruce Langley, a neighbor.

Before his death, Whittaker claimed responsibility for the murders of 34 other women across the country and in Canada.

The killing spree, the likes of which never seen previously and hopefully never seen again, was the most horrific of its kind in Horry County's long history.

But another was on its way.

The following is an excerpt from the next installment of the Myrtle Beach Crime Thriller series.

THE SCALE TIPPERS

East Aurora, New York – November 18, 2018

Rocco Riccardi had been standing in the cold night air for well over two hours. Having traveled from Sicily, the home of his Mafia family, his instructions were to kill six people residing in the United States. The first of those lived in the Cape Cod styled house on Hamlin Avenue, in the town of East Aurora, located 20 miles southeast of Buffalo, New York. It was nearing midnight and his target, a 50-year-old post office worker, who now went by the name of Ed Rucker, inhabited the house with his wife Denise.

Ten years earlier Rucker was Salvadore Testa, a ruthless hitman, and a member of the Genovese crime family who controlled New York's Manhattan district. Facing life in prison for attempting to assassinate a New York City district attorney, Testa saved his ass by turning against the organization. His damning testimony sent numerous members of the family to lifelong prison sentences.

For his cooperation, the Federal government placed Testa into the Federal Witness Protection Program.

The mob, however, never forgives or forgets. It may have taken ten years and many bribes, but they found him.

Hidden in the shadows of trees lining the street, Rocco watched the man walking back and forth between his living room and his kitchen.

Shortly after midnight, a neighbor who was walking his German Shepard around the block, yelled out, "Hey, Mister, what the hell are you doing there!"

Unaffected by the sudden emergence of the neighbor, Rocco calmly removed a Heckler&Koch MP5SD machine gun with an attached silencer from beneath his long coat.

Turning toward the man, he said, "I'm here to kill the man in that house." Then he fired two muted bursts. One knocked the neighbor out of his shoes as the bullets ripped through his body. The second ended the snarling Shepard's life.

"Sorry about that, fellas," whispered Rocco, before turning his attention back toward the house.

Hearing the ruckus outside, the inquisitive, but careless, Rucker peered through the living room window into the darkness. The opportunity Rocco had been waiting for had presented itself. Quickly taking aim, the gun popped once, twice, and a third time.

The first bullet cracked the picture window and blew the left portion of Testa's head against the living room's far wall. The second removed Testa's jaw, and the third caught the already dead Testa in the throat.

Testa's wife, having gone to bed long ago, would find a mess when she awoke in the morning.

Calmly removing the now warm silencer, Rocco put the weapon back under his coat and made his way toward the vehicle he had parked a few blocks away.

He had five more targets. One in Chicago, another in Houston, and the remainder in Myrtle Beach.

ABOUT THE AUTHOR

James Robert Fuller was born in Rochester, New York in 1944. His mother moved to Buffalo, New York shortly after he was born. There she met and married a man whose last name, Wing, was an alias.

James Robert Fuller, involuntarily, became Ronald Wing. This name change did not become known to the author until he was in his mid-forties.

Ron grew up in Western New York, spending many of his younger years living with his maternal grandparents, James, and Maud Fuller, in Salamanca, New York, a small city nestled in the Allegheny foothills. It was there that he had experiences that fostered his *Bay Hollow Thriller* series.

Ron married Barbara Bowman in 1967. They have two children, Jennifer, and Jason, and four grandchildren.

Ron worked for Bethlehem Steel in Lackawanna, New York, until 1978 as a computer programmer and systems analyst.

The family moved to Greenville, North Carolina in 1978, where Ron worked for Burroughs Wellcome, a pharmaceutical company, until retiring in 1995.

Ron and Barbara moved to Myrtle Beach, South Carolina in 1998, where Ron began his writing career, penning the *Bay Hollow Thrillers* which are more in line for young adults and those older adults who are young at heart.

Customers of the Bay Hollow series, asking if the Bay Hollow stories involved Myrtle Beach, led Ron to write the *Myrtle Beach Crime Thrillers* , using his given name on his birth certificate, **James Robert Fuller**, in honor of his grandparents.

"Paradise: Disturbed," Ron's initial venture into adult thrillers, is the first of 11 *Myrtle Beach Crime Thriller series.*

THE MYRTLE BEACH CRIME THRILLERS
By James Robert Fuller

Paradise: Disturbed – Book I

It was announced in January 2024, that "Paradise:Disturbed" would be made into a major motion picture or mini-series with an anticipated release date of December 2025.

The Scale Tippers – Book II
Falano's Findings - Book III
The Cobo – Book IV
The Dispatcher – Book V
Dancing Dead – Book VI
Deadly Connections – Book VII
The Cicada List – Book VIII
The Men of Kabul – Book IX
Dead Money – Book X
Water Hazard – Book XI
Mister Finito – Book XII

For money saving purchases, contact the author at:
RONWING44@GMAIL.COM

RON'S WEBSITE:
MYRTLEBEACHTHRILLERS.COM

ALSO AVAILABLE UPON REQUEST
IS THE 13 BOOK YOUNG ADULT SERIES
"BAY HOLLOW THRILLERS"
by Ron Wing

Volume #1 – Books 1-3
Volume #2 – Books 4-6
Volume #3 – Books 7-9
Volume #4 – Books 10, 11
Volume # 5 – Books 12, 13